D0047951

**Also by *New York Times* bestselling author
B.J. Daniels**

For a complete list of books by B.J. Daniels,
please visit www.bjdaniels.com.

Visit the Author Profile page at Harlequin.com.

B.J. DANIELS

NEW YORK TIMES BESTSELLING AUTHOR

When JUSTICE RIDES

HQN

ISBN-13: 978-1-335-53005-9

When Justice Rides

Recycling programs for this product may not exist in your area.

HQN
22 Adelaide St. West, 41st Floor
Toronto, Ontario M5H 4E3, Canada
www.Harlequin.com

Printed and bound in Barcelona, Spain by CPI Black Print

I've dreamed of being a writer since I was a girl.
I'd never met a writer, had no idea how to write a book,
but I'd always had stories in my head.

With you, dear reader, about to read my 119th book,
I want to thank all the people it takes
for one of my crazy ideas to turn into a published book.

This book is dedicated to everyone at Harlequin and
HarperCollins who made this book happen—from
editing to cover art, printing, promotion and distribution.

Thank you for all your hard work and dedication.
You keep making my dream come true.

When
JUSTICE
RIDES

CHAPTER ONE

JOHNNY BERG DIDN'T see the blood. Nor did he hear the killer quickly hide as he came in the back door of Buckhorn, Montana's general store. He had his earbuds in, rocking out to a new band he'd just discovered on TikTok. His arms full of a towering stack of packages to be delivered, he'd shoved aside the partially open rear door of the store and come in dancing as usual.

Vi Mullen always liked to get to the store an hour before it opened so he often dropped off her packages first. Today, he was ahead of schedule, which made his day. Priding himself on delivering packages quickly, he liked to joke to friends that he drove the truck like he'd stolen it. He always made record time and as the youngest employee, he received some of the best performance reviews from his customers. They referred to him as Johnny on the Spot.

He called out, "Hello, Vi!" like he always did, even though she usually didn't answer. He didn't see her, but the light had been on in the storage room and the back door unlocked, so he knew she was here somewhere. She seldom if ever answered, which was fine with him.

Early on, he'd tried to make conversation with her like he did with his other customers.

"I don't have time for your foolishness," she'd snapped. "And don't forget to wipe your feet before you come traipsing in here, tracking up my wood floors. They're original from the 1800s when my family first settled here in Buckhorn."

"Yes, ma'am," he'd said, hoping to avoid one of her history lessons.

This morning, he'd made a point of wiping his feet on the mat just outside the door before he entered the store—not that she would notice. She'd find something else to nag him about unless he got out of here quickly.

So often it was a blessing if he got in and out of the store without seeing her. Still dancing to the music booming from his earbuds, he made his way through the store, the tall stack of boxes balanced precariously in front of him. He also prided himself on being able to carry everything in one load.

The days Vi had packages to go out, he'd find them ready and waiting for him. With almost relief, he saw this morning that the spot where she would leave anything to ship out was empty. He placed the packages down, straightening the stack. Vi was a stickler on how she wanted things done.

He had worse customers, but Vi still made the top three, he thought as he turned to leave—and froze. His music still blaring in his ears, but his arms free of the tall stack of packages he'd brought in, he stared at the floor—and the bloody footprints. *His* bloody footprints as he'd danced his way through the store.

What the— He popped out one earbud feeling a sense of panic.

"Vi?" No answer. He popped out the other earbud, letting them hang around his neck. In the quiet of the cavernous filled-to-the-rafter store, the music still coming out of his earbuds made it feel even creepier. "Vi?" Still no answer.

Heart pounding, he slowly followed the trail he'd left,

avoiding spreading any more of the blood, terrified of what he was going to find. He tried to throw off the chill that wound around his neck, making him shiver. It wasn't until he reached the storage area at the back that he stopped short. A puddle of blood had pooled in a low spot in the middle of the floor. He slowly turned his head to follow the river of blood to its source.

A slightly built older woman, Vi Mullen lay on her back, blank eyes staring up at the ceiling, mouth open as if in a silent scream. A brand-new ice fishing spear, its price tag still dangling from the handle, stuck out of her chest like a giant fork. Her cap of obviously dyed dark hair made her eyes look like dull black marbles in her bloodless face. One arm was extended, the hand lying in the blood darkening on the floor.

"Vi?" He hesitated. The last thing he wanted to do was touch her. Carefully he stepped closer, but he could tell even before he hunkered down to hurriedly check for a pulse that she was dead. She wasn't the first customer he'd found dead on his route, but she was the first with a spear sticking out of her.

He shoved to his feet, fighting to catch his breath as his stomach roiled and he thought he might be sick. He needed fresh air. Now! As he rushed out to his truck to make the call to both his boss and 911, he didn't even notice that he'd gone through the puddle of blood again until he reached the back steps. He tried to wipe the bottom of his sneakers clean, but gave up, leaving traces of blood on the back steps and the gravel in the alley.

For a few moments safely inside his delivery truck, he could only gasp for breath in an attempt to rid the stench of death from his lungs. His hands shook as he pulled out his phone and dialed 911, then the call to his boss.

That over, he turned up his music as he waited, unable to sit still, unable not to look back toward the open doorway of the store knowing what lay inside. All he wanted to do was get out of there, but the marshal had told him to wait.

It was early enough that the tiny town of Buckhorn hadn't woken up yet. He didn't see anyone around. He tried not to think about Vi and that open-mouthed silent scream he'd seen on her chalk-white face.

It never crossed his mind that whoever "smoked" Vi might have still been in the store with him earlier. Could still be in there. Or that if the killer had seen him, he would be easily recognized with his company jacket on.

Johnny never imagined that he'd seen something incriminating.

And that the killer was now coming after him.

Instead, he was thinking about how this was going to mess up his entire schedule for not just today but the entire week.

CHAPTER TWO

LUNA DECLAN HAD just come down from her apartment over her Buckhorn hair salon to get ready for her first client of the day when she got the call. She ran a hand through her short dark pixie cut, the numerous tiny silver loops at her ears glittering in the morning light. She'd been considering letting her hair grow. Not that she probably would. She was just trying to keep her mind off Jaxson Gray, the young deputy marshal she'd been seeing—until lately.

Her phone rang again. She checked, hoping it would be him with a good explanation as to why he'd been ghosting her the past couple of weeks.

To her surprise and instant concern, she saw that it was her father calling. He *always* called on Sunday afternoon at 2:00 p.m. Routine had been Lawrence Declan's life for too many years. For him to call now on a Tuesday morning...

"Dad?" She couldn't help the tremor in her voice. Something was wrong. She knew it. He never varied from his routines unless... "What's wrong?"

He cleared his voice. Her first thought was that he was ill. That he was calling about a doctor's diagnosis. That he'd fallen and— "Are you still dating that young deputy, Jaxson Gray?"

She blinked as she reeled back all her errant fears. This wasn't about her father. It was about *Jaxson*?

Luna wasn't sure how to answer. Was she still dating

Jaxson? She thought of his handsome face, those sea green eyes, the way his thick dark hair felt in her fingers when he came in for a haircut.

They'd been dating for months. Jaxson had wanted to take it slow and she'd understood. It hadn't been that long since he'd lost his wife. Lately though, she'd felt a change in him. Whatever walls he'd put up to protect himself, they were coming down. She felt as if she were finally seeing the real Jaxson Gray—and she liked what she saw.

Jaxson was a great listener and often encouraged her to talk about her job, Buckhorn and the residents she'd come to know since moving here. She could tell that he was disappointed she hadn't lived here her entire life.

As a hairdresser to those who had lived here their whole lives, she'd heard her share of stories. What was it about people that the moment she began to massage their scalps they began to talk? And the things they'd told her!

She'd kept Jaxson entertained with stories, never mentioning names—although after a while, he could probably guess—until he had to climb into this patrol SUV and leave. After coffee or a meal, he'd always walked her back to her apartment over the salon, but he'd never come inside—even when she'd invited him. He'd always had to get going, saying he had an early shift the next day or some other excuse.

Then last week, he'd shown up at her door out of the blue.

"Could we go have a drink at the bar?" She could tell that he had something on his mind. But once at the bar, instead of telling her what it was, he'd asked her to dance. In his arms, it had felt like a lot more than just friends dancing. She'd been confused even before the kiss.

When the song ended, he'd pulled her to him and really

kissed her for the first time. Boom! Bang! Like Fourth of July fireworks.

While she had felt chemistry simmering between them before that night, she hadn't anticipated the passion in that kiss. It started a fire inside her. She'd told herself that if the deputy hadn't gotten called to the scene of an accident that night, they would have ended up at her apartment in her double bed.

"Why do you ask?" she queried her father now as she looked out at the two-lane blacktop that cut through the heart of Buckhorn. Why *was* he asking?

The one thing she knew about her father was his inability to completely retire. He'd spent too many years as an insurance investigator. He had an uncanny ability to spot fraudulent claims. Because of that, he had an unblemished record for retrieval of stolen insured goods.

She'd even worked with him on a few cases, one that had brought her to Buckhorn in the first place. In truth, she idolized her father and always had. She'd thought about following in his footsteps since she loved the challenge of a good mystery. Instead, she'd found herself doing what her mother had: opening her own salon.

"There might be a problem," her father said. "If you're still dating him."

Mind reeling, she opened the salon's front door and crossed the sidewalk to her huge flowerpot overflowing with blooms. As she began mindlessly pulling off dead-heads from the petunias, she said, "What have you done, Dad?"

They had a long-standing rule between them going back to her first boyfriend. He was not to investigate anyone she dated. She was sure that it hadn't stopped him over the years—he'd just never admitted it.

It was one reason that she'd always told her father all the pertinent facts about her boyfriends, so this issue never came up. But now she realized that she hadn't told him about Jaxson's deceased wife and didn't even know why she'd kept it from him. It hadn't mattered.

She'd filled him in on everything else, including how Jaxson's mother, father and siblings were all in education, either as teachers or administrators, and that he was the black sheep of the family because he'd gone into law enforcement. That had seemed like enough specifics since at that point, she hadn't been sure how serious she and Jaxson were. How serious he was, especially.

Luna recalled her father saying, *Of course, you'd go for the black sheep.* They'd both laughed because it was true. Jaxson was so down-to-earth normal that he was on the verge of being dull. If it weren't for the chemistry she'd felt at times between them, she'd have said their relationship wasn't going anywhere. Then he'd kissed her that night at the bar and sent her over the moon. She'd been relieved that she hadn't been wrong about the two of them.

He'd called last night and asked her out on a date tonight. He'd sounded excited. She certainly was. Tonight was the night. She could feel it.

So whatever her father had found out about Jaxson, it didn't matter, she told herself now. But she still she had to know. "You actually *investigated* him?" she asked with a groan.

"You're my daughter," he said unapologetically. "I've always done a little checking on your boyfriends."

"Because you can't help yourself." She sighed. "I should

have told you that Jaxson has been married, that his wife, Amy, died a few years ago. I'm sorry. I didn't feel it was important." Silence. Then more silence. It was unnerving. Had he found something more?

She straightened to look down the long highway. With a start, she realized that he wasn't calling because she hadn't told him about Amy, Jaxson's deceased wife. Her voice broke when she spoke. "What did you find?"

"I had no intention of saying a word unless…"

Luna thought of her other boyfriends and realized there must not have been an *unless* in their backgrounds. She felt her heart do a little bump in her chest even as she told herself there was nothing to find. Jaxson was perfect. She'd always thought he was a little too perfect for her. But after that passionate kiss…

A semi was gearing down on the west end of town. Luna looked to the east. Were those storm clouds gathering? She realized her father was speaking as she turned to go back inside her salon. Stepping in, she closed the door and locked it again. She had no clients coming for a while, but she needed to finish this conversation without being interrupted.

"Just tell me," she said into the phone.

"The story he told you about his family… It wasn't quite accurate."

Hadn't she sensed there was something Jaxson was holding back even more than intimacy? "How *inaccurate*?"

Her father cleared his throat and recited what sounded like one of his insurance reports. "He was born in Blackfoot, Idaho, an only child, raised by a single mother. No father listed on his birth certificate. His mother died his senior year in high school. He was a good student who excelled in sports. His senior year, recruiters from numerous schools were interested in him. He'd had offers from colleges. Then just days before graduation, his girlfriend, a young woman named Amy Franklin, disappeared."

Luna thought her head would explode. Nothing Jaxson had told her was true except for the fact that there *had* been an Amy in his life?

Her father cleared his throat again and continued. "The young woman was never found. Jaxson was questioned and released. He left right after graduation and disappeared himself for a time until he turned up in Wyoming, working on a ranch. He later went to Montana State University in Bozeman before attending the law enforcement academy and getting a job as a deputy six months ago—in your county."

She shook her head, remembering the way he'd talked about his family, his brother and sister, his parents. "You're sure you have the right Jaxson Gray?" It was a silly, hopeless question since she knew her father was meticulous with his research. He would never have gotten it wrong.

"I'm sending you photos. See for yourself." She heard her phone beep three times, announcing several texts. She had never taken a photo of Jaxson, let alone one of the two of them, but she knew her resourceful father could get a photo of Jaxson without much effort.

"I'm sorry," her father was saying. "But the last time we talked, it sounded as if you might be getting serious about him." She'd talked to her father the day after the kiss, and while she hadn't mentioned the kiss, she was sure he'd picked up on how happy she'd been after her date the night before. "I didn't want to have to worry."

Well, he was worried now. He wasn't the only one. "Why

would Jaxson lie about something that is so easily proven to be false?" she said more to herself than her father. It was obvious. He would have never expected her to check. And he would have been right. If it hadn't been for her father and his insatiable need to protect her...

"Maybe more worrisome, Luna, is why he turned down several other more lucrative deputy jobs to take the one he has now in *your* county. Also, he's never been married that I can find. If you want, I can dig deeper—"

"No, thanks, I can handle it from here." *One way or another*, she thought. She disconnected and called up the first photo in the text from her dad, telling herself it wouldn't be Jaxson.

DEPUTY KENNETH YARROW shouldn't have been surprised to get the call from Buckhorn. The small Western town in the middle of nowhere seemed to attract trouble. He'd barely taken over as acting marshal in Leroy Baggins's absence and now there was a call about a murder in Buckhorn?

Baggins, who was on his honeymoon, had left him in charge of the county—at least temporarily. Not that Ken shouldn't have had the marshal job in the first place, he internally groused as he took the call. At fifty-two and having spent most of his adult life in law enforcement, he knew that he'd been the better candidate for the job. Being passed over for marshal was still a burr under his saddle.

"Acting Marshal Kenneth Yarrow," he said when the call was forwarded to him by the dispatcher.

"Someone killed her." The young male voice, high and thin, was barely audible over the blare of music. "She was dead when I got here. I didn't see her until—"

"Can you please turn that down?" Ken snapped. "Who's dead?"

"Sorry." The music had stopped abruptly. But was he also chewing gum? How old was this person? "Vi. Someone killed her."

"Vi Mullen?" Ken felt a start. He was familiar with Buckhorn's temperamental matriarch and had heard his share of horror stories about her. But that wasn't what had his heart pounding. A few weeks ago, he'd asked Vi out on a date. He'd been thinking about it for a long time and had finally decided to do it. Call him delusional but there had been something about her that appealed to him. They were the same age, had gone to school together, and he'd thought… He didn't know what he'd been thinking.

When she'd turned him down rudely, he'd lost his cool and said some things that he shouldn't have. Now he wondered if he'd been overheard that day in the store. It wasn't like he'd threatened her, he told himself as his mind raced. And now she was dead?

"You're sure she's dead?" he asked, his throat dry. The last thing he needed was to be a suspect in a murder case right now.

"Checked for a pulse. Dead."

"What makes you think it was murder?"

"She has a friggin' ice fishing spear sticking out of her chest!"

Holy shit. *That could do it*, Ken thought. "And you are?"

"Johnny. Johnny Berg. I deliver packages. You know, all over the county but also for the general store in Buckhorn."

"Where are you now?" Ken asked and Johnny told him he was parked in the alley, the back door of the store open like he'd found it. "Stay right there. Don't go back in and don't let anyone else go in. I'm on my way." He disconnected and swore. Buckhorn. It never failed. What was it about that town? And now, of all people, Vivian "Vi" Mullen had been murdered?

"Deputy Gray," he said into the radio. "Where are you?"

The new young deputy came on the radio. "Just passed mile marker 111."

"Saddle up and get to Buckhorn. Meet me behind the general store in the alley. There's been a murder."

MURDER? DEPUTY JAXSON GRAY felt his pulse jump as he pressed down hard on the patrol SUV's gas pedal and raced toward Buckhorn. He told himself it could be anyone. A vagrant passing through town. Didn't mean that it was a local. Didn't mean it had anything to do with anyone he knew.

His phone chimed. He checked and felt immediately guilty when he saw that it was a text from Luna. After the night at the bar, the dance, the kiss, he'd realized that he was ready to move on with his life. He was looking forward to their date tonight and was disappointed when he read the text from her.

He read her text twice in surprise. *She was going out of town?* She hadn't mentioned going out of town.

Had something happened? He hoped it wasn't bad news regarding her father. Jaxson knew how close they were.

As he raced toward Buckhorn, he'd have to answer the text later. He just hoped her leaving so unexpectedly wasn't something seriously wrong. Meeting Luna had been the best thing that had happened to him in a long time. Besides being distractingly attractive, she was intelligent, witty and fun with an insatiable curiosity. She had a way of seeing below the surface when it came to people. She said it was because her father had been an investigator, now retired, and that she'd worked with him for a while on a few cases.

The closer he'd gotten to her, the more he'd worried that she would see through him and his lies. After that kiss the other night, he knew he had to tell her the truth. He couldn't keep holding her at arm's length because it was the last thing he wanted to do. He pocketed his phone as he saw the small Western town appear on the horizon ahead.

He'd tried to keep Luna at a safe distance. But it had been getting harder and harder as he'd gotten to know her. How was he to know that he would end up caring this much for her? Probably because he'd never met anyone quite like her.

He tried to put her, and worry about why she'd left town, out of his mind. There'd been a murder. That's all the information Yarrow had given him. No surprise there. The older deputy, now acting marshal, had been a jerk to him the moment he'd taken the job. Yarrow had told him that he had little respect for deputies who he said were *green behind the ears.*

Jaxson had wanted to correct him and say that the expression was *wet behind the ears,* but out of the corner of his eye he'd seen the dispatcher shake her head in warning, and he'd held his tongue. He didn't need to arouse any more disdain from Yarrow.

Unfortunately, Yarrow only thought he was a lot better at his job than he was. Otherwise, the man would have gotten the marshal job instead of the much younger, much less experienced, Leroy Baggins. So now Yarrow carried around a chip on his shoulder the size of a redwood.

Get to Buckhorn. Meet me behind the general store in the alley. Jaxson braced himself for what might be waiting for him. It felt too early in the morning to see a dead body.

The thought made him let out a bitter chuckle. He often wondered if he had the stomach for this job.

Slowing, he drove into Buckhorn. An hour from the nearest other town, the tiny burg's roots ran deep in the Montana soil. How it had survived to celebrate its 125th birthday was a mystery to anyone who had blown through and not even realized they'd passed it. Yet recently, it had begun to draw people looking for an escape from the larger cities, from the traffic, from the rat race. It had drawn Jaxson, even before he'd met Luna Declan.

But as he headed for the alley behind the general store, he did wonder. There were a surprising number of murders for such a small town in the middle of Montana, in the middle of nowhere.

CHAPTER THREE

AS KEN PULLED UP behind the delivery truck, he saw the new deputy pull in right behind him. He would have preferred any other deputy than Jaxson Gray, who didn't know his ass from a hole in the ground.

But Gray had been close by, and if Ken were being honest with himself, he preferred the deputy over the other cocky cops who thought they knew it all. At least Gray was smart enough that he seemed aware that he didn't know squat. With Deputy Gray, he didn't have to worry about the young man getting in his way.

This was going to be his show, Ken told himself, and no one else's. When he solved this murder, it would prove to everyone that the county had made a mistake making Leroy Baggins marshal. Not that Ken felt he should have to prove himself, but he needed a win. Lately, he'd been feeling like life was repeatedly kicking him in the teeth.

Picking up his Stetson, he climbed out of his patrol SUV, well aware of what kind of day it was going to be even before the deputy walked toward him asking, "Who's been murdered?"

Ken should have known those would be the first words out of the deputy's mouth. This was Gray's first murder while on the payroll. Ken wondered if the green deputy had ever even seen a dead body before? He chuckled to himself at the thought of how the deputy would react to what was waiting for them inside.

"You're ambitious, aren't you, Gray?" he asked in lieu of an answer.

"Yes, sir," the young man agreed as he joined him.

"Thinking you could be marshal of this county one day, right?"

"No, sir."

Ken shot him a surprised look.

"I hope to be a US marshal."

The acting marshal couldn't hold back his laugh. "Then I'd suggest you stay out of my way and not screw up your first murder." Turning his back, he walked toward the delivery truck parked in the alley, chuckling to himself. *US marshal, ha!* Over his shoulder, he said, "The murder victim is Vivian Mullen, the store owner."

"Vi?" Gray sounded surprised.

Ignoring the interruption, Ken continued, "Her family pretty much started this town and she's been running it ever since. Well, until today apparently."

He could see the driver in the side mirror of the delivery truck as they approached the rear entrance into the general store. The driver, feet up on the dash, earbuds in, head bobbing, looked young and trying hard to hide he'd been shaken earlier on his call. Or was he trying to hide something more?

"Get a statement from the kid in the truck," he told Gray as he started toward the open back door of the store. He stopped when he noticed the way the young deputy was staring at the ground as he approached the truck. What did the deputy find so interesting?

He stepped over to look and swore under his breath. There

was a faint trail of dried blood smeared on the back steps as well as some in the gravel next to the truck's driver's side door. "Don't let him go anywhere. I want his prints when the crime techs get here and I might want to talk to him," he said and followed the bloody smeared footprints up the back steps, swearing as he went.

Entering the store, the smell hit him first. He'd gotten used to the scent of fresh warm blood growing up on a ranch where something was always being butchered. As a deputy, he felt as if he'd seen it all.

He'd only taken a few steps when he was blinded by a bright arrow of sunlight that shot across the worn floor directly at him. He blinked and swore some more. *The store's front door was standing wide open?*

"What the hell?" he said to himself. Anyone could have come in and out of the store in the forty minutes it had taken him to get to the scene. He'd told the deliveryman to make sure no one entered. True it wasn't the kid's job, but without a lawman in Buckhorn, he'd depended on the caller to contain the crime scene.

He'd taken only a few steps, still avoiding the bloody prints, when he saw the victim. She lay off to the side in the storage area. Her blood had run from her body across the uneven floor to puddle in the middle where the boards were more worn. Which would explain how the delivery kid hadn't only just tracked through the blood but also spread it all over.

With yet another curse, Yarrow took off his Stetson and ran a hand through his hair. He was now in charge of solving the murder of a prominent Buckhorn business owner and he had a compromised crime scene. Too bad Marshal

Leroy Baggins hadn't delayed his honeymoon so he could have gotten this one.

Pulling on disposable gloves, Ken carefully avoided disturbing the scene further as he worked his way to the front of the store. He closed the door and locked it before returning to the body. For a moment, he merely stared at the woman lying there. Vi had been larger than life, a spitfire of a woman. But that had been when she was alive, he realized. Now she looked insignificant, harmless, just a shadow of her former self, a small woman who'd never reached sixty.

As he crouched down, he considered what had killed her. She did indeed have a *friggin' ice fishing spear sticking out of her chest*. The broomstick-like handle of the spear stood straight up from the wound as if the nine barbed stainless steel sharp prongs weren't just embedded in her body, but possibly in the old pine floor under her as well.

Hearing a sound behind him, he rose to find the deputy standing at the back door. "The kid still out there?" he demanded. "Find out if the front door was open when he came in."

"It wasn't," the deputy said, looking down at his notebook in his hand. "Johnny Berg remembered that the front door was definitely shut, locked and the Closed sign hanging on it—just as it is now. He said Vi kept it locked until it was time to open the store at nine, and from the looks of the amount of smeared fresh blood, she couldn't have been dead long before he arrived."

Ken glanced toward the front door, then at Gray as the impact of that news struck him. Someone had gone out that door *after* the kid had found the body? Looking past the deputy, he saw the teenager at the back door behind Gray. He had those stupid headphones on a cord hanging around his neck, a godawful sound coming out of them. "Shut that racket off!" Ken demanded, pointing at them.

In the deathly silence that followed, he said, "You're sure the front door wasn't open?" The kid nodded, wide-eyed as he looked from the door to the dead body.

"If the door had been locked, then the killer must have gone out the front door when Berg exited through the back to make the 911 call," Gray said—just as Ken had already surmised.

He wanted to tell the rookie deputy to keep his theories to himself, but if the kid was telling the truth, then that appeared to be exactly what had happened. "Yeah, I figured that out all by myself."

"What? Wait." Berg's voice was even higher and thinner than when he'd made the initial 911 call. "Are you saying the killer was still in here when I brought in the packages?" He looked from Ken to Gray, all the color draining from his face.

"You sure you didn't see anyone?" Ken demanded. He started to ask if the kid had heard anyone but knew that was a wasted question since Berg would have had that infernal noise blaring in his ears.

With an even more stunned look, the kid shook his head adamantly. "I didn't see *anything*." His voice broke. "I swear. But what if the killer thinks I did?"

BEFORE LOOKING AT the photos her father had sent her, Luna found herself making excuses for why Jaxson hadn't told her about his real family history. He was ashamed, embarrassed, didn't want her sympathy?

Fabricating the perfect family was one thing, but how did she explain the dead wife he didn't have? She swallowed, wishing she didn't also wonder why as part of his lie he had said Amy was dead. Because he knew she was?

She shuddered and told herself whatever had happened to his old girlfriend, Jaxson hadn't had anything to do with it. He'd been questioned and released her father had said. As if she didn't know that being questioned and released didn't mean he was innocent. But her gut-level instincts told her that he wasn't a killer.

He was, however, a liar. Therefore, she couldn't trust anything he'd told her. But could she even trust her instincts when it came to him?

Taking a calming breath, she let it out and finally looked at the first photo her father had sent her. The young man in the button-down white shirt and tie with the short buzz cut looked nothing like the man who'd walked into her salon a few months ago wearing a Stetson, jeans, boots and a deputy uniform jacket, looking for a haircut. Yet, it was the same Jaxson Gray—just a whole lot younger.

Luna moved the cursor down to the next photograph. Senior photo. Then random shots of Jaxson, one in his football uniform, holding a trophy and smiling. He did have a great smile. A team photo. Another of him in class, looking bored. The last was a photo of him and his mother? Luna looked closely at it. The woman had been pretty, slightly built. There was something haunting in her eyes as she stared at the photographer while her son looked over at her with…concern?

The question was why lie about a mother he'd obviously cared about?

She knew from working with her father that one of the problems with knowledge was what to do with it, especially when that new information concerned someone in your life who you'd come to care about.

Except Deputy Jaxson Gray wasn't really in her life, she reminded herself. Not as *in* as she'd thought anyway, so what would she do when she had the truth? Confront him? Give him the opportunity to come clean? Or open herself up to even more lies? Or simply walk away without a word?

That was just it. She couldn't walk away. She was in too deep. She was falling for this complicated cowboy. There was no way she wasn't going to confront him. Just as there was no way she wasn't going to find out the truth. Her father wasn't the only one who was good at research. She needed to know who Deputy Jaxson Gray really was. The clean-cut cowboy cop he appeared to be or someone responsible for a young woman's disappearance back in high school.

Luna looked again at the pictures her father had sent. The name of the high school was on the wall in the one photo. No question about it, Jaxson had been a good-looking teen-ager in high school. It was no wonder that he'd grown into a drop-dead gorgeous man. While her father hadn't sent a photo of Jaxson with a girlfriend—maybe because he didn't have one or was trying to protect her—Luna knew there had to be girlfriends or friends who would remember Jaxson.

And they shouldn't be that hard to find.

Putting out the Closed sign on her salon, she scribbled a note that she would be out of town for a few days and stuck it on the front door. Then she called to cancel and resched-ule a few appointments.

Afterward ending her last call, she hurried upstairs to her apartment to pack. Before she walked out the door, she texted Deputy Jaxson Gray as if nothing were wrong between them. Have to go out of town. Sorry about tonight. Will talk when I get back.

She waited a few seconds. No response. Was he as disappointed as she was? Or too busy with work to answer?

Pocketing her phone, she picked up her suitcase and carried it downstairs to her SUV parked in the alley. She would find out the truth about Jaxson one way or another. And then what?

Bust him for his lies. But even as she thought it, she hoped there was a reasonable explanation. Blackfoot, Idaho, was a day's drive from Buckhorn. She had to know what kind of man she'd been falling for.

As she drove out of town, she noticed that the Buckhorn General Store was still closed at this hour, a few people were milling around on the sidewalk out front, some looking like they were trying to see what was going on inside.

Strange, she mused, but her thoughts quickly turned back to Deputy Jaxson Gray—and what she might learn about him once she reached Blackfoot.

CHAPTER FOUR

JAXSON TOOK BERG back outside to wait for the coroner and crime scene techs. He felt like the deliveryman knew more than he realized. "Think about when you came into the store. You're sure you didn't hear anything?"

The recently-turned-eighteen-year-old pointed to the headphones dangling around his neck, looking sick to his stomach, and shook his head. Berg had only been working for the delivery company for a few months—just since his eighteenth birthday.

"How about a smell?" If he was right, Vivian Mullen hadn't been dead long. He feared the smell of blood might have hidden any other scents, but he had to try. "Maybe sweat or perfume or cigarette scent from a smoker?"

Berg shook his head again, but he didn't look quite so sure now. "I was just doing my thing. I wasn't paying any attention." He sounded close to tears and Jaxson suspected that the shock was finally hitting home. More than likely, Berg had been in the store with the killer.

That the young man hadn't been paying attention was obvious from the tracks on the floor. Jaxson had also seen the large stack of boxes that had been delivered. "Did you bring in all the packages in one load?" Berg nodded. So it would have been nearly impossible for him to see the floor in front of him. Good thing the victim hadn't been lying in the middle of the floor or Berg would have tripped over her body, he thought.

"Okay, you didn't hear anything, you didn't smell anything," he said. "Did you see anything that was different? Something out of place? Or in an unusual spot?"

Berg let out a hoarse laugh. "You've seen the inside of that store. How would I know if something was out of place?"

Because it was a general store, Vi Mullen had sold everything from groceries to overalls, muck boots to ice fishing spears. The space was packed, the rows of goods narrow and stacked almost to the ceiling. The killer could have been hiding anywhere in the store. But Jaxson wouldn't have been surprised to learn that the killer had been concealed in the storage area. There were plenty of places to hide among the tall stacks of boxes that hadn't been unpacked.

That meant the killer might have gotten a good look at Berg.

"You put the packages where you usually do, right?" Jaxson asked.

"Always. Vi was very definite about the way she liked things."

Jaxson knew he was grasping at straws, but he had to keep trying. He'd learned that people often didn't remember small details until later after an initial trauma—not that Johnny Berg had seemed that traumatized—until he'd realized that the killer might have seen him. "Did you have to move anything to put down the packages?"

Berg thought for a moment before shaking his head. "It was just a normal day. I put down the packages where she likes me to, then I called out to her like I always do."

"Weren't you concerned when she didn't answer?"

He shook his head. "She never answers unless she wants to give me hell about something. Even when she has packages for me to pick up, they're always ready to go right there on the counter so I just take them and leave. Often, I don't even see her. It was always best if she didn't answer. Otherwise, she might slow me down. Didn't want her to start a rant and mess up my schedule. I take pride in getting the packages to my customers quickly." His expression turned forlorn as if he'd just realized that the rest of the packages in his truck weren't going to be just late, they might not get delivered at all today.

"Did she have packages to go today?"

"Not that I saw." Berg groaned and rubbed the back of his neck under shoulder-length hair. "I didn't see anything or *anyone*." He looked scared again. Jaxson watched him glance around. It was still early in the morning, so no one had come to see what was going on in the alley behind the store. Yet. "Can I go now?"

Jaxson got on his radio to Yarrow. Just as he suspected, the acting marshal wasn't interested in questioning Berg further. "You just need to wait until the crime techs arrive. They'll want your fingerprints." And maybe his shoes, Jaxson thought. He had all of Berg's contact information.

He handed him his card with his cell phone number printed on the back. "If you remember anything at all, call me. No matter how inconsequential you think it is. Or if anything comes up." He hoped even if the killer had seen the teenager that Berg wouldn't be in danger, but made a mental note to mention it to Yarrow as the mobile crime scene processing van turned down the alley.

KEN HEARD SOMEONE try the store's front door. He got up to check to make sure the door was still locked. The Closed sign was still turned to the outside. Past it, he could see people trying to see inside since by now Vi would have had the store open for business.

As he walked back to the storage area, he thought he was right about the killer going out the front door—after the delivery kid had gone out back to his truck to make the call. The killer though, he noticed, had been more careful than the kid. The only prints in the blood appeared to be Berg's.

If the killer had been hiding... As he neared the storage area again, he saw a partial footprint in the shadows back by the larger boxes. This one pointed away from the body. He told himself that it could be the delivery kid. But it wasn't the same print as the kid's sneakers.

Carefully, Ken peered behind several of the large boxes across from the body and, turning on his flashlight on his phone, saw drops of blood, some smeared on the floor. He swore under his breath. Gray's theory and his own appeared to be right on. The killer, no doubt covered with Vi's blood, had stood back here out of sight when the delivery kid came in.

Which meant there was a good chance the killer had seen Berg. Then when Johnny Berg had gone back outside to make the phone call, the killer had hightailed it out the front door of the store.

Ken stepped back at the sound of the back door opening again and returned to the body.

"The techs are getting Johnny Berg's fingerprints," Gray said from the back door. "Do you still want to talk to him?" He shook his head. "I was thinking. If the killer saw him, maybe we should—"

"I'm not worried about Johnny Berg," Ken snapped, angry with himself. He had to be at the top of his game. He couldn't let some green-behind-the-ears deputy show him up. "I have a murder to solve and a contaminated crime scene thanks to that kid."

Gray nodded, but he could tell that the deputy didn't agree. Gray stepped outside to let the kid know, but quickly returned.

"Berg told me that Vi always came down here early and left the back door open for him," the deputy said. "It's a pattern I would think anyone in Buckhorn would have known about. The killer must have come in right behind her as soon as she opened the door."

Ken shot him a look. "Based on what evidence?"

"Given where she was killed," Gray said. "It explains why Vi didn't get any farther inside the store other than the storage area. I noticed some large bins in the alley. The killer could have been hiding there. Or not. Either way, it would have been someone she knew and trusted."

The acting marshal ground his teeth. As much as he hated it, he had to ask. "What makes you think that, Deputy?"

"Her purse and keys." Gray pointed to a stack of tall boxes near the body. Ken hadn't seen the leather bag perched up there or the set of keys lying next to it on the cardboard top until now. "If she was startled or concerned, I doubt she would have put down her purse. Wouldn't she have at least kept the keys in her hand? Or pulled out her cell phone? If the phone is still in her purse—"

Ken held up a hand. He'd heard enough. Still wearing the disposable gloves, he started to reach up and take down the bag when there was a flash of light. He turned to see the deputy with his cell phone out, taking photographs.

"I just thought it's placement might be important," Jaxson said with a shrug. "Since the bag is within reach of where the victim was killed. Someone comes in who the store owner knows. She isn't anticipating a need to call 911 so she puts down her purse to deal with the person. She apparently wanted to finish the confrontation back here rather than walk all the way to the front of the store or into her office. Wanted to get rid of him or her quickly maybe."

Ken swore under his breath. "Or she could have pulled her phone and tried to call 911, but the killer took it."

Gray shrugged.

Hoping he was right and not the deputy, Ken took down the purse and ground his teeth as he looked inside, spotting the victim's cell phone. He put the purse back where it had been, wondering how he'd missed it. Too much on his mind even before he'd gotten the call about this case.

As much as it pained him, he had to agree with Gray. "I suppose there could have been an argument," he conceded and waited, knowing he was going to hear another theory from the deputy.

Jaxson nodded and pointed to a box lying on the floor a few feet away. "From what Johnny Berg told me, the store owner was meticulous about everything. That box is lying on its side, but all the other ones near it are not. It would appear the argument turned into a physical altercation that led to Vi being knocked down. The killer must have acted quickly since I don't see any signs that Vi fought back. It also appears that she was impaled while lying on the floor looking up at her killer."

Ken rolled his eyes. "Okay, take it easy, Sherlock." But

he had to admit, the deputy had made some good points. While new at this, Jaxson paid attention. He also suspected the deputy was right about the killer and victim knowing each other. He'd been to Buckhorn enough on other calls that he knew how a lot of people in this town felt about Vivian Mullen.

This had been a crime of passion, he thought. He remembered the fury he'd felt when she'd turned him down for a date. Not just turned him down, laughed in his face.

He stared down at her now, wondering how much rage it had taken to drive an ice fishing spear into Vi's chest like that.

If true, and Vi knew her killer, the suspect list was going to be as long as his arm. "I want the crime tech team in here as soon as they're finished out there."

"I'm guessing the killer hid somewhere back here in these boxes." The deputy had turned on his phone's flashlight and was headed back into the maze of cartons when Ken stopped him.

"Don't do that," he ordered. "Leave it to the crime scene techs. We don't need the area compromised any more than it has been." He was glad when the flashlight beam went out and Gray pocketed his phone.

Ken already knew what was back there.

CHAPTER FIVE

LUNA HAD TURNED OFF her phone for the drive. She figured Jaxson might try to contact her after her text and she wasn't ready to talk to him. Just the thought of the man filled her with conflicting emotions. She thought about the first time he'd walked into her salon needing a haircut. He'd been so shy, her heart had gone out to him at once. Also he was so darned handsome and sweet. She been drawn to him and he apparently to her since he'd asked her out to dinner not long after that.

She'd always prided herself on seeing through people. It was what she'd thought made her a valuable resource to her father. So why hadn't she seen through Deputy Jaxson Gray? She refused to believe it was simply because he looked so safe in his deputy uniform or because he was so damned good-looking and that he could be quite charming and appeared harmless, she thought as she crossed the Montana/Idaho border.

Shaking her head, she thought again of their kiss. Kisses didn't lie. Nor did the look in Jaxson's eyes. For whatever reason he'd lied about his past, she still believed in him. Believed in the two of them. She hoped she wasn't deluding herself as she neared the town of Blackfoot.

She wouldn't let her thoughts go south just yet as she drove, her mind whirling. She didn't have much to go on, but at least she knew the name of the high school Jaxson had attended. She would start there. Someone would remember him, she told herself. Someone would remember Amy, the girlfriend who'd disappeared.

What if Amy was the reason he'd lied? Knowing what she did now, she feared he'd lied because he was in trouble. The thought made her chest hurt as she reached the city limits of the town where Jaxson Gray had apparently grown up.

The high school wasn't hard to find. The huge old classic brick building with large arched windows stood empty and abandoned, the windows boarded up with plywood and Keep Out/Condemned signs.

Luna parked on the street, disappointed but not surprised. This part of town looked as if it had seen better times. About to leave, she spotted an elderly man on a riding lawn mower, cutting the grass. She climbed out of her SUV and approached him.

When he saw her coming, he frowned, but shut off the mower. He didn't climb down though, merely waited to see what she could possibly want. She had the feeling he resented being stopped from his work, but that maybe she hadn't been the first to ask about the school building.

"Hello," she said pleasantly and motioned toward Blackfoot High. "When did it close?"

"Seven years ago. They built a new high school across town." His answer sounded prerecorded as if he'd said these words before.

"I'm looking for someone who went to school here about seventeen years ago. Is there a local library that might have yearbooks?" Luna knew she could have possibly found this online and saved herself a trip. But she hoped to find someone who'd known Jaxson. Known Amy.

"Suppose so." He pointed down the street. "Six blocks, turn right, then turn left for four more blocks."

"Are you from here?" She didn't wait for an answer. "Maybe you've heard of Jaxson Gray?" She knew it was a long shot. But if he was from here, then he might remember Jaxson—especially since his girlfriend had gone missing.

To her surprise, the elderly man broke into a smile— his first since she'd approached him. "*Know* him? I used to help coach him. He was an amazing athlete. Damn shame what happened."

She frowned, deciding to play dumb. "I'm sorry, what happened?"

Now it was his turn to frown. "I thought you said you knew him."

Luna realized she'd made a misstep and quickly corrected it. "I'm asking for a friend who lived around here but moved and lost track of him." She wasn't sure the man completely bought her story, but he looked less wary.

"Then I've got some bad news for this…friend. A few days after his girlfriend disappeared, Jaxson did too. Just vanished into thin air his senior year right after graduation. Far as I know, no one has heard from him since. Made him look guilty when no one in this town thought he had anything to do with Amy's disappearance. He had scholarship offers…" The elderly man shook his head. "This town loved Jaxson. Damned shame. He could have been somebody." He pulled off one of his work gloves and rubbed the back of his neck, his watery gaze in the distance. "I never believed the rumors."

"Rumors?"

He took his time answering, pulling his glove back on before turning to her. "That Amy was pregnant and about to ruin his career and that was why… Like I said, no one believed he did anything to that girl."

JAXSON HAD BEEN shocked when Yarrow had told him the victim was Vi. Just as shocked as he'd been to see her small wiry body lying in a pool of her own blood with an ice fishing spear protruding from her. He'd actually liked the cantankerous woman, but he knew there were a lot of others who despised her.

She'd made enemies, a lot of them, from what he'd heard. But the few times he'd dealt with Vi, he'd found her a fearless force of nature. Which meant that it would have taken guts to even confront her—let alone attack her.

Intrigued, he warned himself against offering any more of his theories to the acting marshal. He could tell Yarrow didn't appreciate it. But at the same time, Jaxson also knew that the lawman did sloppy work, often either ignoring protocol or forgetting it. If he hoped to solve the murder, then the acting marshal was going to need help. The lawman didn't know Buckhorn, had always been contemptuous of the town and its residents and if rumors were true, had a grudge against Vi. He'd heard talk that Yarrow had asked her out on a date not all that long ago. He found that hard to believe. But maybe the two would have made a great pair. Except according to the rumor, Vi had offered no mercy in the way she turned Yarrow down. Apparently he'd given her an earful back before storming out of the store.

Jaxson felt he had come to know Buckhorn through Luna Declan's eyes and ears. The hairdresser had only been in town for less than a year, but she had a keen eye and people seemed to trust her. Not to mention how her clients often relaxed while having their hair done and told her things.

She'd relayed these stories to him, so he had a pretty good feel for the town and the people living here.

The problem would be narrowing down the suspects. He still couldn't believe someone had killed Vi Mullen. Killed in her own store. Who would have the fortitude to confront her and why? Yarrow had to know that it wouldn't be easy to get those answers. While roots ran deep in Buckhorn, so did grudges from what Luna had told him.

Also, he suspected that despite Vi's irascible personality and ability to make enemies at every turn, the residents would pull together to protect one of their own—even a murderer. With the residents standing together, it would make it hard to find the killer—especially if Yarrow was the one asking the questions.

The coroner knocked at the back door, announcing himself. Yarrow went to let him in, saying over his shoulder, "Don't touch anything," as if to remind Jaxson who was in charge. Like he'd forgotten. Like Yarrow would ever let him.

Jaxson quickly took more photos of the crime scene. The crime techs were outside getting evidence from the back steps. The acting marshal would want to solve this one on his own just to show Marshal Leroy Baggins and everyone else who'd thought he wasn't up for the job. Because of that, he might keep things from Jaxson, including important information about the crime.

As Jaxson started to pocket his phone, he looked to see if Luna had tried to reach him again. He answered her text, asking if something had happened with her father. If everything was all right?

He heard Yarrow's cell phone ring as he ushered the coroner in. Excusing himself, the acting marshal stepped outside into the alley as Coroner Bob Langstone entered the back of the store. Jaxson greeted him, anxious to hear what the coroner had to say about the crime, and pocketed his phone.

Langstone was a large robust man whose main job was that of veterinarian, but he filled in as coroner when needed. Jaxson had heard from Luna, who cut Langstone's hair at her salon, that Bob enjoyed reading murder mysteries and discussing old unsolved murder cases.

"Mornin'," Langstone said, giving him a nod before his gaze shifted to the murder victim.

Jaxson nodded and watched the coroner take in the crime scene. He knew from scuttlebutt that Langstone was good at his job and respected by the state medical examiner for his thoroughness. He was relieved that the more local man had gotten this call rather than a coroner from Billings, three hours away.

The coroner wasted little time to glove up and go to work. Jaxson wondered if any of his theories could be backed up by forensic evidence. "Was she standing or lying down when she was impaled?"

The coroner was on the floor next to the victim, gingerly inspecting the wound without touching the handle of the spear. "I'd say down since the tips of the spear have gone all the way through her body and now seem to be imbedded in the worn pine flooring. She's going to have to be pried up. If the barbs have sunk so deep, removing the body might mean pulling up some of the floorboards."

"How much strength would it take to drive a spear though her?"

Langstone seemed to consider the question for a moment. "I don't know if you've ever speared fish, but there is some weight to the stainless steel spear, along with the very sharp barbed points. The implement is made to pierce the scales of a large fish like northern pike, the barbs making it easy to lift the fish from the water without it coming off the spikes. The killer wouldn't have had to put much force into the blow with the victim already down."

That followed Jaxson's theory that there had probably been an altercation that had resulted in Vi being knocked to the floor, just as he'd suspected. Johnny Berg had said that the back door was not just unlocked, but slightly ajar, and the only light that had been turned on was in the storage room. Vi had been expecting the delivery. The back door was often left unlocked after Vi came in, Berg had said. So anyone in town could have known that and just walked in—just as Berg had.

Unless the killer had already been in the store waiting, Jaxson thought with a start. He wondered how many people in town had a key to the store.

"So the killer could have been a woman or someone who wasn't necessarily strong and powerful." The coroner nodded. "Do you think she was conscious when she was speared?"

"I don't see an evidence of a head injury," the coroner said. "Depends on how hard she hit the floor when she went down. Could have been dazed. Or the killer could have acted so quickly she didn't have time to try to defend herself." Langstone glanced up at him and smiled with approval. "You noticed there are no defensive wounds."

He'd already figured that Vi hadn't been afraid of her killer. The attack itself might have been a surprise since Vi hadn't had her keys or phone to call for help.

"It's possible her attacker hadn't planned to kill her,"

Jaxson said. "If it was premeditated, wouldn't the killer have used the weapon he or she brought?"

"Unless things escalated too quickly," Langstone said. "The killer could have grabbed what was handy, afraid the victim was going to put up a fight once she was on her feet again." The coroner glanced at the full rack of spears right next to the body with the price tags dangling from the handles.

"Vi wouldn't have taken the attack lying down, so to speak," Jaxson said. So did that mean whoever had killed her had been afraid of her? Or had Vi been the one who wasn't afraid even after she'd been knocked down during the confrontation? That definitely didn't leave out a female killer. "She would have come up fighting—if she'd gotten the chance or felt the need to." He looked down at the body on the floor. "But once the killer had the spear in his or her hands, there was no doubt of the outcome if the weapon was used."

Langstone agreed. "A deadly act of opportunity," he said, nodding toward the rack of spears. Vi was a slim woman and the sharp spear had been nine-pronged wide. "But given the way the spear prongs impaled her... I'd say the killer was committed. He or she had to have known the weapon would kill the victim."

Maybe the killer had intended just to scare Vi. But once the attacker picked up the spear, things had turned murderous. Jaxson tried to imagine who in the town of Buckhorn would have been driven to murder as Langstone rose to his feet.

"You can let the crime techs in," the coroner said. "Is there a carpenter in town? We're going to need some help freeing the body from the floor."

"Dave Tanner," he said. "He owns the bar. He and his fiancée, Melissa, still live above the business while their house is being built."

"You seem to know a lot about Buckhorn," Langstone noted.

Thanks to Luna, he thought, and again worried as to why she'd left town, apparently unexpectedly—and in a hurry. "I've kind of been dating a woman who lives here. I believe she cuts your hair."

Langstone chuckled. "Luna. That would explain it. I would imagine everyone in Buckhorn bares his and her soul to her."

"She's like a priest or a lawyer anyway," Jaxson said. "She keeps the names to herself."

"Even when it comes to murder?" the coroner asked.

He wondered about that himself as Yarrow followed the crime scene techs in, locking the door behind him. Was it possible Luna's leaving had something to do with Vi's murder? He told himself it had to be a coincidence, but it still bothered him since it had seemed so abrupt.

Stepping out of the way, Jaxson listened as the coroner filled in the acting marshal on the problem with removing the body. Yarrow made some displeased sounds before he got a call and excused himself, again going out the way he'd just come in. Jaxson got the impression that the call was personal rather than business.

On his way out, Yarrow called back over his shoulder, "Gray, stay to make sure no one else comes through here. Then I need you to check any surveillance cameras. If someone entered the store and then left by the front door, they would have been caught on camera."

"If Vi had a security camera," Jaxson said. "Vi didn't

like technology, did everything old-school, still had that old-fashioned cash register her grandparents used."

Yarrow stopped in the doorway and swore. "There must be some surveillance cameras around town. See if any have a view of the front or back of the store." He turned to the crime techs who promised to lock up when they were finished and put crime scene tape on the doors. Focusing on Jaxson again, the acting marshal said, "When you're through, meet me at the café."

"The café?" Jaxson couldn't help his surprise.

Yarrow unlocked the back door, "I have a crime to solve. But first the next of kin have to be notified. Then it's time for breakfast." With that, he was gone.

EARL RAY CAULFIELD was surprised to find an officer of the law standing in his doorway. The town war hero, he'd met Deputy Kenneth Yarrow a time or two over the years. He kept his feelings about the man to himself.

"Deputy Yarrow," he said by way of greeting.

"It's Acting Marshal Yarrow," the man said.

"That's right, Leroy's on his honeymoon. What do you hear from him and TJ?"

"This isn't a social call, Mr. Caulfield," Yarrow said, removing his Stetson. "And I'd prefer not to speak on your doorstep."

"Sorry," Earl Ray said and stepped aside. "Please, come in." He ushered the lawman into the living room and offered him coffee and a seat, but Yarrow said he wouldn't be staying that long.

"Vivian Mullen was murdered this morning."

Earl Ray was seldom at a loss for words. Lowering himself into a chair, he said honestly, "I'm sorry to hear that. *Murdered?*" People had threatened to kill Vi over the years—some with good reason. Earl Ray himself had known the feeling more than once. She'd been a difficult woman.

His initial shock though turned to immediate concern for his daughter, Tina, and granddaughter, Chloe. He'd only recently learned that Tina was his daughter after believing for years that Vi was Tina's birth mother. Instead it had been Earl Ray's own wife who'd given birth to Tina. That baby had been switched with Vi's stillborn after Earl Ray's wife had wanted nothing to do with her infant daughter.

But biology aside, for over thirty years Vi had been the only mother Tina had known. Unless it was too late, he wanted to be the one to tell her of Vi's death.

"Have you notified her family?" Earl Ray asked the lawman still standing in the middle of the room.

"I was hoping you'd help with that," Yarrow said. "I'm told you're the person to speak to about this. That you know everyone in town."

Earl Ray nodded. "I'd be happy to notify the next of kin. I'm close to Vi's daughter." He didn't want to take the time to explain. It was too complicated and only a handful of people knew the truth.

"Also at some point, I'd like to talk to you about who in town might have wanted Vi Mullen dead," the lawman said.

Earl Ray sighed. "A list of suspects could take a while. I'll have to get back to you. Where was Vi killed?"

"At the store." Yarrow put his Stetson back on and headed for the door. Earl Ray had hoped for more information but saw that it wasn't forthcoming. He'd find out everything soon enough, he told himself. Right now he was anxious to get over to Tina's house.

LUNA KNEW THAT the Jaxson Gray the elderly gardener was talking about was the same Jaxson Gray she'd been dating. Still, she pulled out her phone, called up the photos her father had sent her and chose one from high school. "Are we talking about the same Jaxson Gray?"

The man stared at the photo for a long time before handing the phone back. "That's him. Nice kid. Never had it easy but with that scholarship to the university and his skills, he could have done all right for himself." He shook his head. "Terrible tragedy that he didn't go on to play ball. But when Amy disappeared like that, I guess I couldn't blame him. Always wondered what happened to him."

Luna quickly shifted mental gears. "You mentioned an… Amy?"

"Amy Franklin," the man said and shook his head again. "I told my wife that girl was all wrong for Jaxson. She was trouble. Anyone could see it."

"Anyone but Jaxson?" she asked.

"Exactly. He must have had a soft spot for her," the man said, tapping his heart with his right hand. "Why else would he let her move into his house? He probably thought he could help her. But a girl like that…" He shook his head. "Rough, if you know what I mean? If she was pregnant… Well, I wouldn't have been surprised if it wasn't even his." He clamped his lips down as if surprised he'd said so much. Clearly he hadn't thought about Jaxson and Amy in a long time, but he hadn't forgotten that old anger and confusion.

"Someone must know what happened to her," Luna said. "Maybe a good friend of hers or Jaxson's?"

"You sure you aren't one of those reporters?" he asked, eyeing her warily again.

"I'm sure. Please, I came all this way. I just want to find

out everything I can. My friend knew him way back when. Middle school maybe? I guess Jaxson was a pretty good athlete even then." She knew that athletes who were rewarded scholarships to play college ball were often gifted from a young age.

"Right, your friend. I have to get back to work." He started the mower's engine but didn't move right away. Over the noise, he said, "Try the library. Katie might help you. She was Jaxson's girl. Until Amy came along."

Like Buckhorn, the people in this town shared history. They knew everyone's business—especially when two of them went missing.

Luna stepped out of the way as the elderly man shifted the mower into gear. For a moment though, she stood staring at the school, wondering what Jaxson had been like back then. He'd filled out a lot since high school. Could he have had a successful football career? Why had he given it up? So many unanswered questions, she thought as she headed for her SUV parked at the curb.

RELIEVED TO HAVE the next of kin being notified, Acting Marshal Ken Yarrow headed for the café. He was hungry and dying for coffee even though he knew it would only upset his already churning stomach. Gallbladder probably, his doctor had told him. Something about his age, his job, his stressful home life. *Welcome to the real world*, he thought angrily. Like he could do anything about his age or his job. His home life though, well, that was something he was going to have to deal with—but had been putting off.

He radioed Jaxson for an update, getting a longer one than he'd wanted. The crime scene was secure, the techs were at work, the coroner and some carpenter were planning to take a power saw to the floor around the body to transport it when the techs were finished. His deputy was probably asking them dozens of questions. Yarrow was glad to leave him at it. He would read the autopsy and crime tech report when they were finished.

With everyone doing their jobs, he entered the Buckhorn Café and took a seat at the counter. Even before he ordered a short stack, bacon and coffee, he knew he'd come to the right place.

News traveled at a startling speed in these small towns. If you wanted the gossip, you went to the local bar. Too early for the bar? Then you went to the local café.

A large round booth full of old hens were discussing Vi and her murder in hushed tones, but plenty loud enough since most of the women appeared to be hard of hearing. He could tell that this group had probably been gathering here on a morning like this for years. He had a good view of them reflected in the glass of the pie case as he sipped his coffee and, taking out his notebook and pen, began to make a list of suspects, one for him and one for Jaxson to follow up on as he waited for his breakfast order.

"I still can't believe it," said a soft-spoken small grayhaired woman in pearls and what used to be a housedress. "Why it wasn't that long ago that Vi was sitting right there where you are Mabel." She shuddered. "*Murdered*. My word."

"Clarice is right," said the solidly built older woman apparently named Mabel. "I remember that morning Vi stopped by all in a fiddle over Gertrude down at the gas station. It was always something with Vi. Always butting into other people's business, just looking for trouble. Well, it looks like it found her this time if what we heard is true."

"I heard that the young man who discovered her body had tracked her blood all over the store," a shy-sounding woman said.

"Oh, Lynette, don't remind us how Vi was about her wood floors. She would have been so upset," said another woman, her white hair in a tight perm against her head, her pink scalp showing through. "She was always admonishing everyone not to track up her floor."

"I wonder who killed her," Mabel said.

The women all looked around the table at each other, blinking like owls, for a few moments. "None of us," Clarice said as if offended.

"I wouldn't know an ice fishing spear from a shovel," Lynette added. "How about you, Rose?"

The elderly woman with the tight white curls looked taken aback. "I'm not sure I've ever even seen one. What do they look like?"

"About the size of a shovel but with a bunch of sharp spikes for spearing fish," Mabel said. "They aren't lightweight either. It would have taken some strength."

"Are you saying it had to be a man who killed her?" Lynette asked.

"There are women around who might be plenty strong if they were mad enough," Clarice said. "Not that I have anyone in mind."

"Plenty of people probably wanted to kill Vi," Rose agreed. "She could be quite cruel at times."

"She was mean as a mad rattlesnake," Clarice said, making them all turn to look at her. The demure petite woman patted her pearls at her neck. "Not to speak ill of the dead."

"Yes, we shouldn't, but it's nothing we all haven't said

about her when Vi was alive," Mabel said. "Half this town had reason to want Vi dead at one time or another."

The acting marshal thought she was right and wondered how in the devil they would get to the truth.

"But why this morning?" Mabel continued. "Has something happened that I haven't heard about?"

There was a general shaking of heads. But he noticed that one of them seemed to drop her gaze to the table and began wiping the condensation off her water glass. *Lynette*, he thought. Wasn't that her name? She knew something.

He added her to his list and looked up as his young deputy came in. Jaxson removed his Stetson and threw a long leg over the stool next to him.

From the kitchen, the café owner Bessie Caulfield called, "What can I get you, Jaxson?" Bessie, somewhere in her late fifties to early sixties, wore her long gray hair in a braid that fell halfway down her back. A handsome woman, she had the bluest eyes Ken thought he'd ever seen as she smiled at the deputy with obvious affection.

"The usual. Thanks, Bessie." As if realizing his boss had turned to stare at him, Jaxson turned to face him. "I eat here a lot."

In exasperation, Ken said, "Well?"

"Oh," the young deputy said and lowered his voice. "Dave from over at the bar brought a saw from his shop to cut the flooring around the victim before I left. They had plenty of help and the crime techs are going to be there for a while, so I checked on the surveillance cameras. Very few in town. But I did find one on the building Mel owns, Dave's fiancée."

Jaxson pulled out his phone, called up the short clip from this morning, and handed his phone over.

Ken watched it. The resolution wasn't good, but the camera did catch someone coming out of the store. The figure was wearing a Western hat pulled low, a long stock coat and boots. Obviously not wanting to be recognized, the person kept his or her head down as they disappeared from view.

"Man or woman?" he asked the deputy, who shook his head.

"Hard to tell. But I suspect it's our killer."

He handed the phone back as Bessie brought out Jaxson's order and the deputy dove into it. Ken had barely touched his own breakfast. The phone call from his neighbor earlier still had him upset—not to mention Vi's murder here in Buckhorn. The neighbor had called about Ken's live-in girlfriend—and what she'd possibly been up to. He had a bad feeling she was running around on him behind his back.

He heard the café door open, felt the breeze but didn't turn to see who had come in until he heard the first blood-curdling scream. Bessie came barreling out of the kitchen to freeze, all the color draining from her face.

Turning, Ken got the shock of his life.

The dead woman he'd seen not twenty minutes ago with a spear pinioning her to the floorboards had just walked into the café.

CHAPTER SIX

THE HEIGHTS LIBRARY was right where the older gentleman had said it would be in a small brick building. In the glow of the setting sun, a display of books in the window caught her eye. She loved to read so took a moment to check out the titles before pushing open the door and stepping inside. She took in a deep breath, loving the smell of books. As she drank it in, a bell tinkled softly over her head and the door closed behind her.

Luna stood for a moment in the cool quiet before she saw the young blonde woman behind the checkout desk. "Hello," she said quietly, thinking of the hours she'd spent as a girl in her hometown library before coming home with a pile of books each week. She would take them down to her mother's salon, back when they were called beauty parlors, and curl up in a corner to read for hours.

As she approached the desk, she saw the nameplate. Katie Brooks, Librarian. Her gaze shot up to the woman. She was older than she'd appeared at a distance, but still younger than Luna. She was struck by how small, demure and pretty she was. It made her wonder about Amy, the young woman who, according to the gardener, had stolen Jaxson away from Katie and ruined his life by disappearing.

"May I help you?" Katie had a soft Southern drawl, her wide welcoming smile and those big blue bottomless eyes making her even more attractive.

Luna wondered what Amy must look like if Jaxson had dumped this beautiful young woman for her. She found herself tongue-tied. This was Jaxson's girl—until Amy came along. Wasn't that what the gardener had said? She couldn't help the twinge of jealousy almost as strong as what she anticipated feeling when she finally saw a photo of Amy Franklin. She wished she'd known the Jaxson these two women had dated. With at least Amy, he'd cared enough about her to lie about her being his dead wife.

"I'm interested in some old yearbooks from the old high school."

Katie arched one eyebrow. "What year?"

She told the librarian the three years she was most interested in and saw curiosity in the woman's gaze. But Katie said nothing as she came out from behind the desk and led the way down an aisle of books to the back. "If you'd like to have a seat, I'll bring them to you."

Taking a chair at a small table, Luna sat down. A few minutes later, Katie brought her three school annuals. "Just leave them on the desk. I'll put them away later." She noticed that there didn't seem to be another soul in the library.

Luna waited until the woman had returned to her post at the front desk before she opened the first yearbook. It took only a few moments to find Jaxson's photos. Class photo and five other ones of him, most dealing with sports, a couple like the ones her father had sent her. She was struck by how handsome Jaxson was at such a young vulnerable age and how obviously popular he'd been. He could have had any girl he wanted.

She opened the next yearbook. Older, but still drop-dead gorgeous. Again, a nice class photo. More sports photos and... She slowed, her heart squeezing a little, at a junior prom photo of Jaxson and a very young Katie. It was the starry-eyed way Jaxson was looking at the girl, his arm around her, his smile so sweet and innocent. But it was Katie's expression of raw naked love that squeezed her heart painfully. How much longer after this photo was taken had Amy come into the picture? she wondered.

Luna closed the annual, feeling uneasy at having witnessed the intimate moment between the two. She tried to imagine what could have happened to come between them. Surely it was more than Amy Franklin. She reminded herself it was high school, a very emotional, hormonal, unpredictable time in all their lives.

In the next annual, she found Jaxson's senior photo. Her heart did a little bump in her chest. He really was too good-looking, but also even in the photo she could see the sweet, considerate man she'd come to know. There was a generosity about him. A caring that she'd found touching.

She had to remind herself that she couldn't trust any of that since he'd lied about everything. She found the senior prom photo, only this time there was a dark-haired girl standing next to Jaxson. She had big brown eyes and was looking directly at the camera, almost in challenge. Jaxson seemed almost bored and definitely appeared uncomfortable as he looked toward the camera. There wasn't that touching raw love she'd seen in Katie's photo. Instead she saw what the gardener must have seen. Amy Franklin looked like trouble and Jaxson looked as if he already knew it.

Luna closed the annual and sat for a moment, knowing she was going to have to ask Katie about Jaxson.

HOPING HE WASN'T too late, Earl Ray went straight to his daughter's house. He knew Tina would be up. Mothers of young children, especially a new baby who was only a few months old, didn't get to sleep in and Tina's husband, Lars, would already be gone to work. Lars was Buckhorn's handyman and had several employees who he could call when needed. He saw that the streets were plowed in winter, that fallen trees from storms were hauled away and did general maintenance.

Tapping on the front door, Earl Ray could hear the patter of small feet even before he heard his granddaughter Chloe's delightful voice on the other side of the door. Chloe was opening the door even as Tina was calling for her to wait. While most Buckhorn residents didn't even bother to lock their doors, he could see how Tina might be wary after everything she'd been through. A recent visitor had been her cousin, Jennifer, who was now again safely behind bars in the criminally insane ward at the state mental hospital.

"Good morning," he said the moment he saw Chloe's smiling face and heard her say excitedly, "It's Grandpa." She had only recently started calling him that and each time he heard it, his heart soared a little higher. Tina though hadn't called him dad yet and he could understand. It would be hard to find out the man she thought was her father wasn't—especially in her thirties.

His daughter appeared around the edge of the door, holding his grandson in her arms. "Good morning," she said, opening the door wider with her foot.

"Good morning," he said as he scooped up Chloe with the other arm. As he stepped in, he set his four-year-old granddaughter down and met Tina's gaze.

She must have seen something in his expression. He was surprised how much his daughter was like him. They read each other well, which pleased him. They'd bonded much faster than either of them had expected.

"Chloe, I don't think your grandpa has seen your new shoes that light up." Instantly the girl raced toward the stairs. The moment she was out of earshot, Tina turned back to him, motioning him in and asking, "What's wrong?"

He saw no reason to beat around the bush. "It's your..." He had started to say *mother* since Tina still called Vi *mom*. Vi had been heartbroken to find out that Tina wasn't the biological daughter she'd given birth to. Her daughter had been stillborn. "It's Vi."

Tina sighed as she cradled her son, Lars Earl Ray Olson or L. Ray as he was called, to her chest, rocking him as she headed for the kitchen. "I just put a pot of coffee on. I might need a cup before you tell me what Vi's done now."

He followed her into the neat cheery kitchen and took his grandson from her arms. "There is no easy way to say this." Tina had been reaching for a mug when she stopped to look at him. "I'm afraid she's dead. Murdered. Down at the store." Holding L. Ray with one hand, he quickly reached for his daughter as she suddenly swayed. Catching her, he led her over to a chair at the table as Chloe came racing into the room with her new shoes on her feet.

His granddaughter danced around to show him how the shoes lit up when she moved as he placed L. Ray into Tina's arms and watched her struggle to recover from the shock.

"I love them," Earl Ray said to his granddaughter. "Do they make them in my size? Because I want a pair."

"Grandpa, don't be silly."

"Could you get me a glass of water?" Tina asked.

Earl Ray started to turn toward the sink, but his daughter placed a hand on his arm as Chloe yelled, "I'll get it, Mommy."

"How? I mean, who?" she said to him as he took a chair next to her. She was looking down at her son, clearly finding strength in his cherub face.

"I don't know. I spoke with Acting Marshal Kenneth Yarrow. At this point, they don't know much. But I'll tell you anything I find out."

Tina nodded and took the glass of water her daughter had brought her, then Chloe told her grandpa that she also had a new doll. She raced away to get it.

"Vi made so many enemies," his daughter said with a shake of her head. "But I still can't imagine anyone would…" She took a drink of her water before she said, "I'll have to make arrangements."

Earl Ray shook his head. "There will have to be an autopsy so it will be a while before you need worry about any of that. I'll be happy to help any way I can."

Tina smiled, tears springing to her eyes. "Of course they won't be releasing her body yet." She began to cry, leaning into Earl Ray as he put an arm around her, thankful he was there for her. The man she'd called father for most of her thirtysomething years had deserted her and Vi some time ago.

With a start, he realized that Vi's ex, Axel Mullen, should be at the top of the suspect list after all the threats he'd made against the woman during the divorce.

This was going to get ugly, he realized. All of Buckhorn could be dragged through the dirt. He knew everyone in town and had for years. He couldn't bear the thought of how bad it was going to get for everyone—especially Tina.

He hated for her to have to go through this. He just hoped the killer was caught quickly.

JAXSON SHOVED BACK his almost-empty plate and shot to his feet as confusion in the café became chaos. He couldn't believe what he was seeing any more than anyone else. At the sight of the woman standing in the doorway, Clarice Barber had fainted and slid to the floor under the table of the large round booth. Lynette Crest was crying and crossing herself.

Mabel Aldrich was muttering, "I told you to never speak ill of the dead."

Still shocked himself, Jaxson stared at the woman who'd come into the café. She was the spitting image of Vi Mullen. If he hadn't known for a fact that Vi was dead... Whoever this doppelgänger was, she was enjoying this, he realized.

It was Bessie who recovered first. She hurried to the large booth and stooped down to help the woman who'd fainted. "Here, Clarice, let me help you up. Did she hit her head?" she asked the group.

"Rose, get your smelling salts out of your purse," Mabel ordered even as they still stared at the woman in the doorway. Rose Hanson dug hurriedly in her purse.

"I knew Vi couldn't be dead," one of them said. "She was too mean to die."

"So why has she come back from the dead?" another asked.

"That's not Vi," Bessie snapped as she took the smelling salts from Rose. Clarice took a whiff, her eyes flying open. Handing the salts back, she helped Clarice up and into the booth again, and turned to face the woman still standing just inside the café door. "That's Vera."

"Vera?" several of the older women echoed.

"Vi's twin," Bessie said, glaring at the woman who gave her a salute and what could be taken for a smile.

"Vi told me she was dead," Mabel said accusingly.

"She told everyone her twin was dead," Bessie said, sighing as she walked toward Vera. "I'm guessing you've heard about Vi?"

The identical twin nodded. "I heard the moment I drove into town, just minutes ago. There's a crowd outside the store. You know how word travels in Buckhorn." She mugged a face. "But I can't believe that Vi told you I was dead." She sighed dramatically. "Karma is such a bitch, isn't it?"

"What are you doing here after all these years?" Bessie demanded. "You're timing might be considered…suspicious, wouldn't you say?"

"I just had a feeling my sister needed me." Vera sniffed and drew a handkerchief from her pocket to dab at her dry eyes. "I drove all night from the coast. I couldn't shake the feeling that she was in trouble and needed me. I've always been a little psychic when it came to Vi. It's a twin thing."

"Don't you mean psychotic?" Bessie said.

Vera smiled at that. "I just knew that something was wrong, but unfortunately I arrived too late."

"Is that right?" Bessie glanced toward Jaxson and the acting marshal. "I'm betting the law officers here would like to hear all about it."

Jaxson had watched all of this play out before him, unsure what to do. Yarrow hadn't even risen from his stool at the counter. Had Luna ever mentioned that Vi had a twin? He didn't think so. It probably had never come up because apparently the woman had been gone for years and was believed dead.

"You're certainly a dead ringer for Vi," he said, still recovering from the shock.

"Identical in more ways than you can imagine," Bessie said over her shoulder to him as she headed toward the kitchen where something was burning. He heard her angrily banging pans around in there moments later.

Jaxson agreed with Bessie. It seemed more than a coincidence that the twin would turn up now. "How long did you say you've been in town?" he asked the woman, thinking she'd just been moved up to prime suspect in the murder investigation.

"I just arrived and heard the news, Deputy," she said, sniffing and dabbing at her eyes again. "If you're thinking I might have harmed my sister…" She shook her head. "I was miles from here when she died." Before Jaxson could ask how she knew the time of her sister's death, Vera put her hand over her heart. "I felt it the moment life left her."

Jaxson could hear the older women at the table whispering among themselves. No one seemed happy to see Vi's twin—especially after hearing from Vi that Vera was dead. According to the gossip now whirling round the café, Vera had left Buckhorn years ago after a fight with her sister when they were both young. She'd never returned. Until now. *Quite the coincidence*, Jaxson thought, not sure he believed it any more than he did in the twin thing Vera had mentioned.

Behind him, he heard Yarrow finally rise from his stool. "I'm Acting Marshal Kenneth Yarrow," he said as he stepped past Jaxson to address the woman. "What is your name?"

"Vera," she said with a flirtatious grin. "Vera Carter. I was named after my mother since I was the first one out of the womb, something Vi could never get over." She laughed, cocking her head to the side a little as she took in Yarrow.

She was dressed much like Vi had always dressed and had the same haircut, a dark bowl cut, that emphasized their mirror image, Jaxson noted. He wondered how long Vera had worn her hair like that or if she'd had it done that way just for this reunion. Or maybe it really was a twin thing.

"I'm going to want to talk to you about your sister and her murder," Yarrow said, apparently unfazed by the woman's obvious flirting. "How long are you planning to be in town?"

"Funny you should ask," Vera said with another sniff and dab with her handkerchief. "I was planning to surprise my sister with the good news. I've come home. I'm back in Buckhorn as long as it takes for my sister's murderer to be caught. Also to make sure she gets the burial she deserves."

"Then I shouldn't have any trouble finding you to ask you a few questions," Yarrow said.

Vera grinned. "I look forward to it, Marshal."

CHAPTER SEVEN

JOHNNY BERG HAD been too shaken up to finish his route. Not to mention the fact that the crime scene techs had taken his fingerprints as well as his new Vans sneakers because of the blood on them. They'd also taken photographs of his jean pant legs and his hands and shirt.

With each passing minute, he felt more spooked, his nerves shot. It was bad enough that they were treating him like he'd killed Vi. But the worst part was that the killer might have seen him and thought he'd seen something.

"You've had a shock. Take the rest of the day off," his boss had said as the other drivers unloaded his truck and divvied up his packages.

He'd almost argued that he was fine, but he couldn't very well make his deliveries without shoes. As he'd driven his beat-up old sedan away from work, it dawned on him how alone he was. His friends were all at work. He was basically barefoot, which meant there was only one place he could go.

Home.

Just the thought of going back to his empty apartment sent a ripple of terror through him. Normally he couldn't wait to get off work and go home. His apartment was large and roomy and cheap. Real cheap since he had a whole floor to himself in the dilapidated apartment house. When he'd heard about the place, his friend had told him that it was haunted.

Johnny had scoffed. "Oooooo, I'm scared," he'd joked with a laugh. When he'd seen the place, he understood why his friend had said that. The apartment house had definitely seen better days. The bank had foreclosed after the last owner had gone delinquent on the payments, but even the bank hadn't been able to sell it and the rent was dirt cheap. There was talk of it being torn down. Or burned down.

But until then Johnny had the whole third floor to himself. He called it the penthouse since it was the top floor. He'd taken the largest of the upstairs apartments and used the other two smaller units for storage. It had been ideal. His friends loved it since they could be as noisy as they wanted.

There were only two other renters. Both lived on the first floor. The male renter traveled and was hardly ever around. The female was somewhere in her late eighties and, from what he'd gathered, deaf as a doornail. He'd heard her moving around in there with her walker or her cane as he passed each day and headed for the stairs, but he'd never seen her. She kept to herself, which was fine with him.

Now though, the spooky-looking place held no appeal. Still, with nowhere to go without shoes, he headed home, all the time trying to convince himself that he wasn't in any danger. The deputy had told him that he doubted the killer would come after him since, as he'd said, he hadn't seen anyone. Yet he found himself watching his rearview mirror.

Maybe worse, he couldn't quit thinking about the dark shadowed places inside the Buckhorn General Store and who might have been hiding there, watching him. He shuddered, feeling as if he'd barely missed a bullet. Only in this case, it could have been an ice fishing spear to the back.

He shuddered as he realized that with his music blasting in his ears, he wouldn't have heard the killer coming.

VERA CARTER COULDN'T wipe her smile off her face as she left the café. She'd caused a stir even better than she'd hoped. All those old ladies had thought they'd seen Vi's ghost. They'd also thought they'd seen the last of Vi's twin.

Well, surprise! Vera loved that she'd even made one of those old bags faint. They deserved it. The way they used to gossip about her and look down their noses at her when she was a girl. Vi had excelled at everything. Was it any wonder that Vera felt she couldn't get out of Buckhorn fast enough—especially after what had happened between her and her sister?

"I get the feeling that you've never felt guilty—not even for what you did to your sister?" Strangely it had been the first man she'd ever confessed her sins to who'd asked her that.

"Why would I? I didn't do anything that my sister wouldn't have done to me."

"You sure about that?"

Vera had dumped him and hadn't shared her reasons for leaving Buckhorn all those years ago with anyone else. She wasn't sure why she'd shared it in the first place with some man she'd picked up in a bar. Because she *had* felt guilty?

She scoffed at that now as she climbed into her rattletrap of an SUV and headed down the road to where she'd been told her sister had built a house for herself in the mountains. She didn't feel the least bit guilty about anything, she told herself. Vi had stayed in Buckhorn and taken everything that their parents had left them. Vera had never gotten her share. Until now.

She looked to the mountains, caught a glimpse of gleaming windows and towering stone walls. Vi was dead and the way Vera saw it, everything was now hers. *The store, the antique barn, the family property and Vi's new house*, she thought as it came into view.

Vera didn't expect there would be any legal battles over Vi's estate. She was her twin sister. True, there was a daughter, she reminded herself, but not by blood. She smiled again at how fateful it had been running into Vi's ex-husband recently and finding out that Tina Mullen wasn't really Vi's birth daughter at all. Their father had made sure that everything he'd built in Buckhorn couldn't be lost in a divorce or a sibling squabble. He'd put his holdings into a trust. As long as both sisters were alive, nothing could be sold without the other one agreeing.

Vi would never have agreed. Only on her death would Vera finally get what she deserved.

No, she told herself, she felt no guilt at all. She was back and everyone in town might as well get used to it—for as long as she stayed. As she pulled into the drive of Vi's house, she let out a whistle. The house was larger and more beautiful than she'd even imagined and there was a brand-new fancy SUV sitting in the driveway. Vi must have walked to work this morning to save on gas. What a cheapskate.

Vera laughed. She'd hit the jackpot in so many ways with Vi's death. No wonder everyone thought she'd killed her twin. It seemed they were both getting what they deserved.

Vera's smile broadened as she opened the door to her sister's house—her house now—and saw that it was just as nice inside as out. It was just like Vi to build herself a nice house after Axel left her. During their marriage, Vi and Axel had lived over the store for years before renting a house in town. It took Axel leaving before her sister spent the money to have a house built. And what a house it was.

"This will do nicely," Vera said out loud as she closed the door behind her and, dropping her purse on the entry table, stepped into the living room.

"What took you so long?"

She smiled as Axel Mullen appeared from down one of the hallways. "Sure didn't take *you* long."

He moved to her, taking her in his arms. "I'm betting you had to go downtown first to let everyone know you were back."

She smiled at the memory. "Clarice Barber fainted and slid under the table at the café. Took smelling salts to bring her around."

Axel laughed, kissed her and turned to walk into the kitchen. A wall of glass faced to the west with a great view of Buckhorn in the distance, she noted as she joined him. "I'll have whatever you're having," she said to Axel as he helped himself to Vi's liquor.

She glanced around, pleased. This would work perfectly— at least until she sold off everything that the family—and poor Vi—had built in Buckhorn all these years. There was no way she was staying here longer than she had to.

This house and everything else should bring in a pretty penny.

Axel handed her a cocktail. "To us," he said as they clinked glasses and he gave her the smile that she knew had stolen her sister's heart. "And our bright future."

If he only knew, she thought as she took a sip of her drink. Vera had it all, everything that Vi had once owned— including Axel. At least until she sold everything—and left Axel like the way she'd found him, broke and down on his luck.

But in the meantime, she couldn't wait to get him into Vi's bed.

She made a silent toast to her sister. *To you, Vi.*

LUNA LEFT THE high school annuals on the table just as Katie had told her to do and walked to the checkout counter. She wasn't sure exactly how to broach the subject of Jaxson Gray.

"Did you find what you needed?" the attractive blonde asked.

Had she? Not really, but if she asked about Jaxson, how could she avoid telling this woman that he was alive and well in Montana? If Jaxson wanted Katie and the rest of this town to be aware of his existence, he would have let them know.

But that did raise the question of why he'd left as he had and why he apparently hadn't been in touch since then. Or had he?

She met the woman's guileless blue eyes and felt a twinge of guilt for the lie she was about to tell. "I was curious about a former athlete from here," she said. "I'm a sports reporter for a online news service. I'm doing a follow-up on—"

"Jaxson." The name came out with just enough regret that Luna knew Katie didn't know he was in Montana.

Luna nodded. "I spoke with an older man mowing the lawn at the high school. He told me that you used to date Jaxson." Katie nodded. "Is it true that he just disappeared?" Another nod. "You never heard from him?"

Katie shook her head and busied herself with some papers on the counter for a moment before looking up. "Why would anyone be interested in Jaxson after all this time?"

"There are those who thought he was on his way to the

NFL, that he had an amazing career in front of him, that he could have gone all the way," she said, thinking that at least the gardener at the school thought so. "Do you have any idea why he left or where he went?"

Another shake of the head.

Luna realized that she'd made a rookie mistake in her inquiry. She'd asked questions that required only a nod or head shake in answer. "I would imagine you were the last person he spoke to before he disappeared."

Katie let out a bitter laugh. "I wouldn't have been the last person he told. We were no longer seeing each other."

"But you were close. He had to have told someone what was going on with him." The young woman shook her head. "You loved him." It wasn't really a question. She could see that even after all these years it was hard for Katie to talk about him. The sympathy Luna felt must have come through in her voice.

Tears welled in the young woman's eyes. "I did. I thought like everyone else that one day, Jaxson and I..." Katie looked toward the front door as the bell tinkled and an elderly woman came in. "I really need to put those annuals back."

"Please," Luna said, touching the woman's hand to detain her. "I know about Amy Franklin. Off the record, what do you think happened to her?"

Katie stayed behind the counter and seemed to wait until the elderly woman was out of earshot before she spoke. "Jaxson didn't harm her. He felt sorry for her. He made a mistake...and then I think he had trouble getting out of it since by then he'd seen a side of her that...scared him."

Scared him? "When did he tell you this?"

"The last time I talked to him, a few weeks before he

and Amy disappeared." She looked away. "He said he was afraid of what Amy would do if he broke up with her."

"He worried that she might kill herself?" Luna asked.

"Or kill them both. I really shouldn't have said that. You aren't going to print any of this, are you?"

"No," Luna assured her. "So he felt bad about your breakup," she guessed. She'd spent enough time with Jaxson that she'd glimpsed into his heart after all these months.

"We'd decided, mostly Jaxson, that since we were going to different universities, we didn't want a long-distance relationship. Had we been engaged, it would have been different." Luna heard a yearning in the woman's voice. Jaxson hadn't been ready for that apparently.

"Not long after that, he'd been drinking at a party and ended up with Amy, her doing." Katie's eyes glazed over as though seeing everything like it were yesterday. "Jaxson had big plans for his future. He wanted to make his mother and his coaches proud. He was excited about his prospects and a little afraid too, I think. He never drank, but that night…"

"He ended up with Amy."

Katie nodded, clearly fighting tears. "It was just one time, that one night, but Amy began to stalk him. He told me he came home one day and she was in his house, talking to his mother, pretending that she and Jaxson were dating. He wanted her out of his life but then she got kicked out of her house and his mother let her move in with them."

"And then she disappeared?"

Katie nodded again. "But he didn't harm her. It wasn't in him. If anything, Amy Franklin disappeared to hurt him, to destroy his life. She was that kind of person."

"If Jaxson had come back…" She saw the answer in Katie's expression even as she shook her head.

"It was over. I saw him at graduation with his mom. But we didn't talk. I never saw him again."

"Do you think Amy's still alive?" Luna had to ask.

The woman seemed to think about that for a moment before she said, "I don't know. She could have taken her own life just as he'd feared. Or she could have killed him." She shrugged again. "I just don't know."

Luna knew that Jaxson was still alive and if Amy was alive and using her real name, the missing person case would have been solved years ago. There was one more question she had to ask, but Katie spoke before she could ask it.

"I haven't thought about all this in years." She wiped at her eyes. "You aren't going to put this in your article?"

"No, but what you've told me might help me solve the mystery of what happened back then, so thank you." Luna had to ask. "If you ever saw Jaxson again…"

Katie shook her head and looked down at the ring on her left hand. It was the first time Luna had noticed the small diamond engagement ring. "I'd be glad that he was okay, but I've moved on. I've put all of that behind me a long time ago."

"Best wishes on your engagement," she said, sorry to have brought up a painful subject even after all these years. First loves were hell, she thought. "Thank you again for your help."

As she left though, she felt sick at heart for what not only Jaxson had gone through, but Katie. She'd loved Jaxson. Luna knew the feeling.

But it still left the question what had happened to Amy

Franklin? Did Jaxson know? She knew there was only one way to find out—straight from the horse's mouth as her mother would have said.

But how dangerous would that be if he'd killed Amy?

CHAPTER EIGHT

Vera took in the house as she drained her glass. She was anxious to explore and just as anxious to get Axel into Vi's bed. "I wonder what this place is worth on the open market?"

"You do realize that everyone including the law is going to think that one of us—"

"Or both of us," she interjected with a grin.

"Killed my ex and your dear sister," he continued before finishing his drink and pouring them both another.

"Let them prove it," she blustered and told herself she would have to watch his drinking, but other than that, she wasn't worried. "Fate did us one hell of a favor, wouldn't you say?"

He laughed and he opened a bottle of champagne. "To finally being with the right sister," he said as the cork blew off, spewing champagne everywhere.

Vera laughed with him even as the old bitterness came to a slow boil in her stomach. All those years ago, she'd seen Axel first. She was the one who'd flirted with him, the one he said he would see later. But that night, he'd stood her up—because he'd been ambushed by her sister, Vi. Axel, fool that he was, couldn't tell them apart. "You got the wrong sister pregnant that night."

He nodded solemnly over the rim of his glass. "I'm sorry about that."

She looked away. "I don't blame you, after all Vi and I were identical—at least physically."

"I realized my mistake but by then it was too late," he said after draining his glass and setting it down. He stepped to her, cupping her shoulders in his hands and sending a fissure of pleasure through her. "Fortunately, it all turned out like it should have."

Vera smiled. Yes, it had. Not to mention how she'd gotten her revenge against her sister by having her own child with Axel. The thought of Jennifer locked up in a mentally insane ward though almost dampened her good spirits. She shoved the thought away.

But it wasn't as easy to tamp down her bitterness.

Vi had gotten everything—Vera, nothing—when their parents died. True, Vera had left Buckhorn secretly pregnant with her sister's husband's child and without a goodbye, running off with a fast-talking man with about as few prospects as she herself had had.

And it wasn't like there had been any real money to be split. Her parents had poured everything into the store, the antique barn, the land around town. Vera had seen Buckhorn as a dead end. She'd expected the town to die and blow away a long time ago.

Her parents had left Vi a whole lot of responsibility and work. Vi being Vi, had taken the challenge by the horns and ridden it like a wild bull. Vera grudgingly admitted that she would never have done it. She would have sold the whole kit and caboodle and never looked back—if she had been able to. Work in that store all these years? That would have been a death sentence.

She chuckled, realizing that as it turned out, the store had been a death sentence for her twin—and a lottery win for her. Plopping down on her sister's couch, she rubbed her hand over the soft expensive fabric. Feeling like a kid in a candy store, she marveled at her good luck. Too bad it had to come at Vi's expense. She shrugged the thought off.

They should celebrate because Axel was right about one thing. Before long the law would come knocking. Clearly, she and Axel had more to gain by Vi's death than anyone in town. For the first time in her life, she was number one—*the number one suspect*, she thought with a laugh.

JOHNNY BERG PULLED UP in front of his apartment house. The place looked worse than he remembered it, paint weathered off, porch railing hanging, two of the front steps rotted away. No wonder kids never came down here to the end of the street to trick or treat. The building *was* scarier—much scarier than when he'd left it early this morning.

He looked around, seeing no one, which came as no surprise. Ethel, the elderly woman who lived on the bottom floor, seldom left her apartment. Gabe's vehicle was gone so he was no doubt on the road again.

There had never been much traffic with the apartment being the last place on the dead-end road. Today was no different. Still Johnny waited for a few more moments before he cut the engine on his small older sedan.

This wasn't like him, he thought as he pulled out his earbuds and turned off his music. He normally came home in the same way he'd left—music blaring, feet dancing, feeling *dope*. He'd felt young, confident and happy with his job and his life since he'd known it was just beginning.

He swallowed and told himself that there wasn't a killer waiting for him inside the old apartment house. Logically the killer probably didn't even know his name, let alone where he lived. Maybe the killer hadn't even seen him at the Buckhorn General Store this morning. Or even if the killer had, didn't mean that the person had any reason to want to kill again.

Johnny considered those arguments for a moment before he opened his car door and stepped out. He thought about turning his music back on. It felt strange not to have it blasting. He listened, heard the sound of a vehicle in the distance, a television was on somewhere down the street, closer a meadowlark broke into song. Even closer his blood thumped in his ears.

Suddenly he felt as if his hearing was too sharp. The porch steps groaned loudly under him. He avoided the missing boards as usual and opened the front door with a creak that sent ice slithering up his spine.

"Is that you, Johnny?" came a high-pitched scared elderly woman's voice from behind the closest door.

"It's me, Ethel," he called back.

"Doesn't sound like you."

He shuffled his feet some, not in the mood for his usual dance up to the top floor.

"Is everything all right?" she asked.

"Rough day," he admitted. "Anyone been around?"

No answer. He realized that she must have moved away from the door. Glancing up the stairs, he was surprised at all the dark shadows. The entryway was lit by only one bare bulb. Slowly he began to climb, all the time listening and thinking how easy it would be for a killer to hide just about anywhere inside this rambling apartment house.

It was a thought he hadn't had before as he suddenly burst into a run, taking the stairs three at a time. At his door, he fumbled with the key, convinced someone was directly behind him, breathing down his neck, and that any moment… He finally got the key in and turned, shoving open the door and practically falling inside. He slammed the door, locked it and leaned against it as he fought to catch his breath.

His life had been going so well, he thought just an instant before he heard one of the floorboards in his bedroom creak. There was someone in there.

Johnny had only an instant to wonder why he hadn't checked every room and whether or not he had time to open the door and run. He realized he didn't have time as he heard the footsteps growing closer. Any moment the person would be coming around the corner.

Looking around wildly for anything he could use as a weapon, he heard another creak, a thump and, grabbing his skateboard by the door, raised it over his head, terrified of what he was about to see.

His former girlfriend stepped out of his bedroom and shrieked when she saw him, covering up his own sound of alarm. "You scared me half to death! What are you doing?" He slowly lowered the skateboard, his blood still pounding wildly. "I thought you were at work. What are you doing here?" she cried, her free hand over her heart.

She had no idea how terrified he'd been, he thought, growing angry as he demanded, "What am *I* doing here? What are *you* doing here?" That's when he noticed what she had in her other hand and saw the answer. "You're *robbing* me?" he cried, thinking that this day couldn't get any crazier.

"I wasn't stealing it," she snapped indignantly. "I was just borrowing a few things." She shrugged and gave him that familiar innocent look that said, *But I'm cute and you like me, huh.*

"Not anymore," he said under his breath. "Put it all back!" he said, advancing on her. His heart was still drumming violently in his chest. If she'd had any idea the kind of day he'd had so far... "All of it." She held some of his favorite band T-shirts, a jean jacket signed by a female guitar player who'd gone on to play in an almost famous band and a silver belt buckle that had belonged to his grandfather. In other words, his most prized possessions. He had no doubt that if he hadn't caught her, all of it—and his skateboard—would have ended up on eBay.

"And give me my spare key," he said as she dropped the loot on the sagging sofa. Her look was insolent as she dug in her pocket and produced the key. Plunking it down in his outstretched hand, she frowned. "You lose your new shoes?"

He realized as she said it, that she'd been looking in his bedroom for his new Vans, planning to sell those as well. Had he not decided to wear them today and worked a full day, they too would be gone.

"You really are a piece of work," he said, shaking his head as he pocketed the key, wondering how many more of his apartment keys were out there in the world. Knowing Bristol, she had probably made duplicates.

"I guess this is it, then," she said, meeting his gaze with a questioning one of her own.

As much as he hated to admit it to himself, for a moment he actually thought about asking the thieving woman to stay at least for the night, maybe even until the killer was caught. It had been on the tip of his tongue as she shrugged and started past him toward the door. Was he really that desperate though?

He let her walk out, leaving the door standing open and him all alone.

THE HIGH WHINE of the saw ripping through the store's floorboards suddenly stopped. Jaxson had been standing close by, the smell of death mixing with that of aged pine flooring turning to sawdust. Dave Tanner warned them that Vi's body, now wrapped in a bag but still attached to the wood, was about to drop into the crawl space and for everyone to be ready. Crime scene techs, the coroner, Jaxon and even Yarrow, who'd just returned, stepped forward. Dave had made handholds on all four sides in the pine floor before he'd sawed all the way around the body.

The saw began to whine again, sawdust flying and, as Jaxson grabbed hold, he felt the floor under Vi drop away a few inches before they were able to raise her on the planks under her. Adjusting their holds, they laid the body and the boards down on a stretcher to be taken out to the waiting coroner's van.

The body covered, Yarrow walked them to the door. Past him, Jaxson could see that a crowd had gathered, but was being held back by the extra law enforcement called in. No camera crews that he could see, but there was one reporter he recognized in the crowd, Darby Cole, from the local online newspaper. Vi would have been disappointed there was so little fanfare, he thought as he and Yarrow closed the door and walked back inside to where the large rectangle hole had been cut in the floorboards. Vi would also have been having a conniption fit to see the mess they had made.

As Jaxson stepped closer to the rectangular hole they'd

made in the floor, he looked past the sawdust and rough edge of the sawn wood to the exposed earth below. His eyes widened in alarm, blood pumped wildly in his ears and bile rose up his throat.

"What the hell is that?" Yarrow said next to him.

Jaxson felt the room begin to spin.

"You look like you could use some air," the acting marshal said.

He nodded, his body vibrating with the shock of what he'd seen as he rushed out the back door, his hands going to his knees as he gasped for air.

Behind him, Yarrow must have finally looked in the hole under the floorboards. Jaxson heard the acting marshal yelling for the crime techs and coroner to come back inside.

CHAPTER NINE

THE ACTING MARSHAL had laughed as the young deputy had raced out. Ken liked seeing proof that Gray wasn't as tough as he thought he was. After all the hassle with extricating Vi Mullen's body, the shock had finally gotten to the deputy, he'd thought. He enjoyed seeing the cocky young man looking like he was about to pass out.

Now though, Ken was staring into the hole left by extricating Vi's body and feeling sick himself. At first he couldn't believe his eyes. For just an instant, he thought it was a doll. The body had shrunk as it mummified in the warm, dry space beneath the store floorboards. The dark hair had continued to grow and now spread out in a dust-coated fan around the shriveled, sunken face like one of those autumn apple dolls that were always on sale at farmers markets.

Repulsed, he felt the contents of his own stomach float up to his throat. Snapping his eyes shut tight, he fought it back down with every ounce of his determination. He'd choke to death before he would find himself puking out in the alley on his knees in front of the young deputy.

But the image remained on his retinas. The body of a small woman in a faded dress, a red patent leather high heel lying next to her on its side and a compact flowered cloth suitcase on the other. What the hell?

He opened his eyes but turned away as the coroner and

crime scene techs returned. Behind them, he saw his deputy, shamefaced though still pale. Gray had pulled himself together faster than Ken would have expected.

They all looked expectantly at him. He pointed into the dark rectangle of exposed earth at what had been under the now missing floorboards as he mentally cursed Marshal Leroy Baggins. If the fool hadn't gotten married and picked this week to go on his honeymoon...

"Seems we have another body," he said and stepped away from the macabre sight, desperate for some fresh air.

"BUCKHORN." JAXSON SAID the word like a curse as he lay on the uncomfortable motel room bed, staring up at the ceiling. It would be daylight soon. Yarrow would be knocking at his door. He hadn't been able to sleep a wink. How could he? He was a lawman. He'd sworn to uphold the law.

Yesterday had been a nightmare making him question what the hell was he doing here. He'd thought himself a fool for even coming to Buckhorn to begin with—let alone going after this deputy job. But all trails had led to this isolated Western town in the middle of nowhere, hadn't they?

Now he knew why.

He closed his eyes to shut out what he'd seen—what he could no longer unsee—the hidden mummified body of a girl lying on the exposed ground below the store floorboards. The cheap flowered cloth suitcase. That one scuffed, dust-coated red patent leather high heel lying in the dirt next to her as if she had just kicked it off.

Another murder. How else had those remains and that girl's belongings ended up under the store's floorboards otherwise?

Rubbing his eyes, he still couldn't believe it. He'd wanted

to stay as the coroner and crime scene techs processed the scene—the second crime scene of the day.

But the acting marshal wouldn't hear of it. "We can take it from here. Find me another surveillance camera. There has to be more in this godforsaken town. A home security system, something."

So he'd hit the streets, what streets there were in this tiny burg. Security didn't seem high on anyone's list. Vi's contempt for technology meant there were no security cameras on any of her businesses so that didn't leave much in the heart of Buckhorn.

But he got lucky when he expanded his search and saw a camera at Durham's Garage and Gas. The problem was that Gertrude's husband, the former FBI agent, had installed the system and he was out of town. She promised to let him know when Ike returned.

Worn-out and still reeling from the events of the day, he'd returned to the motel as darkness dropped like a cloak over the town. He ached for sleep, but when he closed his eyes, he kept seeing that small mummified body and all that dark hair.

He knew he shouldn't, but he couldn't help himself. He tried Luna's number again. She hadn't answered his earlier text. The call went straight to voice mail. He didn't leave a message. *Where was she?* He worried that she'd had a worse day than he had.

What he needed to do was shut it all out, but all he could think about was Luna. He needed her, had needed her for some time, but he'd held back because of what he'd feared. And now all his fears had come true.

Even as he reminded himself that he should never have gotten involved with Luna, she was the only person he wanted to talk to about this, the only person he could trust. He had fought his growing feelings for her, hating himself for lying to her. If only he had told her the truth right away.

Now it felt as it was too late. Where had she gone? He had no idea. All he could think about was that night at the bar, holding her in his arms, and that kiss. That amazing kiss. After it, he knew he couldn't keep lying about his feelings for her. He'd planned on telling her last night. It would serve him right if she was off somewhere with Tucker Price.

He knew that Tucker had asked her out to his ranch for a horseback ride. Word traveled like a wildfire in Buckhorn. Marjorie Keen had gone out of her way as if she couldn't wait to tell him that she'd seen Luna and Tucker together. "Laughing and having a great time down at the café."

He didn't even know if it had been a date or if the two had just run into each other and shared a coffee at the café. Not that he could blame Luna. He'd been a damned fool for not following his heart. Hell, she and Tucker could be away somewhere together right now. That image did nothing for his quickly disintegrating mood. He cursed the thought.

His cell phone chimed with a text. He hoped it wasn't the one he'd been dreading from Yarrow.

His heart bumped in his chest. It wasn't Yarrow. It was from Luna. I need to see you.

Relief washed over him. He stared at the text for a moment, knowing that if he saw her, he would tell her *everything*. He had to. He should have told her a long time ago. I need to see you too. Are you home? I'm in Buckhorn.

LUNA HAD DRIVEN straight back to Buckhorn. It was late when she'd pulled in. She remembered turning off her phone and pulled it out, shocked to see texts from friends about Vi Mullen being murdered? She'd hurriedly checked the others.

I think there was a second body, but can't confirm, one friend had said. Where are you? Look what happens when you leave town.

She couldn't believe it. That explained why Jaxson was in Buckhorn. She'd thought he was probably an hour away in his apartment in the next town, snug in his bed, or on patrol somewhere in the very large county.

As anxious as she was to talk to him, she had to do this in person where she could see his face. It's the only way she would know the truth when she called him on his lies. Nor could she put it off any longer. It wouldn't be that long before her first client came through the salon door this morning.

She texted him. I'm at my apartment.

To her surprise, he texted back immediately, sounding as anxious to see her as she was him. I'm on my way.

I'll leave the back door open.

Luna put down her phone and hugged herself against a sudden chill. Vi had been *murdered*? A possible second body? What *had* happened while she was gone?

And now she was about to confront Jaxson. She felt tears sting her eyes. She cared about this man more than she'd wanted to admit even to herself. The first time she'd met him she'd told herself that he was all wrong for her. Too shy. Too normal. Too perfect.

She let out a bitter laugh. As it turned out, he was more like her than she'd ever expected. Still waters run deep. Wasn't that what her father used to say? The question was how deep did Jaxson Gray's run?

He'd run out on the girl he'd supposedly loved and the

town that had loved him. He'd passed up a career he'd apparently been gifted at. He'd lied about so much. Then there was Amy, the girl who disappeared right before Jaxson had. There had to be more to the story, her investigative mind told her. But was she going to want to hear it? She felt sick—just as she had when she'd gotten the call from her father. She realized that Jaxson wasn't the only one who'd been holding back over the months they'd been dating. She'd been hurt once before when she was much younger. Had she instinctively known that Deputy Jaxson Gray could break her heart if she opened herself up to him?

Going downstairs, she unlocked the back entry door from the alley and hurriedly returned to her apartment. Right now she just wanted a few moments to herself before he arrived. That's about all she got because she'd barely taken a breath before she heard his boot soles as he mounted the back steps. He sounded in a hurry.

She reminded herself that, despite her feelings for him, she could be opening her door to a killer. Taking a deep breath, she threw the apartment door open before he could knock.

CHAPTER TEN

JAXSON'S APPEARANCE SHOCKED HER. He looked as if he'd had a worse day than hers. His face was pale and drawn, his eyes bloodshot and filled with something she'd never seen there before. Fear.

Had he somehow found out that she'd gone to Blackfoot? Was he that afraid of being busted? No, she thought, it was something even worse.

She felt a pull toward him stronger than gravity. Her heart ached to see him like this, even as she reminded herself that he was a liar—and maybe far worse.

"Luna." There was so much pain and emotion in that one word that she thought he might try to take her in his arms. She stepped back and watched him swallow before he entered the small apartment. She shut the door and locked it, before turning to him.

He'd stopped in the middle of the floor, his back to her. He appeared to be looking at her overnight case where she'd dropped it. She hadn't been sure how long she'd be gone. As it was, she'd been so anxious to get back to Buckhorn, that she'd driven straight through. She hadn't taken the time to unpack it and put everything away.

"Have you heard?" he asked, his voice rough.

"About Vi? She really was murdered?"

When he turned to face her, his expression was so grim there was no doubt. Yet she couldn't believe he was tak-

ing Vi's murder this hard. He was a lawman. Nothing had
rattled him with his job in the past. So it had to be more
than Vi's murder.

A lump rose in her throat as she asked, "I heard there
might have been a second…body?"

His expression darkened, growing even more grim. He
swallowed and asked, "Can we sit down? There's something I have to tell you."

She nodded, the gravity of his words forming knots in
her chest. All her instincts told her that she didn't want to
hear this. "Do you want…coffee?" She suspected they both
were going to need something stronger, but it was way too
early in the morning for alcohol. Not to mention the fact
that she had clients coming soon.

He declined the coffee as he dropped onto her couch and
bent over to bury his face in his hands.

She felt her heart break at the sight of his anguish and
was suddenly terrified of what he was going to tell her.
Making a pot of coffee had its appeal just to postpone the
inevitable. Whatever it was, it had to be far worse than what
she'd already found out about him.

Heart pounding, she realized there was no putting this
off. Clearly there was something he was ready to tell her.
She had to know what was wrong, maybe what had been
wrong between them all along.

Taking a seat on the other end of the couch, she turned
to face him. "What is it you have to tell me?"

He lifted his head, his gaze falling again on her suitcase.
"Your trip. It wasn't bad news about your father, was it?"

"No." Luna couldn't help being touched that even as
upset as he obviously was, he'd been worried about her.

He knew how close she was with her father. "What's going on, Jaxson?"

"I've wanted to tell you the truth for a while now," he mumbled before turning to look at her. "I was afraid of losing you."

Losing her? Was this about Tucker Price? She wanted to tell him that her upcoming so-called date was only a horseback ride on his ranch. There was only one man she was interested in. Jaxson Gray. Or at least the Jaxson Gray she'd thought she'd been falling in love with.

She watched him swallow again, her own throat suddenly dry. No, this was something much worse than her "date" with the local rancher's son.

"That story I told you about my perfect family? It wasn't true."

There's more, she thought bracing herself. But why was he telling her this now? Something more must have happened.

His gaze returned to her overnight bag. She saw him frown. "So your trip…" he said. "You didn't say where you went."

He was clearly stalling. She crossed her arms over her chest, hugging herself against what she feared was coming. "Blackfoot, Idaho." She saw his startled expression. "Maybe you've heard of it."

Jaxson looked as if she'd punched him in the stomach. "Why would you—"

"I wanted to find out why you lied to me."

He looked down at his boots and then back up at her. She felt the tension thick as Montana mud between them. He must have felt it too because he didn't seem to know what to say or do next. "If you'll let me explain…"

She couldn't have denied him, not given the way he was looking at her. She had to hear him out, to give him a chance because she couldn't keep pretending what she felt for him wasn't serious. "Why pretend you had the perfect family?" she asked, even as she worried he might still lie to her.

He sighed. "After you told me about your mom and dad, I couldn't bear to tell you the truth about my family. I'm sorry I lied to you."

"Being raised by a single mother isn't anything to be ashamed of."

"If only it were that simple." He looked away for a moment. "My mother had problems. Back then, no one talked about bipolar disorder, at least not in the town where we lived. I never knew who I was coming home to after school. She could be in the kitchen, making ten different things, not finishing any of them, the radio blasting, her dancing around, flour everywhere." He closed his eyes for a moment as if he could see what had become a familiar scene in his youth.

"Or I could come home to find the house dark, and her bedroom door closed. I was always afraid to open it for fear of what…" He rubbed a hand over his face. "When she was in one of her *down* episodes, she would stay in bed for days. She refused to see a doctor, saying she was just tired. Maybe if I had convinced her to see a professional who could have helped her…"

Luna reached over to touch his shoulder. He placed his hand over hers for a moment. It was warm, strong, his touch tender. "I'm so sorry." She could understand why he'd made up the stable, loving, overachiever family. "But that's not all, is it?" She took a wild guess. "This is about Amy, isn't it?"

"Amy." He said her name like a curse. "It's always been about Amy."

She decided to give him a minute and maybe herself as well. "I saw an old friend of yours when I was in Blackfoot," she said as she got up, went into the kitchen and began to make a pot of coffee. She couldn't imagine his childhood. It broke her heart. Nor could she imagine what more there could be unless he had killed Amy. Her hands trembled as she grabbed the can of coffee from the shelf.

Startled, she realized that Jaxson had come into the kitchen and now stood directly behind her. He took the can from her, easing it out of her trembling hands.

"Katie seemed nice," she said, stepping away to let him make the coffee. His back was to her. She saw him tense at the name.

He rubbed the back of his neck, head down. "Did you tell Katie—"

"About you? No. She's now a librarian. She's engaged."

"That's good," he said. "I never wanted to hurt her."

Hurt her? Hurt her like he had Amy? She watched his hands. They were large strong hands, the fingers long. She looked away, hating that her thoughts had veered off to regret. She'd often wondered what those hands would feel like exploring her body. Now she feared those hands could have done serious harm. Yet, even as she thought it, her heart argued that this man couldn't seriously hurt anyone.

Her pulse hammered in her ears as she asked the one question that had haunted her since learning the the truth. "Why, in the lie you told me, did you say Amy was dead?"

He reached to turn the coffeepot on. "I don't know. I

guess because I knew she was dead," he said, his back still to her, his voice rough with emotion. He turned slowly to look at her.

She felt her heart bump in her chest, her breath catching even as she told herself she knew this man, knew what he was capable of.

"I didn't kill her, and I didn't lie to you about *everything*. That kiss the other night after our dance—"

"Yes, what was that kiss about? For months you've kept me at arm's length until that kiss."

"I'm sorry. I should never have gotten involved with you."

"Why did you?" she demanded, his words hurting more than she'd thought they would. "Why were you so interested in Buckhorn and the people who live here?" She saw that she'd hit a nerve. Heart racing, she said, "You used me, pumping me about Buckhorn and the people who live here. Why?"

"I was trying to find out what happened to Amy," he said and turned to take down two mugs from the cupboard.

"It was always about Amy," she said, the words tasting bitter in her mouth.

"No, it wasn't like that. When I met you…" He shook his head. "I couldn't tell you." He turned to fill the mugs then motioned to the living room. Like a sleepwalker, she followed him back to the couch, cupping the mug in her hands to soak up the warmth since her body had gone ice-cold. At least she'd been right about one thing. This had been about Amy.

SOMEHOW, JAXSON HAD to get the whole story out. He stared down at the mug in his hands and began at the beginning, his voice breaking as he recounted the story. "After Katie and I broke up… We were both going away to separate colleges and I didn't know what my future held. With my mom sick…"

"You met Amy," Luna said, sounding resigned to hear this.

He looked miserable. "Old story. A party. Too much to drink. Looking up to find a girl standing in front of me with a gap between her teeth wearing a pair of red high heels." He closed his eyes for a moment, remembering the one red high heel he'd seen under the store floorboards.

"I asked about her shoes since she was so small and the heels so red, she looked like she was playing dress-up. She said they were her lucky shoes. Later she said because she met me that night, it proved just how lucky they were." He shook his head. "I was drunk and angry and upset that night. My mother had been having an episode, Katie and I had argued in English class earlier that day, my coach was on my ass, warning me not to screw up and lose a college scholarship and my bright future." He groaned at the memory, and he looked over at Luna. She appeared to be holding her breath.

"I've replayed that night so many times, wishing I'd never gone to that party." Amy Franklin had been there, appearing in front of him, need and want in her brown eyes, and he'd been young and foolish and in just the kind of mood to do something stupid. In an instant he had ruined his life.

"My coach used to say that it was all about the split-second decisions I made on the field. Turns out, it's true of life as well." Amy Franklin had landed in his world like a live bomb he couldn't defuse. All he'd been able to do was wait for it to go off. And then it had. Now it was too late to change any of that, he reminded himself.

"A one-night stand turned into my coming home to find Amy sitting in our living room, visiting with my mother. My mother liked her, probably because she saw herself in Amy, in her neediness. When Amy got into a fight with her parents, my mom insisted she move in with us." He shook his head again. "Things got complicated quickly. Amy knew that there was no her and I. It had been just that one time, a mistake.

"But my mom had filled her head with a story about the only man she said she'd ever loved—my father, Owen Henry, the man who ran out on us. Amy became obsessed with finding him." He raked a hand through his hair. "She thought it would save my mother if she found him and brought him back to Blackfoot."

LUNA HAD EXPECTED to hear him tell her a love story. Instead he'd told her a sad tale of a disillusioned, needy young girl who'd fallen for a fantasy. "Surely you tried to stop her."

"Of course I did. It was a ridiculous idea. My father had been gone for years. I barely remembered him. For all I knew, he was dead. I tried to reason with her." He cleared his throat. "When I couldn't, I'd had enough and told her she had to go home. It was late. My mother was upset and so was Amy, but I couldn't take any more. I told her she could stay the night but that was it. She had to leave in the morning."

He took a breath and continued, "Amy had been staying on the floor in my mother's room. I feared my mother was encouraging her, making her believe that if she could bring my father back, she would get well and we'd all be a family. That night I heard Amy promise my mother she was going to find him. The next morning Amy was gone. A few days later, cops showed up at our door. According to her parents, Amy hadn't gone home. She'd disappeared. Everyone thought I'd done something to her. I lost any chance for a scholarship. My mother died not that long after her disappearance. It was a nightmare."

"You told the police all of this?"

He nodded. "They didn't believe me. It did sound ludicrous. Had they known what Amy was like… Anyway, if they looked into the information I gave them, they never said. Nor did they find her. My mother had told her that my father was a cowboy who'd been born and raised in Montana on a ranch. According to my mother, he'd promised to take the two of us there one day. But first he had to straighten out some things with his family." He scoffed and took a gulp of his coffee. Like hers, it was probably now lukewarm, but he didn't seem to notice.

Luna considered what she'd learned about Jaxson. Jaxson had worked on several different ranches in Wyoming before attending MSU in Bozeman and the law enforcement academy and then getting hired on at the marshal's department as a deputy in this county. Had all of that just been about finding Amy by tracking his father? "A ranch, huh," she said, finally finding her voice. "That's not much help given the size of Montana and the number of ranches."

"I had a pretty good idea of where to start," he said. "My mother had this ceramic bird figurine that apparently my father had given her when they'd first met. She'd broken the stupid bird a few times in one of her manic states and glued it back together, always adhering the sticker on the bottom that said it was purchased at the Buckhorn General Store, Buckhorn, Montana."

Luna felt a start. She saw it all now. The job as a cowboy, then a deputy. All the questions he'd asked about Buckhorn and the people who lived here. "Amy knew about the ceramic bird and where it had been purchased," she said. "You think she came to Buckhorn?"

His eyes shone. "I know she did."

Luna felt her pulse jump. "Did she find your father?"

"I have no idea. I never heard from her after she left Idaho."

She frowned. "Then how can you be sure she came to Buckhorn?"

His gaze locked with hers again and she saw the pain and fear she'd seen earlier. Looking into his eyes, seeing the darkness there, her words came out a whisper. "Why are you telling me this now?"

"*I found her.* After having this hanging over my head all these years, I found her." His voice broke. "She was buried under the floorboards at the Buckhorn General Store where I suspect she's been all this time."

Luna felt goose bumps race across her flesh. She was too shocked to speak. She listened as he explained how Dave from the bar had sawed around Vi's body to remove both it and the flooring. "It took Vi Mullen's murder for Amy's remains to turn up," he said.

Still in shock, she asked, "How can you be sure it's Amy? I mean after all these years…"

"The body had mummified, but I recognized her suitcase and one of her…red high heel shoes. It has to be her."

"How did she—"

"Die?" He shook his head. "Maybe the coroner will be able to tell."

She finished what she had been trying to ask. "How did she end up under the floorboards of the old store?"

"Apparently the flooring in the storage area was replaced about the time when she came here looking for my father seventeen years ago."

Luna's mind whirled. She felt sick to her stomach as she fought to make sense of this.

"Why she thought my father might still be here…" He rubbed his neck.

"You've never found him?" she asked.

"I never looked. I had no interest in finding him. I never bought into his cockamamie story about making things right with his family. My mother was the only one who believed that. Except for Amy and look where it got her." He shook his head. He looked exhausted but not as scared as he had when she'd opened the door. "I was just looking for Amy and some indication of what had happened to her. I followed her to Buckhorn seventeen years ago, but couldn't find anyone who'd seen her. But I just had this feeling in the pit of my stomach that Buckhorn held the answer."

"That's why you took the deputy job here," she said. "Maybe there's something in her belongings that will provide a clue as to what happened to her and whether or not she found your father."

He shrugged. "You see now why I lied to you, why I did my best not to get involved with you? Yes, I did need your help. I needed to know about Buckhorn and the people who live here. I just had this feeling that Amy had made it this far. Now do you see? This has been hanging over me for seventeen years…"

She realized with a start what would happen now. "Once the coroner identifies her and finds out that she went missing all those years—"

"It will lead them straight to me. I'm a lawman, I've sworn to uphold the law. I need to tell Yarrow what I know."

"If you do that, you know what will happen. If you're serious about finding the killer, you can't tell anyone."

He put his head in his hands for a moment before looking up at her and nodding. "I want more than anything to find her killer and clear my name. To prove to you that I'm the man you wanted to believe I was."

Her mind was reeling again, but one thought wouldn't go away. "Would you have ever told me if Amy's body hadn't been found?"

He turned toward her. "I've almost told you everything so many times... But now that you've heard the whole story—"

"The whole story?" she snapped. "You have to know how suspicious this looks. You just told me that you were in Buckhorn seventeen years ago. How do I know that you didn't kill her and impulsively put her under those floorboards? That the only reason you're in Buckhorn is because you knew her body would be found and what you'd done would be exposed unless as the law you could protect yourself somehow?"

His gaze met hers, held it, his green eyes pleading. "You know I didn't kill her."

Did she?

"I never planned to fall for you. But I did." He cleared his throat. "The more I was around you, it became harder and harder not to want...more." She looked into his eyes and felt a stab of heat rocket through her veins like liquid nitrogen. Dragging her gaze away, she reminded herself that he'd lied to her once. Could she trust anything he'd just told her?

He raked a hand through his hair again. "I didn't want to lose you." His gaze locked with hers. "But I've already lost you, haven't I?"

The words, his voice, the look she'd seen just moments before in his eyes made her heart ache. She tried to swallow the lump in her throat. Her eyes burned with unshed tears as she turned to face him again. He looked scared, but not half as scared as she was for him, for them.

"I don't know," she said finally. "How can I trust you?"

"I'll prove it to you. I just need time to find out what happened to her," he rushed on. "I'll clear my name. I'll find out who killed her. But I can understand if you don't want anything to do with me until I do," he said after a few electrified moments. "In fact, it is probably best if you put as much distance as possible between us until I do."

Luna knew that her father would agree. Jaxson had lied to her. She wasn't all that sure he would have told her the truth if Amy's body hadn't been found. But he'd already stolen a chunk of her heart. She either had to go all in— or try to get that piece back by proving he wasn't the man she thought he was.

"I'll help you," she said, surprised by the emotion she heard in her voice. "But, if you're lying to me, I will help the law put you behind bars."

"No, Luna, there's a killer out there. You don't want to get any more involved," he said with a shake of his head.

"I'm a trained investigator."

"You're a *hairstylist*."

"That too," she said as she rose from the couch. Did he

really think he could tell her all of this and she would leave it alone? "I majored in criminology, and I've worked with my father on cases. That's how I ended up in Buckhorn to start with. Someday I'll tell you about it. In the meantime, I'm going to find out who killed Amy, which means starting with finding your father—and discovering whether or not Amy did the same."

"It's too dangerous," he said, getting to his feet. "Come on, Luna, someone *killed* her and stuffed her under the floorboards at the store. For all we know, that someone is still around. Not to mention, now someone has murdered Vi Mullen."

"You aren't suggesting that the two murders are connected, are you?"

He shook his head. "I can't see how. But if you start asking questions around town…"

He had a point. One her father would have mentioned as well. But she'd never been able to resist a good murder mystery. This one was more than intriguing since it involved a man she wanted desperately to believe in. Helping him solve it could mean clearing his name and finding out if there was a chance for them.

Or finding out he was still lying and guilty as hell, she reminded herself. Which would put her in even more danger.

She told herself that she was good at this stuff, and it wasn't like her to turn down a challenge. She was also invested more than she wanted to admit. She had to know the truth.

However, there was that one thing that worried her a little and had from the moment her father told her what he'd found out about Jaxson Gray. *If I'm so good at read-*

ing people and uncovering the truth, how is it that I didn't see through his lies?

He took a step toward her. His gaze locked with hers again. "I'm so sorry I kept all of this from you." The air between them seemed to pop and sizzle for a few moments. His phone chimed, announcing that he had a new text. He glanced at it and swore under his breath. "It's Acting Marshal Kenneth Yarrow. I have to go."

"How much time do we have before he finds out your connection to the corpse under the floorboards?" Luna asked.

He shook his head. "This is another reason I didn't tell you even when I knew I could trust you." He hesitated, but just a moment before he said, "Yarrow has two murders to solve. I don't think I have to tell you which one will take priority. But once they get a DNA sample and ID Amy, I will be lucky if I don't find myself behind bars. Maybe I should just tell Yarrow now. I don't like another lie."

"No," she said. "Use this time to prove your innocence. I'll help you any way I can. Yarrow doesn't know you were in Buckhorn seventeen years ago?"

Jaxson shook his head as he picked up his Stetson, but before putting it on, he said, "I'm glad you know the truth but, Luna, don't do anything to put yourself in danger, please. This story is tragic enough. I can't bear the thought of you getting hurt or worse, killed because of me."

"I'll need all the information you have on your father and Amy as soon as possible," she said as if he hadn't spoken. He groaned as she rose to see him out. "But lie to me again and—"

"I won't. I *promise.*" He held her gaze and she felt sparks even before he said her name, his voice breaking. "Luna."

She felt a live wire jolt. Had he reached for her then, she might have stepped into his arms. His phone chimed with another text, the moment gone. He checked it and said, "I have to go."

She nodded and watched him leave, shaken by what he'd told her, what he hadn't and what she feared. But what scared her the most was that she would have stepped into his arms moments ago had he tried to hold her. He was right about one thing. She needed to keep her distance from him until this was solved.

Closing the apartment door after him, she leaned against it, realizing the sun had risen up over the mountains to paint the town in gold. She questioned what she was getting herself into as the sun rose higher. It was going to be another bright and sunny Montana day.

But Jaxson had left behind a dark shadow that she couldn't throw off. What if he was still lying to her? What if he had only told her because he knew she would do everything she could to help him?

All her instincts told her that she could trust him. But could she trust her instincts?

CHAPTER ELEVEN

JUST AS THE SUN ROSE, Johnny Berg shot bolt upright in bed, his heart hammering. At first, he'd thought he'd heard something in the creaky old huge apartment house. Footfalls? The creak of a door opening?

He wouldn't have been surprised if Bristol came back. But in the new light of day, he saw that his bedroom door was closed and locked. There was no one in his room. He'd left the closet and bathroom doors wide open so there was nowhere for anyone to hide. He'd even checked under his bed, embarrassed to admit it, but other than some dust bunnies, there was nothing. No monster waiting to spring out and grab him.

Straining to hear over the thunder of his pulse—he heard nothing amiss. Not even the old apartment house had anything to say. No footfalls, no creak of a door, no moan and groan as the old place settled and decayed on its way to falling down.

So what had awakened him?

As his pulse began to slow, he felt the remnants of the dream he'd been having when he'd jerked awake. He'd been at the Buckhorn General Store delivering packages. Everything was just as he remembered it. Or was it?

He frowned. Only this time...

His pulse took off like a startled jackrabbit. He gripped

the covers as he realized he'd lied to the cops. He *had* seen something yesterday morning when Vi was killed. He just hadn't remembered it until right now.

CHAPTER TWELVE

YARROW WAS WAITING for Jaxson when he walked into the Buckhorn Café. He knew he looked it as if he hadn't gotten any sleep. He hadn't, he thought as he slid into the booth opposite the acting marshal. Yarrow didn't look all that good himself.

"Where have you been? I knocked on your door before I called your cell," Yarrow said, studying him across the table.

"I woke up early, went for a walk."

"I thought maybe you were staying at your girlfriend's place."

Jaxson shook his head. He knew what Yarrow was asking. He would resent the county paying for a motel room that wasn't being used. "You thought wrong," he said simply.

As tired as he was from worry and lack of sleep, he wasn't looking forward to the motel bed tonight. The county had paid for them to stay at the Sleepy Pine Motel on the edge of town rather than the new hotel. At least Yarrow had gotten them separate rooms, not that Jaxson couldn't hear the older man snoring through the thin walls.

But it hadn't been snoring that had kept him awake before Luna's text. Jaxson was still shocked by what they'd found under the floorboards of the storage room. It was Amy. A part of him still wanted to tell Yarrow now. He knew waiting could make things worse. But if he could find out how she'd ended up there....

He tried to feel relieved that Luna now knew the truth finally. But he should have known she would be determined to help him. Or at least determined to get to the truth. Oh how he wished he'd never lied to her. He couldn't bear the thought that no matter how this all turned out, he could have lost her, something he knew he would regret the rest of his life.

"The coroner confirmed that the remains were that of a young woman," Yarrow was saying. "It's been there for years. So we'll wait on forensics for more information."

Jaxson had known the moment he saw the red high heel—and the flowered suitcase. He'd also recognized the dress Amy had been wearing. It was his mother's favorite. Amy had either borrowed it or just taken it. His mother could also have given it to her since she'd encouraged Amy to go on this ridiculous quest. He'd been shocked to see the dress, worse to know that the mummified remains were Amy's.

Hadn't he hoped he would find some trace of her here? But not like this.

Yarrow pushed a handwritten list of names across the table to him after they'd eaten. "We have to concentrate on Vi Mullen's murder. Start questioning these people. I've taken the other half of the list. You didn't get anything more on security cameras?"

Jaxson told him about the one at the gas station. "Ike should be back in a day or two." He looked at the list and let out a whistle when he saw all the names he alone was to question. "Looks like we're questioning everyone in town."

"Just about. The sooner we get this one solved, the

sooner we can find out why the hell there was another body under those floorboards. We might never get out of this damned town. In the meantime…"

In the meantime, it was the Sleepy Pine Motel.

"Are we just asking about Vi Mullen's murder or—"

"For now, we're not mentioning what was found under the floorboards. Not that we can keep a lid on it. But until we have an ID on the remains…"

Jaxson didn't think the suitcase or the remains would offer up much as far as how Amy had ended up there. He hadn't seen a purse or wallet in the shallow grave. He could have given the acting marshal a name, but then he would have also had to explain how he knew Amy Franklin. At the least, he would be pulled off the case. At the worst, he would be arrested.

He desperately needed this time. Unfortunately the one person who would probably know how Amy had ended up under the floorboards was dead. Murdered. Vi would have had to know, wouldn't she?

All he'd had to go on was that Amy had probably come to Buckhorn, Montana. That was seventeen years ago, and she'd never been heard from again after disappearing. Had she found his father? He hadn't believed it. He still didn't. But finding her dead and buried under the store floorboards had him believing that she'd found something she shouldn't have.

He'd never understood why his father had left the way he had. Maybe the last thing he'd wanted was to be found. All Jaxson knew was that he had to know—and quickly. Maybe it hadn't just been about finding Amy that had brought him to Montana, to Buckhorn as a deputy, to Luna Declan, he thought with a pang of guilt. Maybe he too had wanted to find his father.

"You sure you're up to this?" Yarrow asked.

Jaxson looked up from the list he was holding in his hand, confused since his thoughts had been so far from Vi Mullen's murder. "Didn't sleep…well."

"Try not taking walks before sunrise," his boss said as he reached for his wallet to pay for their breakfast bill. "We have a job to do. Someone in this town knows what happened to our murder victim."

Jaxson nodded, thinking the same thing about Amy.

"Why did that young man look so familiar?" Clarice Barber asked after losing the thread of the conversation the women had been having in the Buckhorn Café the next morning.

They'd exhausted the subject of Vi Mullen's murder and twin Vera's return to Buckhorn and had gone back to talking recipes, diet tips, craft projects and each of their aches and pains as they finished their coffee.

"Didn't he look familiar to you?" Clarice asked, nudging Mabel beside her.

"*What* young man?" Mabel asked a little irritably. Clarice had noticed that her friend had less patience with her lately, but let it go.

"The one at the counter."

Mabel glanced at the empty café counter. "There's nobody there."

"Not now, earlier this morning. The young one with the gun."

"Are you talking about Deputy Jaxson Gray?"

She nodded as she struggled to retrieve the memory. "I'm sure that I've seen him before."

"Of course, you've seen him before," Mabel snapped. "He comes in here all the time with our hairdresser, Luna."

"No," Clarice said, shaking her head. "That's not where I saw him."

Mabel grumbled something under her breath and turned to talk to Lynette, leaving her to continue trying to remember.

"He was much younger," Clarice said to herself because no one was listening to her now. They were all talking about some recipe they'd seen on Pinterest. It didn't sound good to her, not that she did much cooking anymore. "Yes, he'd been much younger," she said as she recalled what had jarred the old memory—seeing him talking to Vera. Except when she'd seen him before, when he was young, he'd been talking to Vi.

How could she have forgotten that Vi had a twin sister? She remembered Vera as a girl, a shameful wild child with a nasty mouth. Vera had been rude when Clarice came into the store.

"That's where I saw him!" Clarice cried with delight as she plucked the old memory out. "I saw him in the store talking to Vi, not Vera. He wasn't that old. Although I've never been able to tell them apart until Vera opens her mouth. That girl needs her mouth washed out with soap."

"Clarice, what are you talking about?" Rose demanded on her other side in the large round booth.

"That young man," she said, feeling better now that she'd remembered. "Only he was different back then. He wasn't a deputy." She took a sip of her now cold tea. Vera had given her such a scare yesterday. It was yesterday, wasn't it? "I knew I'd seen him before." Rose had lost interest and turned away.

The group moved on to another topic, but Clarice found herself thinking about the deputy. It had been the first time she saw him in the Buckhorn General Store, hadn't it? She frowned. Or someone who looked like him? Was his kin from here? She didn't think so. She thought about asking Mabel. Her friend had a much better memory, especially when it came to people who'd lived here, but Clarice could see that Mabel wasn't interested.

She told herself that maybe she'd ask the young deputy the next time she saw him. If she remembered.

LUNA HAD HURRIED downstairs to the salon, arriving only moments before her first client—Gertrude Durham. She thought it fateful that the woman who'd brought her to Buckhorn in the first place also brought with her all the latest scuttlebutt about Vi's murder and what had been found under the floorboards at the store.

Working for her father's insurance retrieval business, she'd come to town looking for a jewel thief and had suspected Gertrude. Luna had opened her salon business as a cover and ended up staying after the case was solved.

"I'm sure you've probably heard," the fiftysomething woman said. Gertrude had the most beautiful long gray hair, which was usually in a braid tucked under a trucker cap. The local mechanic, she had inherited Durham's Garage and Gas on the edge of town. "Vi Mullen's been murdered."

Gertrude said it like a woman who'd been harassed by Vi from the moment she hit town. Not that Vi hadn't harassed a lot of people, Luna reminded herself.

"Who do you think did it?" Luna asked. She'd learned in the short time she had lived here that a lot of people despised Vi and certainly some had wished her dead.

Gertrude laughed. "Take your pick. But using an ice fishing spear on her? That's cold." She chuckled at her joke.

It had been difficult to get Gertrude into the salon the first time, but since then Gertrude had become a regular client. The older woman sat down in the salon chair and Luna began to unbraid the thick gray hair. Only recently married to a former FBI agent, the older woman's hair wasn't the only thing that had changed since they'd met. Once a loner who hadn't spoken two words to anyone, Gertrude had thawed out—especially toward Luna—and now let her do anything she liked with her hair.

"The marshal have any idea who did it?" she asked as she leaned Gertrude back against the sink so she could shampoo her hair.

"Marshal Leroy Baggins is on his honeymoon. That's left Deputy Kenneth Yarrow in charge." Gertrude's views on the capabilities of Yarrow were clear in her tone. "He's got that young deputy of yours helping at least. But I suspect you already know that."

"I've been out of town," Luna reminded her noncommittally as she began to rinse the suds out of Gertrude's hair and reached for the conditioner. Few people knew her background. While she'd gone to cosmetology school, following in her mother's footprints, at university she'd majored in criminology, also tiptoeing into her father's investigative part of his business.

There was nothing she loved delving into more than a good mystery, and now there'd been a murder right down the street—and a cold case under the floorboards. She would have wanted to get involved in the cases even if Jaxson hadn't been neck-deep in at least one of them.

"I heard people are taking bets down at the café on who did it," Gertrude said as Luna massaged the conditioner into her scalp. Her client laughed. "Right now, my money is on the ex who I heard was back in town."

"Axel is back?" He would probably be at the top of the marshal's list as well, but from what Luna had heard about him, she didn't see him as a murderer. Then again it sounded as if the killing had been impulsive rather than premeditated.

With the victim being Vi Mullen, the suspects were limitless, she thought as she began to rinse Gertrude's hair again.

"But to cover my bets, I'd put money on suspect number two, Vera Carter, as well," Gertrude said.

Luna frowned. "Who's Vera Carter?"

"Vi's twin. She hit town the morning of the murder."

"Vi had a twin sister?" Luna recalled hearing something about a sister. "Wait, I thought her sister was dead?"

"That's what Vi told everyone. Must have been wishful thinking," Gertrude said with a chuckle. "Vi lied about her *identical* twin being dead because of some bad blood between them. I guess Vera caused a real stir when she walked into the café right after everyone heard that Vi had been murdered." She let out a bark of a laugh. "All those old hens were in the café. They all thought Vi had returned from the dead. One of them even fainted."

"I can't believe how much I missed," Luna said.

"Remember how Vi was with people?" Gertrude said, sobering. "I've heard that Vi pales next to Vera and apparently the latter is staying in Buckhorn."

"I can't wait to meet her." She was already mentally adding the twin to her list of suspects. But what any of them might have to do with Amy's murder, she couldn't imagine.

KEN HEARD FIRST THING in the morning that the crime techs had worked through the night at the store. Suspecting there might be more bodies buried under the floorboards, they'd searched the crawl space. But they'd found no other remains. After collecting the second body, along with the victim's belongings, they'd finished up this morning and taken the evidence to the crime lab to be processed.

The coroner had taken both Vi's body and the unknown female's back to his office for autopsies. Now all Ken could do was wait for the reports.

The body under the floorboards had obviously been there for a while. It could wait while he found Vi's killer, which required more immediate investigation, he told himself. But right now that seemed like an impossible task. The general store had been full of fingerprints. So far, there was no evidence to point him in any specific direction other than people who had an obvious dislike for the town's matriarch.

Vi was his top priority, even before the press had gotten hold of the story. Now the governor was clamoring for the killer to be caught. So far they hadn't heard about the second body. That was the only good news.

The handle of the ice fishing spear had been dusted for prints. None. Even if the killer had been wearing gloves, there should have been fingerprints on the handle belonging to whoever had opened the box of spears. Had the killer taken the time to wipe the handle clean? It would appear so.

He'd been glad to hear that Johnny Berg's prints hadn't

been on the spear. The kid had been smart enough not to touch it. He couldn't see Berg killing Vi. He could however see Vi murdering the kid for tracking up her store floor—had she still been alive.

With a sigh, Ken realized that he had no evidence to go on. That surveillance camera video was their only lead and it had led nowhere. Maybe they would get lucky with the camera at the filling station.

He had taken the list of those he considered the top suspects and given the deputy the rest. After meeting Vera in the café yesterday, he had moved her to the top of his list—especially since he'd learned that she'd moved into her sister's house just outside of town. That seemed a little fast.

Ken drove the short distance to the former mountain home of Vi Mullen east of town. It was a beautiful Montana spring day, all blue sky and sunshine. He parked, took in the view of the valley and Buckhorn for a moment, then climbed the steps and rang the bell. He hadn't called ahead, hoping to catch Vera off guard.

But if anyone was caught off guard, it was him as the door was opened by a man he recognized—Vi's ex, Axel Mullen, wearing a robe that clearly wasn't his since it was flowered and appeared to be silk. *Vi's?* Directly behind him, Vera appeared, wearing a fancy negligee in the same flowered print. It left way too much flesh showing even though he could appreciate how good she looked for her age—a woman about his own age.

Ken cleared his voice. "Sorry to catch you both so early." He wasn't sorry. But he was surprised. "You're staying here too?" he said to Axel, who didn't answer, just held the door open for him to enter.

"Coffee, Deputy?" Vera asked coyly.

He didn't bother to correct her. "I'd love a cup while you get dressed."

"We wondered how long it would take you before you stopped by," she said as she told Axel to get him a cup of coffee and started down the closest hallway.

Axel poured him a cup and motioned to a stool at the breakfast bar. Sitting down, he took a sip of the coffee and looked around, noticing three empty wine bottles and one champagne bottle sitting on the counter. "Had a little party last night?" he asked as he nodded toward the empties.

Axel smiled. "No law against giving Vi a decent send-off is there, Deputy?"

"Acting Marshal," he said as he pulled out his pen, notebook and phone. "I'll be recording this." But before he could ask his first question, Vera returned, wearing a tight T-shirt and an equally tight pair of jeans. She was pulling on a pair of leather sandals that, from the way she was admiring them on her feet, had belonged to her now-deceased twin.

"I see you've made yourself at home," Ken commented.

"Vi would have wanted me here," Vera said she helped herself to a cup of coffee.

"You sure about that?" Ken asked.

She laughed. "I am. It's a twin thing."

Right, he thought, and looked at Axel. "I'm sure she would have wanted her ex-husband here as well." *With you*, he thought but didn't add.

Vera chuckled. "Now that might be a stretch."

"I should probably get dressed," Axel said. "I would imagine you want to talk to Vera alone." He started down the hall.

"I'm going to want to talk to you too," Ken told him before he could escape. "But you're right, I do want to talk to Vera alone first." He turned to the woman as Axel left. Damn, but she did look so much like Vi, it was unnerving. He took another sip of coffee, hit Record on his phone and then picked up his pen. "When exactly did you say you arrived in Buckhorn?"

She stepped into the attached living room and made herself comfortable on the couch. "Please make yourself at home," Vera said and laughed. "Like you said, *I* have."

He got up to move into the living room, glancing in the direction of the hallway that Axel had disappeared down. All the doors were closed. He took a chair rather than join her on the couch in the spot she'd patted, indicating he should sit next to her. He put the phone on the coffee table between them. "You were about to tell me when you arrived in Buckhorn."

"Was I?" she asked with a grin. "You saw me. I'd just gotten in. I went straight to the café."

"Really? So how is it you heard about Vi's murder?"

"Axel. I believe he stopped by the store and heard." She shrugged. "We came in separate cars."

"You and Axel, huh?" She nodded. "How long has that been going on?"

"Not that long," she said with a grin. "We just happened to run into each other out in Spokane and realized how much we had in common."

He figured he knew exactly what they had in common. "You sure you didn't arrive earlier that morning and stop by the store before it opened?" Vera smiled and shook her head, wagging a finger at him. "If you could respond verbally for the recording, I'd appreciate it."

"No, I didn't get in earlier."

"And Axel?"

"You'd have to ask him, but I didn't see him until later yesterday," she said. "He was waiting for me here."

"What brought you to Buckhorn after all these years?"

She glanced around for a moment before she spoke. "I just had a feeling. I'd thought that it was time Vi and I put our differences aside and tried to be sisters again. Unfortunately, I didn't get here soon enough."

"You have to admit it is quite the coincidence that you just happened to decide to return to Buckhorn—you and your twin's ex—on the day Vi was murdered."

"It's eerie, isn't it," she said and shivered.

He noticed that she hadn't corrected him on when Axel had arrived. How long had he been in town? "Who do you think killed your sister?"

"Gosh, I wouldn't know. Like you said, I haven't been back here in years, so your guess is as good as mine. I assume you'd met my sister at some point?" She didn't wait for an answer. "She was…difficult." She laughed again. "That's what my mother used to say about me, that I was difficult. The irony. Our mother named me after herself because I was born first and her favorite—at least for a while. I don't think she really liked either of us. But Vi was definitely a mama's girl. I'm sure you've heard the story about the broken vase. Vi thought she'd broken it. Our mother never let her forget it or ever forgave her and it turned out that Karla Parson had broken the vase out of meanness and let Vi take the blame for years."

"Where were you?"

She looked startled. "Sorry?"

"Where were you when the vase was broken?"

"I was probably in the tree house. Vi wouldn't let me

play with her and her friends so I spent a lot of time alone as a child."

Ken wondered what to believe. "Spying on your sister and her friends?"

Vera laughed. "It's almost like you know me."

"You're telling me that you and your sister didn't get along."

"Everyone in town knows that."

"How was it that your sister ended up with your daughter?" He saw at once that he'd hit a nerve as he was vaguely aware that Axel Mullen was certainly taking his time getting dressed. He wouldn't slip out the back door, would he?

Vera shrugged, avoiding eye contact. "Why are you bringing up Jennifer? She has nothing to do with this."

He waited, seeing how uncomfortable she had become.

Finally she sighed and said, "Jennifer was a lot like me growing up. She ran away. Vi took her in. At some point, she preferred to be a Mullen. She and Tina were like sisters. I'm sure that's why Vi let her change her name from Carter to Mullen."

"Your maiden name was Carter?"

"Still is. I've never married."

"Jennifer's father is…?"

"You really want all the sordid details, don't you," Vera said shifting on the couch. "Okay, why not? That's the irony of Vi changing Jennifer's name to Mullen. She really is a Mullen. Axel is Jennifer's father." She raised a brow. "I slept with my sister's husband before I left Buckhorn for good. Satisfied? Jennifer was the product of that night of unbridled passion."

Axel came back into the room. As if on cue, Vera rose. "I have things to take care of. If that's all, Marshal."

"Did you kill your sister?"

She gave him an impatient look. "How could I? I wasn't even in town."

"Can you prove that?"

Her gaze narrowed. "Can you prove I was?" With that, she walked out.

He turned off the recorder until he heard her leave. "I'd like to ask you a few questions," he said to Axel as the man poured himself a fresh cup of coffee and topped it off with bourbon. Ken turned the phone recorder back on.

"I didn't kill Vi. I wanted to often enough though." He smiled. "Does that count?"

"When did you arrive in Buckhorn?"

"Not until yesterday, late in the morning. Vera told me to meet her here, so I did."

"Did she also tell you that your ex-wife was dead?"

"I was shocked." He didn't look shocked. He looked like he was lying about something, probably everything.

"Vera said you got to town before her and stopped by the store. She said you were the one who told her that Vi had been murdered."

Axel frowned. "I can't imagine why she would say that. I didn't arrive until late morning. She's the one who told me about Vi." He shook his head, but he didn't look happy.

"How long have you two been together?"

"Not long. Ran into each other in a bar in Spokane." He shrugged. "I can't seem to get away from the Carter women."

If Ken had to guess, he'd say the man was thinking how much Vi would have hated him not only being with her twin but living together in his ex-wife's house. "Revenge is sweet, huh."

For a moment Axel looked startled, but then laughed. "It is strange how things turn out."

Ken couldn't agree more. But he could tell that Axel was still concerned about why Vera had told a different story. "Vera said she's planning to stay in Buckhorn. I was wondering about your plans."

Axel glanced around the room. "I think I just might stay as well."

"How would you describe the nature of your relationship with your ex-wife's twin sister?"

The man grinned. "Friendly."

"The two of you are a couple?"

"Do you have a problem with that?" Axel asked.

"Only if the two of you murdered Vi Mullen," he said bluntly. "One more question. The flooring in the storage area. I've heard that it was replaced seventeen years ago."

Axel laughed. "So it's true. You found a body under there? Well, then, Vi put it there. Not me."

"Do you know who did the work?"

"Vi was in charge of that, like everything else that had to do with her store, her antique barn, her property." His words reeked of bitterness.

"But you were around. You must have seen men working on the flooring," Ken persisted.

"Sure, it was just some cowhands she'd gotten cheap."

"You happen to remember who they were?"

Axel shook his head. "I think they were in from either the Eaton or Price ranches or maybe both. They're the closest to town. So who was under there?"

Ken stopped the recording on his phone and rose. "I'm sure we'll be talking again." He wasn't worried about Axel leaving town. Clearly he was also making himself at home.

But he did wonder if the reason Vera's story was different from Axel's was because she was planning to throw him under the bus.

Now Axel was probably wondering the same thing.

LUNA WAS DEAD on her feet and her day was just beginning. Earlier Jaxson had texted her what information he had on Owen Henry, his father. Taking a break, she called her own father. She quickly told him everything that had happened and what she'd found out in Idaho along with what Jaxson had told her.

When she'd finished, he said, "Are you sure about this man, Luna?"

She knew it was foolish to hang her heart on one passionate kiss especially from a man who'd lied to her—not to mention who could be arrested for murder at any time.

"I am sure I want to find out the truth," she said. "I have to know what happened, both to the father and the former girlfriend."

"I don't like this, but I'll do what I can to help. What do you need?"

Luna smiled to herself, knowing that her father was just as much a sucker for a good mystery as she was. Add to that his concern for his daughter's feelings for the deputy, Lawrence Declan would do everything in his power to help solve this case. "Jaxson's father was going by the name Owen Henry. He would be about fifty-seven now, if he's still alive." Owen would be about Vi's age, she realized. "Supposedly born in Montana on a ranch, later worked as a carpenter down in Idaho. I know it's not a lot to go on."

"No, but at least it's not a really common name. Any siblings?"

"Sorry. Jaxson was seven when his father left. His mother apparently didn't know much about Owen either, Lillian and Owen never married, she never met his family—if he had any—and she never apparently stopped loving him." Luna couldn't imagine anything worse. Was that love? Or obsession mixed with a big helping of denial and fantasy.

"How will this help the situation if I find him?" her father asked.

Luna considered that for a moment. "Maybe Amy found him and if so, he might know who killed her."

"Or she did find him, and he didn't want anyone else to find him. You do realize how dangerous this is in so many ways."

She did. "Unfortunately, the clock is running. Once they have DNA and realize it's the missing Amy Franklin, then it's going to lead them to—"

"Deputy Jaxson Gray," her father said.

"I should have gotten a photo of Amy Franklin from her yearbook."

"I'll see what I can do."

"Thanks. I need a photo of Owen Henry too."

"If he had a Montana driver's license, I should be able to get one."

"I'm hoping someone here might remember one of them or both."

"Once you start showing the photos, you'll have no idea if you've also shown the killer that you're coming for him. Or her."

"Don't worry, I'll be careful," she added quickly before he could warn her what she was getting herself into. She already knew. "Thank you for helping me. This means a lot."

"What I'm hearing is that Jaxson means a lot to you," he

said, but he didn't sound happy about it. "I'm trusting your instincts, but his name is going to come up in this investigation. I'm sure you've considered advising him to come forward before that happens."

Luna had thought about it. "He doesn't have much faith in the acting marshal who's handling the case." He heard her father make a disgruntled sigh. "Please, help me find Jaxson's father and I'll take it from there. In the meantime, I'll see if any of the old-timers might have known him. If he was a real cowboy from the area…"

"Just promise me that you'll be careful."

"Always. Thanks, Dad."

"I hope Jaxson Gray is worth it."

"I'm pretty sure he is." She realized that she was betting her heart on it.

CHAPTER THIRTEEN

JAXSON FELT AS IF he were underwater. He tried to breathe. Telling Luna everything had done little to relieve his fears. He should have known that once he had, she would try to help him.

I'm good at this, she'd texted him after he'd left her apartment. Trust me.

He did trust her. But he couldn't understand why she still trusted him. At least enough to help him. Not enough though to trust him with her heart. She'd made that perfectly clear.

When had he realized he was falling in love with her? He smiled to himself remembering a day on the river. They'd been hopping from one rock to the next trying to cross to a spot Luna knew about to have a picnic lunch.

It had been one of those amazing Montana summer days, all sunshine, crystal-blue sky and the scent of pine. The river had glistened so invitingly that he should have known they would end up in it before the day was over.

Luna had turned to say something to him, lost her footing and the next thing he knew she was floating downstream. He dropped the picnic basket on the rocks and dove in without a second thought.

When he caught up to her, she was soaking wet and laughing. He'd pulled her to him as they struggled to get to their feet in the moving water.

He could still remember the water droplets on her lashes, the brightness of her eyes, her smile as he held her. That day he'd lost a huge chunk of his heart to her.

But it was desire, something he hadn't felt in a very long time, that surprised him. He'd wanted her. Not just for an afternoon, but for a lifetime.

That realization had stunned him since he'd known he couldn't have her. Or that she wouldn't want him after she learned the truth about him. Yet, he couldn't stay away from her after that day. He'd said that he'd rescued her, but he knew that she was the one who'd rescued him.

He'd wanted to put the past behind him—whatever it took. He wanted a future with this woman.

That's when he should have told her the truth. He should have trusted her. Now she knew the truth and at least she hadn't walked away. Instead she wanted to help find out what had happened to Amy, maybe more out of curiosity than saving him. But he could hope that she might share his feelings. All he had to go on was that kiss and her response to it.

He smiled to himself. Also she wanted to help him. Not that she'd ever made it a secret that she loved unraveling mysteries. But he worried this was one that not even Luna Declan could unravel. He'd given her what information he had on his father and Amy, which wasn't much. That Luna was looking for his father made him uncomfortable. He feared her finding Owen Henry—especially if Amy had found him and she was now dead. As much as he'd despised his father for years, he still didn't want to believe he was a killer.

Why would Owen Henry have killed Amy? Because

she'd found him? Because she was going to expose him? Was what Owen Henry had run from that dangerous?

If so, then the last thing Jaxson wanted was Luna involved in this whole mess. Not that he could stop her.

All he could do was his job. Right now he was supposed to be concentrating on Vi's murder. He couldn't see how her murder and Amy's could be related, but Amy had been found in her store under the new flooring.

His head ached. He rubbed his temples. He would do his best to find Vi's killer. He started with the first name on the list, Mabel Aldrich, a longtime Buckhorn resident. She answered the door of her house just off the main drag in a flour-dusted apron. He caught the scent of what smelled like apple pie emanating from deeper inside.

Mabel, who was of indiscriminate age, was a large-bodied woman with dyed dark hair and intelligent brown eyes. She cocked her head. "Deputy Gray, you're just in time. I have an apple pie cooling on my kitchen counter. Come in." With that, she turned and walked deeper into the house. He closed the door and followed her.

The kitchen looked like a 1950s remake except that this one was original from the long rectangular yellow Formica table to the matching padded metal chairs. The wallpaper, though faded, was yellow daisies.

"Sit!" she ordered and busied herself cutting him a piece of the pie.

He didn't put up an argument. Luna had told him that there was a little jealousy between Bessie Walker, now Caulfield, and Mabel. Apparently, before Bessie started her café, the two women used to compete, baking for blue ribbons at the county fair.

"I need to ask you a few questions," Jaxson told her as

he pulled out his phone. "Do you mind if I record your answers?"

She glanced over at him after placing a large piece of pie onto a plate. "Go right ahead. You recording yet?" He nodded. "I didn't kill Vivian Mullen."

He smiled at that as she slid the pie-filled plate in front of him along with a fork. "What time did you go down to the café that morning?"

She looked pointedly at the pie on his plate. He picked up his fork and took a bite. "Have you ever tasted a better apple pie?" Mabel demanded after he'd swallowed.

"Never," he said, thinking it might be true.

"Five fifty-five. We like to go right before the café opens so we can get our booth. We've been sitting in that booth every morning except Sundays as far back as I can remember."

"Did you happen to see anyone on your way to the café?"

Mabel put her hands on her hips. "Saw Lynette coming up the street from her house."

"She lives on the other side of town?"

"If you're asking if she slipped into the store and killed Vi on her way to the café, she did not."

He had to smile. "How do you know that?"

"Blood. She had on brand-new sneakers, white, of all colors. I just happened to notice. That woman is so fastidious. If she had scuffed those new shoes, she would have had to go back home and change them."

"Maybe that's exactly what she did."

Mabel shook her head. "She also is religious about being on time. She couldn't have killed Vi since Vi Mullen opens the back door of the store at six on the nose every morning."

"Everyone in town knows this?"

"Everyone who's paid any attention does. So Lynette wouldn't have had time to go home and change." Mabel gave him a top-that look.

"Maybe she just put the bloody shoes in her purse after she removed the new sneakers."

The woman shook her head. "Lynette always brings a coin purse with just enough money for breakfast and a tip and not a penny more. Her coin purse is too small for an extra pair of shoes and no, she didn't take off her shoes before killing Vi. Have you ever seen her feet?" Mabel made a repulsed expression. "She'd rather die than let anyone see them, especially Vi."

He'd had his fun with Mabel. It was time to move on. "So we can assume Lynette didn't kill her. See anyone else that morning?"

But Mabel seemed to have something else on her mind. "You know about Vi's online site she added on her website, right? *All About Buckhorn*, she named it. More like All About Vi." She laughed. "Just Ask Vi, some people call it. The town know-it-all starting a forum so she could go on about how much the town owed her? You can imagine what people thought about that."

"It hasn't been up that long, right?" He remembered Luna mentioning it, but hadn't been that interested at the time.

"Not that long, but sure has stirred up some people."

There was always something going on in Buckhorn involving Vi Mullen. He wondered what the townspeople would talk about with her gone.

Then with a jarring start, he realized it would be Amy—and his connection. At least until that story died down and he was long gone from Buckhorn. Probably in prison.

"If you want to know who hated her most, you should check out the comments at *All About Buckhorn*," Mabel was saying. "People got pretty nasty and Vi got pretty nasty back. She even put the worst comments about her and her site on that board of hers at the store where she put the bad checks. Recently, she stopped posting on the site. I think I heard she had tried to take it down. She was pretty angry that people hadn't used it like she'd intended and she'd riled up a bunch of people who'd pushed for her to take down the site—and the comments she'd posted on the Hate Board."

Jaxson was familiar with the corkboard at the back of the store near the old post office boxes, but he'd never paid it much mind and figured locals didn't either. Maybe he was wrong about that.

OWEN HENRY LOOKED a little like his son in the photo. Luna stared at her phone and the headshot her father had sent her. It appeared to have come from an old Montana driver's license. New licenses and photos were required every eight years. This one was more than twice that long ago.

"Just because he let his Montana driver's license expire," she'd said to her father, "doesn't mean that he's dead. He could have just moved to another state. You said you didn't find a death certificate."

"No, but don't get your hopes up. The last record I could find of him was seventeen years ago. I would imagine if he was still alive, he would have used a credit card, licensed a car, had a job, gotten married or applied for a loan during that time."

She knew he was right, but still a part of her wanted to believe that he was still alive and would have some answers for her—as well as his son. "Fifty-seven isn't all that old.

He could have changed his name, gotten a new social security number, moved to another country."

"Luna," her father said. "You're grasping at straws."

Sighing, she said, "But he was alive seventeen years ago, right? Was it anywhere near Buckhorn?"

"It was. He'd gotten a check for apparently some work he did on the Eaton Ranch just outside of town. He and Amy Franklin could have crossed paths. The last income I've been able to find for him was in the spring seventeen years ago. It was a rather large check. Five-thousand dollars."

Severance pay? From a ranch? Didn't sound likely. Or for a contracted job? There was only one way to find out— talk to Tom Eaton. "Thank you. This is a great help," she said, feeling her earlier excitement return. "Amy could have found him."

She realized what that might mean. "If he hadn't wanted to be found for whatever reason, he could have left, changed his name, gotten a new social security number, even moved to another country."

"He could have," he said, a smile in his tone at her continued need to believe the man was still alive. "But why didn't he want to be found?"

"Back child support?"

"I believe he did pay child support. Someone was making a monthly deposit into Lillian Gray's bank account for five-hundred dollars until the account was closed."

Luna suddenly liked Owen Henry a whole lot more. "So he wasn't a deadbeat dad." She wondered if Jaxson knew that.

Still her heart broke for Jaxson at just the thought of the childhood he must have had—especially when she thought of her own happy one.

"What now?" she asked.

"I'll keep looking. Any news at your end?"

"No. I haven't heard from Jaxson yet, but the key has to be Owen Henry, his biological father. Why would he disappear about the time Amy came to Buckhorn looking for him?"

"Maybe the real question is did she find him and that's why she ended up under the floorboards at the store?"

Luna refused to believe the man was a killer. She just hoped she was right.

MABEL TOOK HER time answering Jaxson's last question. "Who else did I see that morning? Saw Lars Olson drive past in his truck that morning. Then I saw Clarice hurrying to catch up to me. That was it. And don't get any ideas about Clarice. She will be late for her own funeral, but I can testify that she didn't have a drop of blood on her that morning."

"Notice anyone parked in front of the store." She shook her head. "Please answer for the recording."

"I saw no one else. But why would the killer have been parked out front when he went in the back door?" Mabel said.

"He? You don't think it could have been a woman?"

"I suppose. Make a woman angry enough and she can commit murder just like a man."

"Why the back door?" he asked.

She made an impatient face. "Now you're just messing with me. Everyone knows the front door is locked until Vi opens the store at nine. So the killer had to go in the back door, which is left open for deliveries once Vi gets there."

He smiled at her and took another bite of his pie before he asked, "Have you ever used an ice fishing spear?"

"When Frank was alive. There might even be one in the garage. You're welcome to look." She wiped her hands on her apron and looked again at his plate. "Did I use one on Vi? Already told you I didn't kill her. As much as Vi irritated the devil out of me, I'm not sure I could have used one on her."

He took another couple of bites. "This pie really is delicious. Have you heard about Vi getting into a disagreement in town lately?" He noticed her hesitate and finished his pie, giving her time. His phone chimed, announcing that he'd just gotten a text. He saw it was from Luna. "Excuse me a second." He opened it and felt his heart slam against his ribs at the sight of his father looking up from the screen at him. Luna had written that the photo was from his father's driver's license, the last one he'd had—seventeen years ago.

He quickly pocketed his phone, not wanting to think about why his father wouldn't have had another driver's license since then. Maybe it just hadn't been under the name Owen Henry. That too brought up a thought he didn't want to deal with right now.

"Mabel, we're going to talk to everyone in town. If you've heard something…"

She sighed as she reached to take his plate and fork. "Dave Tanner." Dave owned the bar and steak house in town. "I'm not even sure what it was about, but I heard Dave's fiancée, Mel, mentioned. Melissa's been trying to buy some land from Vi and you know Vi, she dug her heels in. You'd have to ask Dave, but I heard he and Vi had a row a couple of days ago. But Dave wouldn't hurt a fly." She looked guilty for even bringing it up.

"Thanks," Jaxson told her, sensing that she wasn't going to tell him anything more as she turned and began to rinse his plate. "Thanks for the pie. It was the best I've ever had." He saw some of the tension release from her shoulders.

He thought about the photo Luna had sent him of his father. There was no reason he couldn't show the local residents he questioned Owen Henry's photo. If there was any chance that the murders were related, Jaxson had to know.

"I can let myself out but if you think of anything else that might help…" He made up his mind and said, "There is one more thing. Not to do with Vi's death." She turned from the sink.

He pulled out his phone and called up the photo as he stepped closer. "Do you recognize this man?"

Mabel dried her hands on her apron and carefully took his phone. She squinted at the photo. "Looks familiar, but then again so do most of the cowhands around here. Who is he?"

"Owen Henry. That name ring any bells?"

She shook her head and handed back his phone. "Sorry."

"But you think he was a cowhand?"

"I'm not sure why I said that." She frowned. "You said he isn't connected to Vi's murder?"

Jaxson shook his head. "It's another case I'm working on." He pocketed the photo. "Thanks for your time and that amazing pie."

Mabel blushed. "Anytime, Deputy."

Once inside his patrol SUV, he considered the rest of the names Yarrow had given him. Dave Tanner was way down the list. He scratched off Mabel and mentally moved Tanner up. For a moment, he thought about calling Luna, but he knew she would be busy at work. At least with her at work, he didn't have to worry about her moonlighting, he told himself since she was right on the main drag with large windows that looked into her salon.

When and if she found out anything, she would let him know. Even as he thought it though, he had to remind himself that Amy hadn't put herself under those floorboards. The person who killed her probably had.

Now he'd involved the woman he was falling in love with. He reached for his phone, wondering what he'd been thinking. "I can't help worrying about you," he said the moment Luna answered. "It's too dangerous. Please don't do any more investigating. Just…don't get any more involved."

He could hear the smile in her voice when she spoke. "Do you know me at all? I couldn't walk away from this if you put a gun to my head." He cringed at the mental image. "I just spoke with my father. If it makes you feel any better, he feels the same way you do, but he knows that once I set my mind to something… He's going to help, so stop worrying. It was seventeen years ago. What are the chances that the killer is even still around? My next client just walked in. Later." She disconnected.

He continued to just sit in his vehicle, holding the phone. *What were the chances that Amy's killer was still around?* Maybe the same as Vi's. He took a moment to see if Vi had succeeded in taking down her internet site, *All About Buckhorn*. It was still up but there hadn't been a comment for some time. He scanned the comment section.

Mabel was right. There were some nasty exchanges between Vi and locals. They seemed to grow more contentious with Vi responding with threats that she was going to tell each of their secrets.

"Wow," he said to himself. "Vi really knew how to stir

the pot." But was this why she was killed? Was someone afraid she would make good her threat and tell their secret?

Pocketing his phone, he started the engine and drove to the bar to talk to Dave Tanner.

BEING PRESSURED TO solve this case quickly, Ken drove out of town to what had once been a small trailer park. Some of the trailers still remained, but were clearly abandoned, doors open, roofs caving in. There were abandoned cars, some up on jacks, others stripped and left to rust.

An older model sedan and a chopped motorcycle were parked in front of one of the newer double-wides. He parked beside the sedan and got out to the sound of a barking dog and a yelling woman inside the mobile home.

Before he reached the door, a middle-aged man came out, slamming the door behind him as he yelled for the dog and the woman to both shut up. He moved past the acting marshal as if he hadn't even seen him. A moment later, Yarrow heard the man kick-starting the bike. After a few attempts, the motor caught and he left in a hail of dirt and dust.

Ken knocked. He could hear what sounded like things being thrown around inside. He knocked harder and the sound stopped. The door opened. A woman's tearstained face filled the doorway and she was wearing a large faded sweatshirt over a pair of cutoff jean shorts.

Karla Parson brushed back a mass of tangled greasy-looking hair, licking chapped lips, as she took in his uniform. He caught the scent of marijuana that seemed to be coming from the fake wood walls as well as her pores.

"I'm Acting Marshal Kenneth Yarrow," he said. "I need to ask you a few questions about—"

"I don't know anything," she interrupted. "You should have asked Butch before he left. I stay out of his business."

"You're the one I need to speak to."

She blinked. "Then I guess you'd better come in." She stepped back and he noticed that her feet were bare, and the floor was covered with what might have been breakfast dishes. None were broken it appeared because they were plastic. "I was just cleaning up a few things," she said as she bent to retrieve the mess. "Why do you want to talk to me?"

He stepped in, closing the door behind him, then cautiously worked his way to the couch, avoiding both food and dishes. He considered sitting down but changed his mind given the disrepair of the couch. He told himself to make this quick. The trailer had a sweet smell of something rotten.

"I need to ask about Vivian Mullen," he said.

She looked up from where she was bent over, a dirty plate in her hand. She chucked it into the overflowing mess in the sink as she rose.

He pulled out his phone. "I'll be recording this."

"Why are you asking me about Vi?"

"You saved her life recently."

She let out a bark of a laugh. "Don't remind me. We both regretted it. You should have seen her at the hospital. It about killed her that she had to thank me." Her eyes narrowed. "But that was months ago. So what's this about?"

"You didn't hear what happened to her?"

Karla waited, looking at him blankly.

"Someone murdered her." He waited for Karla's reaction. Surprise? Shock?

It took a moment for the woman to even react at all. When she did, it wasn't what he'd expected. She reared back, tilting her head toward the ceiling and laughing, open-mouthed, for a good fifteen seconds. When she stopped, she looked at him in surprise. "You don't think I..." That made her laugh again. Wiping her eyes, she said, "Sorry, wasn't me. But when you find out who did it, I want to congratulate him or her. Meanest woman who ever lived." She frowned. "Vi's really dead?"

He was surprised she hadn't heard but living this far out... "Did you happen to go into town yesterday?"

"Is that when she was killed?" She shook her head. "My car isn't running."

"Your boyfriend didn't give you a ride into town on his bike?"

She sighed, anger pinching her features. "Butch wouldn't throw water on me if I was on fire let alone let me use his bike and I don't ride in the bitch seat." She shook her head as she began to pick up more dishes and food from the floor. "Vi's dead. I guess her time was up. I needn't have bothered to save her life then, huh? What do call that? You know..."

"Irony? You saved her life, and someone killed her not all that long afterward."

"That's it. Irony." She considered the floor for a moment. "I'm going to have to get the mop bucket out." Her gaze came back to him. "So who do you think killed her?"

"I don't know yet," he said. "You care to speculate?"

Karla wagged her head. "Anyone who knew her. But if I had to guess... Lynette Crest."

Ken remembered one of the old hens at the café was named Lynette. He also remembered thinking that he wanted to talk to her. "Why her?"

With a shrug, she said, "Bad blood between them for

years. Lately? Vi threatened to sue her son for not paying his bill at the store. She put one of his insufficient-funds checks up on a board in the back, saying not to take his checks, not to let him charge. Heard Lynette was livid, thinks she's so much better than everyone else in town." Karla swore. "I've been on that board so many times it isn't even funny. So what's the big deal?" She coughed and looked at the dirty floor again. He could tell she was anxious to get her mop out and get busy. He was just as anxious to get some fresh air.

"If you think of anything…" he said, turning off his phone and pocketing it. He handed her his card with his cell phone number on it. She barely looked at it before tossing it onto the cluttered counter.

"Yarrow, right?" she asked before he could reach the door.

"Acting Marshal. I'll be staying at the motel in town."

"You had a thing for Vi, I heard?" The humor in her voice made him turn back.

"I beg your pardon?"

She waved a hand as if to brush it off. "I heard you asked her out one day in the store not too long ago. She really put your ass down. If I were you, I wouldn't care who killed her."

She'd heard about his humiliation at the store, but she hadn't heard that Vi had been murdered? He didn't know what to say, but Karla didn't give him a chance.

"Careful, the floor's slick." He nodded, feeling her watching him. "You think she's burning in hell?"

Her question surprised him. He reached the door, opened it to let in fresh air and light, and looked back at her. "Quite possibly."

Karla laughed. "Well, if she is in hell, then it won't be

long before she'll be running the place." She shook her head and said with almost urgency, "I've got to get this cleaned up before Butch comes back."

Yarrow hesitated, thinking he should ask if she was afraid of her boyfriend, if she was in danger, if she might need help. But she must have been asked before because she said, "He's okay. I've known worse." Her gaze locked with his for a moment and he feared she'd say something more about what had been overheard that day in the store between him and Vi. Had he threatened her? He honestly couldn't remember. Maybe.

But all she said was, "Life's funny, isn't it?" He saw so much regret in those eyes that it made him ache. At that moment, he thought that he and Karla weren't that different. It was a frightening notion.

"Yes, life is funny." But neither of them was laughing as he left. On the way back to town, he passed the boyfriend on the motorbike headed home.

CHAPTER FOURTEEN

WHILE VERA HADN'T returned to Buckhorn after she'd left years ago, she'd stayed in touch. She'd known what had been going on. Just as she knew where to get anything she needed once back here. It hadn't taken her long to connect with a thirtysomething pot distributor simply named Butch. She'd met him in an area outside of town by the creek and they'd done their transaction. Even though marijuana had become legal in Montana, she preferred to get hers old-school. Also, it was cheaper.

She'd waited until he'd left on his loud black smoke-emitting motorcycle before she smoked a joint out in the pines like old times and then headed back into town. She had business to attend to concerning her twin, she thought as she drove.

As she felt the drug smoothing her rough edges, she thought of her sister. It had been easy to know what Vi had been up to all these years. The woman had to be the most hated person in town, always going on about what she'd done for Buckhorn. It had been enough to make Vera gag.

But while Vi had painted a rosy picture of herself and Buckhorn, there were things that not even the former reigning self-pronounced empress of this town could sugarcoat. There'd been the death of their oddball brother. Vera had always known there was something not quite right about him. Then Axel had left Vi. That had to have crushed her. Not even Vi could put a pretty spin on that.

Not that Vi hadn't bounced right back by throwing a big 125th birthday celebration for the town. Single-handedly, according to her, Vera had heard. But then the governor had almost been killed. Still Vi had recovered from even that—until someone put her out of her misery.

As Vera drove back into Buckhorn, she looked around the in-the-middle-of-nowhere-town her sister had lived her entire life and thought how different she and Vi had been— and yet how alike. They'd fallen for the same man all those years ago and gotten pregnant, producing two daughters— at least that's what she'd thought until she'd run into Axel in that bar in Spokane.

Vi's birth daughter had died. Jennifer had lived, but Vera had to wonder if there wasn't something wrong with their genes. Also their choice in men if Axel was an example. When she'd first seen him in that Spokane bar, it had seemed like anything but good luck. It had been after his divorce and Buckhorn's 125th birthday celebration. He'd looked beaten down, showing his age. She'd felt sorry for him and offered to buy him a beer. That's when he told her about his visit to Buckhorn and how poorly Vi had treated him.

None of that was anything new. She'd been treated badly by Vi as well. Her twin had stolen her daughter, even gone so far as having Jennifer's last name changed to Mullen, which ironically was appropriate since Jen *was* Axel's daughter. Had Vi ever figured that out?

The night at the bar, Axel had actually tried to hit her up for money. She'd laughed in his face, but she'd bought him a beer, curious to find out how he'd ended up in such dire straits.

The story he'd told riveted her to her bar stool. *"Tina isn't your biological daughter?"* That had been the only part of his tired story that she had grasped onto with both hands.

"She's not mine," he'd said and laughed bitterly. "And here's the kicker, she isn't even Vi's." Vera had thought he'd had too much to drink. She'd been skeptical until Axel had shown her the DNA proof—and Vi had admitted it to him that it was true. Tina wasn't his anymore than she was Vi's.

Babies switched at birth? Tina wasn't Vi's legal heir. Not that it mattered. The trust their father had made of the properties in Buckhorn hadn't taken in account children or grandchildren. Even if Vi had left a will, Tina couldn't break the trust even if she tried. Which meant that if Vi died, everything would be Vera's.

Vera had been so delighted by the news that she'd bought Axel another beer and one thing had led to another. Axel had always been good-looking. But he now looked a good twenty years younger than the man she'd run into at the bar. In his late fifties and only a little older than Vera, he should have been hers. Vi had stolen him from her all those years ago, but thanks to her sister's timely demise, the two of them were enjoying a reunion of sorts.

"How do you like this, sis?" Vera said now as she drove back to the house. "I have it all, including Axel, and you got what you had coming to you." Apparently there was someone meaner than her sister who had an axe to grind— or an ice fishing spear so to speak.

Revenge was something Vera knew intimately. She had enough grievances built up against her twin, she thought, to make it next to impossible to shed a real tear for Vi. Her twin had stolen everything—including Axel and later their daughter, Jennifer.

Just the thought of Jennifer made her wonder what Vi's daughter, had she lived, would have been like. More unstable than Vera's daughter, Jennifer?

The irony of the situation was priceless. Too bad Vera had waited so long to share the truth about Jennifer's father with her sister. Now Vi wasn't around to appreciate it. She had often imagined the expression on her twin's face when she told her the truth. Axel had been Vera's first. Vi had taken him away from her all those years ago by getting pregnant.

But before Vera left, she'd gotten her revenge by sleeping with Vi's husband. In another twist of fate, Vera had gotten pregnant. Not even Axel knew that Jennifer was his.

Now she and Axel were together—at least temporarily—and their daughter was in a mental institution for the criminally insane. Vera wouldn't be in Montana long enough to visit her since the thought gave her the willies.

Worse, that annoying voice in her head that sounded like her mother's was always trying to make her feel guilty for the way her daughter had turned out.

She wanted to remind her dead mother that when Jennifer ran away, she ran to Vi. So why wasn't Vi responsible for how the girl had turned out?

As she drove back to town, she ground her teeth. Vi might be dead, but she wasn't forgotten. Vera was almost angry that someone had killed Vi before she could get revenge against her sister. *Almost*, she thought. Now everything her sister had worked her entire life for was hers.

DAVE TANNER STILL lived over the bar while building his and Melissa's home outside of town. He would have had it finished if not for Buckhorn's 125th birthday celebration. He'd pulled workers off the house to add on to the bar, building a steak house on the back.

Jaxson knew all this from Luna. Most everything about Buckhorn and its residents he'd learned had come from her. She was right—he had used her. At least at first, at least until he found himself falling for her.

He parked out front at the bar, regretting the mistakes he'd made that had him at this point in his life. Luna was at the top of that list.

Like most everything that had changed in Buckhorn, the old sign that had read only Bar had been replaced before the town's 125th celebration with a larger one that read Buckhorn Saloon and Steak House. The weathered rustic log structure had been painted a dark brown.

The front door that had been thick planks of wood, covered with flyers and hand-printed notes from people looking for jobs or used cars and appliances, was gone. Buckhorn was growing, something Vi Mullen had started, but she would never see how it all turned out.

Jaxson pushed open the huge log and glass door and stepped inside, glad to see that little had changed inside from the first time he'd been there. A small television droned at the far end of the bar where a couple of older regulars were propped up on stools. Both turned as he came in.

"Mornin', Ralph. Wilbur," he said to the two and nodded at the owner standing behind the bar. All three responded in greeting, their curiosity clearly piqued as he said, "Dave, could I have a moment. Maybe in your office?"

Dave, who was about his age with a tanned shaved head and a friendly smile that lit up his entire face, wiped his hands on a towel, asked the regulars to keep an eye on the bar and motioned Jaxson back.

Once inside the small office with the door closed, Dave offered him a chair.

"This shouldn't take long," the deputy told him, pulling out his notebook as he sat down. "I just need to ask you a few questions about Vi."

"I still can't believe someone killed her and in such a brutal way," the bar owner said as he sat down behind his desk. He seemed shaken and Jaxson realized that having to saw the floorboards around the body must have been a traumatic experience for him.

"I'm asking everyone if they noticed anyone around the store that morning or in the alley behind it."

Dave shook his head. "I had a late night at the bar. I wasn't awake until I got the call about assisting with getting her body out."

"I heard you and Vi had an argument a few days ago," Jaxson said, getting right to it.

The bar owner looked chagrined as he dropped his gaze and ran a hand over his shaved head. "I shouldn't have gotten into with her. I'm sure I didn't help the situation and I only managed to make Mel angry at me for butting in." He sighed. "If you heard, then you probably know Mel wants a piece of property that Vi owns. She has this idea about trying to get a small health care clinic here in town. She's spoken to some medical personnel who might be interested in manning it a few days a week. But first she wants us to build the facility and has a spot picked out."

"Why would Vi have been against that?" Jaxson asked.

"Sounds like a great idea." With a medical emergency, the only options in Buckhorn were an hour's drive to the next town or a helicopter flight out. Both took valuable time.

"Vi just said she wasn't interested in selling off any more of her property," Dave said with shrug. "And since she owns all the property around the town, she had us land-locked and at her whim."

"You do realize that sounds like a motive for murder, right?"

The bar owner looked shocked. "You can't think that I…"

"You wouldn't be the first person to want to throttle Vi."

Dave shook his head. "It's a moot point. Vi changed her mind. Mel talked to her again, apologized for me and…"

"Vi agreed?"

He nodded. "You can talk to Mel, but Vi was having her attorney draw up the paperwork. Not sure what will happen now though."

"Why did Vi change her mind?" Jaxson asked, surprised. Vi Mullen was notorious for digging in her heels and never backing down.

"Mel can be pretty persuasive. But I don't think it hurt that Mel suggested the business be called Mullen Clinic."

Jaxson chuckled. "You married a smart woman." The deputy shifted gears. "Did you happen to hear anything at the bar the night before Vi was killed? Someone complaining about Vi?"

The bar owner looked faintly amused. "She was often the topic of conversation, but I can't remember anyone going on about her that night. Jory Price was having his bachelor party and his fiancée, Avery Eaton, and her attendants showed up."

Jaxson knew about the wedding that would unite not just the two powerful families but the two huge ranches. Both ranches were run by prominent men in the state. Along with cattle, Tom Eaton raised some of the finest quarter horses in the nation. Everyone knew that Tom's youngest child, Avery, was his pride and joy.

"The men had been drinking heavily before the women showed up. Things got pretty wild," Dave was saying.

What any of that had to do with Vi or her murder, Jaxson couldn't imagine, but he let the bar owner continue.

"I had to call Melissa to come down from upstairs to help," the bar owner said. "As the night went on, I had to pull some truck keys and throw a couple of the worst customers out before closing. I almost had to call for backup when the future groom and his best man got into it."

Jaxson doubted that since Dave had the body type of a bouncer and the temperament of a saint—until crossed. He figured the bar owner could hold his own against the cowboys. "Who's Jory's best man?"

"Carson McCabe. I don't know what started it, but it got pretty physical before I separated them and threw them out."

The name McCabe was familiar since this hadn't been Carson's first bar fight. He was a hired hand on the Eaton Ranch. His father was the ranch manager—possibly the only reason Carson was still employed.

"Or McCabe *was* the best man," Dave said with a chuckle. "Not sure after the other night. The last thing Tom Eaton would want is anything ruining his baby girl's upcoming nuptials. I had to pull McCabe's keys. He left the ranch pickup out front."

"How'd he get home?"

Dave shrugged. "I guess someone took him. He was dropped off early the next morning. Melissa saw what looked like his father driving the other truck. I guess Mc-Cabe brought a spare key to his truck because he didn't try to get the ones I took from him until later that evening. He was still hungover even then."

"Early the morning of the murder?" Jaxson asked. "Before six?"

"Right about then I think. Melissa would know."

Thanking Dave, he pocketed his notebook and got to his feet. "If you think of anyone who might have been upset with Vi recently…"

"I'll give it some thought. Melissa is upstairs if you want to go up and talk to her. She might have heard something."

"I'll do that." Going out the side door, he headed up the stairs, thinking about what Dave had told him. Nothing he could see that would have had anything to do with Vi Mullen or her murder. Still he found the argument between the future groom and best man interesting. He wondered what Luna would make of it since he'd heard about her and Tucker Price being seen together at the café. Tucker was Jory's older brother.

Jaxson tried to ignore the stab of jealousy. Luna was right. He'd lied to her, so he had no right to be jealous. But Tucker hadn't had to try to move in either.

BY EARLY AFTERNOON, Luna was already tired and anxious to hear from Jaxson. She feared Amy's DNA report might come back sooner rather than later. She'd shown the two photos, one of Owen and one of Amy, to everyone who'd come into the salon. No one had recognized either one of them.

Tired and discouraged, she'd gotten caught up on the appointments she'd had to cancel and was finishing up her day with Clarice Barber.

A throwback from a gentler time, the soft-spoken small gray-haired elderly woman always wore pearls and what Luna's mother would have called a housedress. Today's dress sported tiny yellow butterflies in a shirtwaist, buttoned all the way up to her pearls.

"Are you all right?" Luna asked, noticing that Clarice didn't seem herself after her wash and set. Normally full of chatter, the woman had responded to Luna's attempt to draw her out in monosyllables.

On closer inspection, the woman looked pale and seemed upset.

As she started to tuck her under the standing drying ring, Clarice touched her arm with trembling fingers. "That boy of yours."

Luna looked at her in confusion. Had the woman had a stroke?

"The handsome deputy," Clarice clarified. Luna smiled, nodded and waited. Evidently the woman had something on her mind. "I've seen him before. At least I think it was him."

Something about the quiet way Clarice said it, looking around the empty salon as if the walls had ears, set Luna's pulse off. "Before what?"

"Before now. I saw him when he wasn't a deputy. He was much younger."

Luna was telling herself that Clarice was probably mistaken when the elderly woman added, "He was in the store, talking to Vi. They were arguing. It got really loud. Then he left in some old ranch truck."

Heart in her throat, Luna pulled out her phone. "Is this the man you saw?" she asked as she called up the photo of Owen Henry.

Clarice took the phone, holding close and gave a startled gasp. "It could have been him." She frowned. "Or the deputy when he was young, but Mabel said he didn't live here when he was young, did he? Mabel is always saying I get everything wrong," she said, handing back the phone.

Luna had noticed a resemblance between Jaxson and his father. It was in the eyes and the shape of their strong jaws. Knowing Clarice, she could have seen Owen Henry, but she also could have seen Jaxson when he came to town seventeen years ago, looking for Amy. "When did you see this man arguing with Vi?"

Clarice shook her head. "I think it was a long time ago, but I'm not sure." She sounded rattled. "He kind of looks like the deputy." It was more a plea.

"Yes, he does," Luna quickly agreed and that seemed to soothe the older woman some.

"After he left, Vi was really upset, cussing and carrying on—until she saw me and looked…scared. She demanded to know how long I'd been standing there and what I'd heard. I said nothing and got out of there." Clarice fiddled with her pearls, looking nervous. "The deputy is such a nice young man. I wasn't sure I should say anything."

Luna called up Amy's photo and showed it to her. "Have you ever seen this young woman?"

Clarice looked confused. "Isn't that Lynette's granddaughter, Sadie?"

"No."

"Then I don't know," she said, handing back the phone and looking tired.

But Luna had to ask, "Do you remember what the argument was about with the man who looked like the deputy?"

She frowned. "He was asking about some girl."

Her heart began to pound. "Was it Amy?"

"Maybe." Her gaze locked with Luna's. "I could be wrong. Mabel is right. I often don't know what I'm talking about. But I know I saw him before now. I know I did. I saw him arguing with Vi and she was really upset."

Had Clarice seen Owen Henry arguing with Vi all those years ago? Or had she been right the first time and it had been Jaxson when he'd come to Buckhorn seventeen years ago? Except Jaxson hadn't mentioned getting into an argument with Vi.

"I'm glad you told me," Luna assured her.

"Vi wasn't very nice to him, but then she wasn't nice to a lot of people." She frowned again, looking confused. "I think it was a long time ago. He looked so young back then."

"You need not worry anymore about it."

Clarice looked so relieved that Luna felt sorry for her. It was obvious that she liked the deputy and didn't want to think badly of him. Was she worried that Jaxson might have killed Vi because of an argument years ago?

With a relieved smile, the woman sat back with a magazine to allow her hair to set. Luna stepped away and thought about Clarice's usual confusion.

Had it been Jaxson arguing with Vi Mullen when he'd first come to Montana looking for Amy? Or his father, Owen Henry? Then again Clarice could be confused and the argument was more recent.

Her phone chimed as a text came in. She stared at it, realizing she'd forgotten about going horseback riding with

Tucker Price. She hadn't ridden in years and had looked forward to it at the time.

It was tomorrow afternoon.

CHAPTER FIFTEEN

AFTER CLARICE, LUNA HAD no appointments and took advantage of it. With Owen Henry's and Amy's photos, she headed over to the café, which she knew wouldn't be busy this time of day.

She found Earl Ray sitting in his usual spot, talking to his wife, Bessie. "You're just the two people I want to see," she announced and joined them at the counter.

Bessie tucked her long gray braid behind her. It fell almost to her waist. "If you're going to try to talk me into cutting my hair—"

"Not a chance," she told the older woman. "I love your hair. No, I have a photo I want to show you." She pulled it from her pocket. "Do either of you remember this man?" She handed it over.

Bessie studied it for a long moment saying, "He looks vaguely familiar," before handing it to Earl Ray.

He studied it for a moment, adding, "I agree with Bessie. Familiar but I don't recognize him. He does look a little like Jaxson though, doesn't he? Who is he?"

"His name is Owen Henry. I believe he worked on a ranch around here just under twenty years ago." She could see that both were curious why she was asking.

"How about this young woman," Luna said and showed them both the photo of Amy Franklin. Bessie shook her head after one glance. Earl Ray took a little longer but finally handed the phone back.

With a knowing look of understanding, he said, "What are you up to, Luna Declan? I suspect you're playing detective," he teased with a twinkle in his blue eyes. His phone rang and he excused himself to take it outside.

"I'm wondering if the man in the photo might have helped put down the flooring in the storage room seventeen years ago," Luna said to Bessie.

"I remember when that floor went down. Don't recall who Vi hired though to do it. She's probably the only person who would know. Except for Axel. He was still around then. And now he's back with—" Bessie sighed "—Vera. How in the world did a body end up under there?" She shuddered at the thought. "Have you heard any more about the identity of the remains?"

"I don't think they know yet," Luna said noncommittally.

"A young woman, I heard. Mummified." Bessie shuddered again.

"I'm sure the acting marshal will get to the bottom of it," she said.

Bessie laughed. "Sure he will."

Earl Ray was still on the phone, so she thanked Bessie and hurried back to work.

WHILE MCCABE WASN'T on the list of suspects Yarrow had given him, Jaxson still wanted to talk to him before his day ended. If Dave was right, then the cowboy had been parked in front of the bar in a spot where he could have seen someone come out of the store on the morning of the murder. He could have seen the murderer and not realized it.

As he drove out to the Eaton Ranch, he thought of his

father. Had he been here seventeen years ago? Had Amy found him? If so, what had happened?

He knew Luna was right. If Amy had found him, then his father was the trail they should be trying to follow. He used to get so tired of hearing his mother talk about Owen Henry that he often hadn't paid any attention. Now he wished he had. In all her talk of romance and love and soulmates, maybe she'd said something that could help him now.

Ahead, he could see the turn into the ranch. He had his father's photo on his phone. He debated whether or not to show it to McCabe. If he kept showing the photo and asking questions about Owen Henry, it was bound to get back to Yarrow.

The acting marshal was on edge enough right now, more than usual with these murders. Jaxson got the feeling that it wouldn't take much for him to completely unravel with all this pressure on him. Two murder victims and Yarrow wanting to show everyone that he shouldn't have been passed over for the marshal job.

Parking in front of the large rambling white house, Jaxson got out. The place was beautiful with a wide front porch and a bright array of flowers growing in pots everywhere he looked. He wondered if the Eatons had a gardener. He wouldn't have been surprised.

He could see a bunch of ranch hands sitting in the shadow of the barn. "Looking for Carson McCabe," he called to them.

A rangy blond ranch hand rose from the bunch and headed in his direction. He'd met McCabe on several occasions, both times had involved breaking up a fight. He wondered if the cowboy remembered him. Or if the uniform jacket alone was the reason McCabe already looked obstinate.

"What's this about?" the cowboy demanded within feet of him. McCabe had a split lip and there was discolored bruising around one of his eyes from his recent fight. Jaxson wondered how Jory had faired since he had a wedding this coming weekend.

"Is there somewhere we could talk? Privately? Or we could sit in my patrol SUV."

McCabe shook his head. "I've spent enough time in the back of your patrol car, thank you very much." He motioned toward the pines by the creek and headed in that direction.

They hadn't gone far into the trees before they were out of sight of the other ranch hands. McCabe stopped and turned. "So what do you want?"

"I'm investigating Vi Mullen's murder."

This was clearly not what he'd expected. Looking relieved, the cowboy let out a laugh. "I thought Jory had called you about the disagreement we had the other night."

"What was that about?" Jaxson asked.

"Nothing." He shook his head. "You want to talk to me about Vi? Well, I didn't kill her. Is that all?"

"You left the ranch pickup you'd been driving at the bar the night before the murder."

He frowned. "So what?"

"You were dropped off early the next morning at the bar about the time of the murder. Did you go to the store that morning?"

His eyes widened in alarm. "I went straight back to the ranch. If you don't believe me, you can ask my old man. He was waiting for me, already mad about having to drive me into town first thing."

"I believe you," Jaxson said, but still planned to check with the elder McCabe. "From where your pickup was parked at the bar, you could see down the street in the direction of the general store."

McCabe frowned. "You think I saw the killer?"

"I think there is a chance you could have."

He shook his head. "I was hungover. I could barely see to drive since I had one eye swollen shut." He turned to spit into the grass. "Even if I had seen someone, I wouldn't have thought anything about it. I didn't know someone had killed Vi until I heard that afternoon."

Jaxson nodded. "If you saw someone in that alley or even leaving the store that early in the morning, you probably didn't even register it. But now that you have time to think about it…" The cowboy was frowning again. "We're pretty sure the killer went in through the back and came out the front before the store was to open. Will you at least think about it?" He reached into his jacket pocket, took out his card and handed it to McCabe. "Call me if you think of anything that might help."

He took the card, still frowning as he looked down at it.

"Thanks for your help." The deputy saw that McCabe was uncomfortable on this side of the law—and found some humor in it as he started to leave. It was a long shot, but one Jaxson had to take. At this point, he didn't feel they were getting any closer to finding Vi's killer.

"One more thing," he said and pulled out his phone. It took him only a few seconds to call up the photo. Another long shot. Seventeen years ago, McCabe was probably ten or eleven. "Do you know this man?"

The cowboy took the phone, looked at the driver's license of Owen Henry, frowned again and handed it back. "Who is he?"

"Name's Owen Henry."

"You think he's the killer?" McCabe asked as he pocketed the card with Jaxson's number on it.

"No," he said. At least not Vi's.

"If that's all, I need to get back."

"Call me if you think of anything that might help." But Jaxson could tell there was a slim to none chance that that was going to happen.

As he climbed into his patrol SUV, he got a text from Ken telling him to come to the café.

From a booth at the front of the café, Ken finished his coffee and watched Jaxson put away his late lunch. He vaguely remembered being able to eat that much at the young deputy's age. "Tell me what you've gotten so far."

The café was empty except for a trucker at the counter back by the kitchen. He listened as Jaxson told him about his interview with Mabel Aldrich, then Dave Tanner and Tanner's fiancée, Melissa Herbert.

It didn't surprise him that Jory Price and Carson McCabe had gotten into an altercation. McCabe was a hothead with a quick-draw temper. He listened as Jaxson told him about interviewing McCabe.

"He could have seen the killer, but he says he was in such bad shape that morning he doesn't recall much. I left my number with him in case he remembers something."

"Anything else?" Ken said when the deputy finished. Jaxson might be young and inexperienced, but he was sharp and eager to learn and seemed thorough. Ken found himself warming toward the deputy.

"Melissa did verify Dave's story. Vi was going to sell her the land. I wonder what will happen now that Vi is dead?"

Ken shook his head. "I interviewed Vera and Axel. They appear to be a couple. Definitely suspicious. Those two had the most to gain from the victim's death. But if the murder was impulsive, heat of the moment like we suspect, then it leaves us with too many suspects. Not that the latter rules out Vera and Axel."

"Anything on the…other one?"

Ken groaned, not even wanting to think about it. "Baggins really left at a convenient time," he complained. "Langstone is working with the state medical examiner. He thinks they might be able to get a DNA sample, but right now the current murder takes precedence. How are you doing on your list?"

"Lars Olson, Vi's son-in-law, is next. How about you?"

"Lynette Crest," Ken said. "She's one of those old hens who hang out here in the mornings." He saw the deputy's surprise. "I don't think she killed Vi. I just have a feeling that she knows something."

JAXSON HAD BEEN surprised by Yarrow's more friendly attitude toward him. The acting marshal had almost been treating him like an equal. For whatever reason, he hoped it lasted.

In the meantime, he couldn't help thinking about the past as he went looking for Lars Olson who, according to local scuttlebutt, hadn't been close to his mother-in-law. In fact, Vi had told anyone who would listen what she thought of Lars, which wasn't much.

He caught up with Lars at the local landfill. A nondescript man in his early forties, Lars had a receding hairline and a growing thickness around his middle. But he had a kind face and, from everything Jaxson had heard about him, he was a good man, hard worker and great father.

The deputy had found him unloading the town's garbage truck out at the town's landfill. He'd motioned to him, and Lars had cut the truck's engine and climbed out a little stiffly.

"I spend my life behind the wheel of either a garbage truck or a snowplow or a pickup," Lars said. "The job's starting to get to me, but if not me, then who?" he continued as if he'd been having this conversation with himself for a while. "Vi tried to fire me numerous times, but she couldn't find anyone who wanted the job." He let out an amused though bitter sounding laugh. "I never thought I'd spend my life here in Buckhorn."

He looked out at the mountains past the landfill before his expression changed as he seemed to remember what had kept him here. "You heard about the baby?" He brightened considerably. "We got our Chloe. Now I have a son." He smiled a faraway look in his eye for a moment before he said, "Sorry. You're probably wanting to ask me about Vi's murder, huh? I heard the law was talking to everyone in town."

Not quite, but Jaxson didn't correct him. "What can you tell me about your relationship with Vi?"

"She hated me and I wasn't fond of her, but I'm sure you've already heard all about it from everyone in town. It wasn't like Vi kept anything to herself. She thought Tina could do better. It was true," he said with a chuckle. "I made some mistakes and almost lost her." He shrugged. "Vi had her reasons for despising me."

"Why was that?" Jaxson asked even though he'd already heard.

"I had an affair when her daughter and I were living together," Lars said. "It was with Shirley Langer, who ran the Sleepy Pine until she left town.

"That was when Tina was pregnant." Lars nodded to himself. "With another man's baby. But Chloe is mine now and always will be," he said fervently. "Tina and I were going through a rough patch. That's all it was. Vi didn't make it easier, but we all survived the scandal and are stronger for it. I think that lately I was growing on my mother-in-law. Another fifty years and she might have even said my name without growling."

Lars was joking, but Jaxson knew about the animosity between the two. He just thought it would have been more likely for Vi to kill Lars than the other way around. "Where were you the morning that Vi was murdered?"

"Working. I get up at five and go down to the town shop," Lars said. "I fix whatever is broken, work on the trucks, get ready to climb behind the wheel of whichever truck needs to be run that day. I pick up garbage once a week. No snowplowing this time of year, but there was a windstorm recently that blew down some trees that I needed to take care of with my chain saw."

The deputy asked, "Did you go by the store on your way to either the shop or to cut the fallen trees?"

Lars frowned. "I did when I had to go pickup my chain saw over at Dave's. He had sharpened the blades on it for me."

The answer took him by surprise since he knew the kind of night Dave had had and how late he'd probably gotten to bed. "Dave Tanner? He was up at that hour?"

The town's handyman laughed. "Not when you own a bar that closes at 2:00 a.m. I didn't wake him. I knew the chain saw was in his shed behind the restaurant, so I picked it up and drove down the alley back toward town."

In the direction of the general store. "Did you see anyone in the alley?"

"Not behind the store, but while I was in the shed, an Eaton Ranch truck pulled into the bar parking lot."

"Did you see who was driving?"

"Looked like George McCabe, the Eaton Ranch manager, but I can't be sure who was behind the wheel. Definitely saw who got out though. Carson McCabe. He looked the worse for wear."

"How's that?" Jaxson asked, even though he knew.

"Hungover for starters. Also like he'd been in a fight. He had a black eye and what looked like a fat lip. He was limping as he unlocked the truck and climbed in."

"What happened then?"

"George left. Carson was still sitting in the other ranch truck when I left."

"One more question. You didn't happen to replace the old flooring in the storage room seventeen years ago, did you?"

Lars shook his head. "Vi trusted me to take out the old flooring. Also I worked cheap since I was young and hungry. But when it came to the new floor, she said she wanted someone who knew what he was doing. That was Vi."

"You remember who she hired?"

Lars shook his head. "I'd taken an extra job over in the next county hauling hay."

"Anyone who might know?"

"Vi kept everything when it came to paperwork. It might

still be in her files. Wouldn't be computerized. She liked doing things the way her parents had—the hard way."

Jaxson thanked him and pocketed his notebook and pen. "Who do you think killed her?"

Lars seemed to think about that for a few moments. "Vi had been getting more irritable over the past few years, couldn't seem to get along with anyone. She was really hurt when Axel bailed on her, even though she tried hard not to show it. She was an angry woman most of her life, but lately..." He sighed and looked toward the mountains. "I think she just crossed the wrong person. Maybe someone angrier at the world than even she was."

CHAPTER SIXTEEN

JOHNNY BERG FOUND himself more scared than he'd been even yesterday. *He had seen something at the murder scene.*

He couldn't believe that he hadn't remembered. It had come to him, a flash of memory that had awakened him and sent his pulse into overdrive. There had been something glittering on the floor at the edge of his vision that had caught his eye just for an instant. Not long enough for him to see it and consciously make a note of it at the time.

The memory had made him bolt upright in bed in terror. Keys. There had been a set of keys lying on the floor next to a stack of large cardboard boxes opposite Vi's body. The flash of silver on the floor on the opposite side of the storage room was why he hadn't seen Vi's body on his way into the store.

The realization came with another jolt. Had the killer dropped the keys in the process of trying to hide quickly and hadn't had time to retrieve them before he'd come into the store?

His blood turned to ice at the thought of who might have been hiding back there. He tried to remember if the keys had been there when he found Vi's body, all the time knowing they hadn't been. He would have seen them. He would have probably picked them up with the killer just inches away. He would be dead now.

The thought drove him out of his apartment and back

to work. He had to keep moving, had to decide what to do. Tell the cops what he's seen or keep his mouth shut and live another day?

The killer had seen him. There was no doubt about that now. He debated what to do. The killer didn't know he'd seen the keys. But if the killer thought he had, he might be afraid that Johnny knew who the keys belonged to.

The artist in him could see the keys clearly now that he'd remembered them. He could describe them to the cops. Hell, he could draw a picture of them. But what if it didn't help find the killer? Instead, once the cops started asking about a set of keys, it would make the killer think that he'd seen something even more incriminating.

He thought he would lose his mind as he drove his route. Nope, he couldn't tell the cops about the keys he decided as the workday wore on. Johnny Berg wanted the killer to feel safe. He didn't want him doing anything rash. He felt better after making that decision, yet he found himself watching his rearview mirror, unable to shake the feeling that the killer was already watching him, waiting to see what he did.

THE ACTING MARSHAL was on his way to Lynette Crest's when he got a call from the neighborhood kid he had watching his house—more accurately watching his girlfriend.

"She left again," Bobby said, making Ken wonder what he'd been thinking when he'd hired the unemployed teenager to keep tabs on Shar.

"Left with a gym bag on her way to Pilates or left all dolled up like she was going shopping?" *Or going to meet someone?*

"Dolled up? Yeah, that."

"Describe what she was wearing. A dress, high heels, hair fixed, makeup?"

"You didn't tell me I had to remember all of that," the kid complained, but after a sigh said, "A blue shiny dress, high heels, bright red lipstick and her hair… Well, it wasn't in a ponytail like it had been yesterday. It was kinda curly and down. Sunglasses! She had on sunglasses," he said as if excited that he'd remembered. "And she was looking at her phone, smiling. She stopped for a minute, sent a text and then left. Better?"

"Much," Ken said grudgingly. From what he could tell, Bobby spent his days since graduating from high school in his room gaming with other teens who would probably never leave home either.

"I probably should get a raise, huh?"

"Don't push it. Let me know when she comes back." He disconnected and swore. For weeks he'd been suspecting something was going on with her. His being out of town was giving her free rein. Was she cheating on him? He still didn't know, but that knot in his stomach he'd had for weeks told him she was. He just needed proof.

Turning his thoughts back to the job at hand, he pulled up in front of Lynette Crest's house and cut the engine. It was a small neat cottage with rows of tulips bordering the sidewalk.

He stepped out into the beautiful spring day feeling heavier under the weight of his suspicions. Shar wouldn't be the first woman who'd cheated on him. But he swore she would be the last as he walked to Lynette's front door.

JOHNNY BERG DROVE his route, not as fast as usual though because he was distracted. Also, he didn't want to go back to his apartment. He couldn't quit thinking about Vi's murder and the set of keys he remembered seeing on the storage room floor on the way into the store.

He was positive that they hadn't been there after he'd found the body and gone outside to make the 911 call. Realizing what that meant had his nerves even more on edge. *The killer had definitely still been in the store.* The killer, having heard him drive up, must have dropped the keys as he or she hurried to hide.

He felt a chill run the length of his spine every time he thought about it. Worse, he kept seeing the keys. Had he seen them somewhere before?

Tell the cops! But then he would talk himself out of it, reasoning that the killer would hear—or might even be questioned as a suspect. His theory was that if the killer was questioned by the cops and not asked about a set of keys, the killer would think that Johnny hadn't seen them on the floor. That he couldn't identify them.

Didn't that mean that the killer wouldn't come after him?

Then again, what if the person was just waiting for the perfect opportunity? How could the killer leave him alive, fearing that he *had* seen the keys, that he could identify them and lead the law right to the killer's door?

As soon as he got home, he pulled out some paper and a pen. Closing his eyes, he pictured the keys for a few moments. Then he began to sketch. He'd always been good at art because he noticed details. His mother was a graphic artist, his father an architect. Drawing was in his blood.

It wasn't until he was finished and looked at what he'd drawn that he realized maybe the cops *could* use the drawing to find the killer. Or not. It just wasn't a chance he could take.

He quickly folded the paper, wrote on the outside "if anything happens to Johnny Berg, give this to the cops," and called his friend Cody. "I have something I need you to hang on to for me."

AS THE DAY wore on, Ken felt as if he were merely spinning his wheels. He was no closer to solving Vi Mullen's murder than he was finding out the truth about his girlfriend, Shar. He was depending on a teenager who couldn't grow facial hair yet.

Shaking his head, he cursed his luck at getting this murder—not even to mention the remains that had been found under the floorboards. Both cases had him in Buckhorn for who knew how long. Living in a town more than an hour away made it impossible to spy on his own girlfriend who was living in his house while he was in a ratty motel.

Both he and Jaxson were putting in long hours, needing to talk to suspects before too much time passed since the murder. Maybe it would be smarter to go home and drive the hour plus each morning and night. But he knew it was cheaper and more efficient to stay at the motel at least until they'd interviewed the main suspects on their lists.

He knew that his sour mood was due to the fact that he suspected Shar had been cheating on him for some time. He hadn't broached the subject with her and admittedly based his suspicion on a look he'd seen pass between Shar and some attorney ambulance chaser at a recent party. But he knew that look, damn it.

Just as he was anxious to talk to Lynette Crest strictly based on a look he'd caught at the café the morning Vi's body had been discovered. He wondered if he were any more right about what he'd seen then than he was with Shar and the lawyer as he knocked on Lynette's door.

She was a tall thin woman in her midsixties or seventies. There was a primness about her, a rigidity, as she opened the door dressed in a crisp and freshly ironed blouse and slacks. He could smell the ironing spray she'd used and see the ironing board through the crack in the partially open door to the laundry room. Past her, the house like Lynette was immaculately clean and uncluttered. He wouldn't have been surprised to find the couch covered in plastic.

"I'm Acting Marshal Kenneth Yarrow," he said, showing his badge. "I'd like to ask you a few questions."

"If this is about Vi Mullen's murder—"

"It should only take a few minutes," he said, cutting her off.

Lynette seemed to hesitate before she stepped aside, saying, "I only have a few minutes. I'm watching my grandchildren this afternoon."

He wiped his feet and stepped in as far as the rubber mat where Lynette had apparently taken off her shoes when she'd come home. She now wore flats, which he suspected were inside shoes. The house didn't feel in the least bit welcoming. He couldn't imagine grandchildren playing here.

"How old are your grandchildren?"

"Four and six. A boy and a girl." She didn't offer him a chair or encourage him to come any farther into the house.

Pulling out his notebook and pen, he decided to make this quick. "You had an argument recently with Vi." It wasn't a question. It was a bluff; one that apparently worked.

Lynette's face was already pale. She definitely didn't appear to be a sun worshipper. His words had turned her skin even more chalky. "Whoever told you—"

"It doesn't matter who told me. I want your side of the story," he said, tired and losing his patience and feeling uncomfortable standing on this small piece of rubber mat, trying to interview her. But for the life of him, he wasn't taking off his shoes. At the same time, he couldn't make himself step onto her pristine white carpet either.

"Do I need a lawyer?" she demanded.

"You tell me? What did you argue with the victim about?"

"Victim?" She spat the word out as if it tasted nasty in her mouth. "Vi was anything but a victim. She was a mean, vindictive, hateful bully." Her color had come back and now infused her cheeks.

"What did you argue about?" he asked again.

She pursed her lips tightly. He waited, determined that he wasn't leaving here until he proved to himself that he wasn't wrong about Lynette's guilty look he'd seen that morning in the café.

"My son has been going through a rough spot in his marriage," she said quietly. "I'm sure it's temporary. The woman can't do better than my son." She waved a hand through the air in front of her mouth as if airing her family's dirty laundry was abhorrent to her. "There was a miscommunication regarding his and his wife's joint checking account." She straightened even more erect. "The check he wrote at the general store was returned for insufficient funds. He didn't know his wife had emptied the account in one of her more irrational moments after an argument. The mistake was corrected. I explained this all to Vi and asked her to take his insufficient-funds check off that board of hers near the mailboxes at the back of the store. She refused."

"You threatened her."

Lynette looked away. "I might have used some harsh words."

"Did it get physical?"

"Of course not," she snapped.

"Did you see anyone else in the store?"

"No, but obviously someone must have overheard the argument I had with her. Was it Marjorie Keen who told you? That woman is the worst gossip. She was probably hiding in that maze of a store just hoping to hear something she could wag her tongue over. You might find even more dead bodies in there if you looked."

He had. "Did you tell your friends about your argument with Vi?"

She looked shocked at even the suggestion. "It was humiliating enough as it was."

"How did you and Vi leave it?"

Lynette looked down at her hands she now had gripped together. "I might have said I was going to come back with a sledgehammer and destroy her hateful board. She has it covered with plexiglass so no one can remove their checks."

"But you didn't."

"Of course not. I just said it in the heat of the moment. But I would imagine you know all this or you wouldn't be here."

"Is the check still there?"

"I don't know. I refuse to spend another dime in that place ever again."

"You didn't go back?"

"No, I was too embarrassed and now I have to drive over two hours just to get a carton of eggs and a quart of milk. My mother must be rolling over in her grave to have a daughter of hers behave in such a fashion. She would have said that I cut off my nose to spite my face and she'd be right." Lynette looked close to tears.

Ken heard a vehicle drive up out front.

"That will be my grandchildren," she said, regaining her composure. "I really need to see to them."

"Of course." He put his notebook and pen away. "Thank you for answering my questions." As he stepped out, he passed a boy and girl slowly walking up the sidewalk toward the house. They looked as miserable as Ken expected given how un-kid friendly that house was.

"Move along now," Lynette called to them.

At the curb, a man in an Eaton Ranch pickup revved the engine and left in a cloud of exhaust fumes.

It took Ken a few moments to put a name to the face. AJ Crest. He was married to the oldest of the Eaton daughters, Dana, Debra, Dixie or was it Deanna? That was it. AJ apparently still worked on the ranch, maybe even still lived on it—at least temporarily. If the marriage was on the skids, then AJ Crest might be looking for not just a place to live, but other employment as well.

He wondered what Tom and Bethany Eaton had thought about Vi posting an overdraft check from their son-in-law so the whole county could see it?

His head hurt and he couldn't quit thinking about what the kid had told him about Shar's comings and goings. He needed to go home. He needed to confront her. He needed one part of his life in order—one way or another.

JAXSON LOOKED AROUND Marjorie Keen's kitchen, fighting a case of claustrophobia. The kitchen, like the rest of the house, was filled with knickknacks on the shelves on the flower-wallpapered walls. There were ceramic frogs and squirrels, dolls and a variety of salt and pepper shakers overflowing onto counters and tabletop. The eyes peered up at him from corners of the room, one giant frog looking ready to jump at any moment.

Known as the worst gossip in Buckhorn, Marjorie welcomed him in, ushering him through the clutter to the kitchen where she was now chatting about the spring weather, her dead husband, her dead animals and the price of bacon as she insisted on making the coffee he'd already declined.

"I need to ask you a few quick questions," he interrupted after several attempts to jump in between subjects. "About Vi's murder. Can you tell me where you were that morning?"

She looked surprised at the interruption as if she thought he'd been hanging on her every word. She was a stout petite woman as wide as she was tall with very short gray hair and furtive small brown eyes that darted here and there as she spoke. "I was home. Where else would I have been at that hour of the morning?"

"I noticed that you have a security camera that faces the store."

"It's just for show. It doesn't work. I don't think it ever did. My son-in-law bought it, but he never hooked it up and I never got around to it. I mean, really, who needs one of those in Buckhorn. I know everyone in town."

He didn't mention that there was probably a killer among them. Instead, disappointed to hear that the camera wasn't operational, he commented, "If you look out your front window past that empty lot, you have a pretty good view of the alley, which leads to the store. I would imagine you weren't looking out that window the morning of the murder."

Marjorie frowned. "What would make you think that? The first thing every morning, I open those curtains to let in the light. I heard that loud delivery truck just like I do every time it comes roaring down the alley."

"Did you hear the truck or see it?" he asked, trying to nail down the time.

"I heard it before I saw it," she said. "I remember the cloud of dust he put up when he got it stopped at the back of the store. He drives way too fast. That dust devil spun in the air long after the driver got out of the vehicle that morning."

So she *had* stood at the window for a while. "Did you happen to see anyone before the truck went by?"

Marjorie scrunched up her face for a moment. He could tell she wanted to have seen someone. Finally she shook her head. "Just the truck, just the dust, that's all." She sounded disappointed.

Jaxson moved on with his questions. "Can you think of anyone who was angry at Vi recently?"

The older woman pursed her lips for a moment before she answered. "Gertrude Durham. I guess it's Shepherd now. I heard her arguing with Vi just the other day."

"What were they arguing about?"

"Cat food."

He stared at her. "Cat food?"

"Vi said, *you buy cat food every time you come in here and I've yet to see a cat at your place. If you can't afford to eat anything other than cat food...* You should have seen Gertrude's face. She was furious, said it was none of Vi's business if she ate cat food for breakfast, lunch and dinner. She finally shut Vi up when she told her that she fed a bunch of stray cats. She'd inherited them along with the gas station, she said and went on to say that if people bothered to neuter and spay their pets—"

"You think Gertrude killed her over cat food?"

"I bet people have been killed for a lot less," Marjorie said. "But if not her, then you might want to talk to Lynette Crest."

"Why would you say that?" he asked, realizing Lynette was on Yarrow's list, not his. In fact, Yarrow had been headed over there to see her right after lunch.

"The Hate Board by the post office mailboxes. Vi put Lynette's son's insufficient-funds check up there after it bounced and refused to take it down."

"Hate Board?"

"That's what we call it. Lynette told Vi she was coming back with a sledgehammer—Vi put clear hard plastic over the board to keep people from taking down their checks. Doesn't matter if you've made it good or not. Vi says it tells a lot about a person so she leaves them up. I think it says a lot about her."

Jaxson had heard stories about confrontations involving that very thing. He made a note to check it and see whose insufficient-funds checks might still be up there. Or if anyone had tried to remove one.

Exhausted, he glanced at the time. Gertrude Durham-Shepherd was next on his list. It felt later than it was. He thanked Marjorie and left, barely escaping her probing questions about the investigation and wanting to know who he thought had killed Vi.

His cell phone rang as he was climbing into his patrol

SUV to head over to Gertrude Shepherd's. Yarrow. "Deputy Gray."

"I need to go back to my house tonight to check on something," the acting marshal said without preamble. "I need you to go down to the store." He explained that there was a plexiglass covered board back by the mailboxes. "See if there is an insufficient-funds check from AJ Crest back there. Take a photo of it. Take photos of anything that's on the board. I'll be back first thing in the morning. Call if something comes up." He disconnected.

Gertrude would have to wait until tomorrow, Jaxson told himself. He'd check the store and then... He wanted to see Luna, but instead he'd go back to the motel. Until the case was over, he didn't stand a chance with her. Even then he wasn't sure she'd be able to trust him again.

Right now though, he desperately needed some sleep. He was almost to the motel when he got the text. Sleep would have to wait.

CHAPTER SEVENTEEN

"You're going to have to accept that you might never find Owen Henry because he's dead." It was the first thing her father said when Luna answered the phone.

"You found a record of his death?"

"No. But the trail ended with that last check from Eaton Ranch seventeen years ago. He got a DUI years before that so his fingerprints and DNA are on file. Even if he changed his name and his appearance with fake documents for whatever reason, he couldn't change his DNA. If he'd gotten arrested or was required to provide a DNA sample as needed by some employers, there would be a record. Also, the discrepancy between his names would have been discovered."

"Come on, you have to admit it's too much of a coincidence that Amy came looking for Owen about the time he got a big check from Eaton Ranch—*both* seventeen years ago. I need to get some dates nailed down," Luna said, thinking quickly. "I need to know exactly when he left his job at Eaton Ranch—and when Amy Franklin might have arrived in Buckhorn."

"I can send you the date of his check, but you're not getting the relevancy of what I'm telling you," her father said.

"Yes," she said with a sigh. "Amy is dead. Owen Henry could have met the same fate but just not be buried under the store's floorboards and if that was the case—"

"Then someone got away with two murders back then.

At this point, it is merely speculation, but the murderer could still live in or around Buckhorn."

"Two murders," Luna repeated, her mind racing. "Or maybe three. Maybe Vi's murder ties in as well."

"Even more dangerous in that case," her father said, but she wasn't listening.

"I have to find someone who knew Owen Henry," she said. "Avery Eaton, Tom Eaton's youngest daughter, is coming in to have her hair done. I'll see if she recognizes the photo."

"I don't know why I don't save my breath sometimes," her father muttered. "Luna, please."

"I love you too," she said and disconnected as Jaxson came through the door.

He'd apparently caught her last words because he frowned. "Anyone I know?"

"My father." She quickly told him why she'd texted him to come by and what she'd learned and why she thought there could very well be three murders that somehow tied in. "Avery Eaton has a hair appointment in a few minutes, but I wanted to see you first. I'm going to show her the photo of your father and hope she can tell me something."

"How old is she?" he asked.

"Midtwenties."

"She would have been seven? Do you really think—"

"She might remember him. He worked on her father's ranch. I still need to know the exact date Amy arrived in Buckhorn," Luna said, not letting his skepticism slow her down. "Then I can check it against Owen Henry's last day at the Eaton Ranch. If the two are tied together—"

"Then it's even more dangerous," Jaxson said. "If you're

right and they are connected and both were murdered, once you start asking questions... Luna..."

He reached out and cupped her cheek with his large warm hand. The look in his eyes brought back that passionate kiss. She felt heat curl its way through her before heading for her center. She covered his hand with her own and caught the flash of desire in his eyes.

He took a step closer, and she felt that aching need to be in his arms an instant before the front door of the salon opened and Avery Eaton walked in.

JAXSON HADN'T WANTED to leave Luna. Hell, what he'd wanted to do was lock the salon door, sweep Luna up in his arms and carry her upstairs to her apartment. He'd spent months ignoring his desire for this woman. He was tired of fighting it. He wanted her. Needed her in ways he'd only dreamed.

And he'd seen something in her eyes that told him she wanted him too.

He cursed Avery Eaton for her bad timing, even though he doubted there would have been any possibility of carrying Luna up to her apartment. She still didn't trust him. She might never trust him again.

He cursed himself for thinking that keeping Luna at arm's length would protect her. They could have been together all this time if he'd just told her the truth a long time ago.

Now she was the one keeping him at a distance. Worse she was like a bloodhound on the scent. There was no stopping her from trying to find out what had happened to not just Amy but his father.

While the last thing he'd wanted to do was put her in

danger, he'd done exactly that. He'd told himself that who-ever had killed Amy would be long gone after seventeen years. But what if he was wrong? He was risking Luna's life—something he'd been determined not to do.

Not that he could stop her, he realized. Luna was her own woman. But he feared that she didn't realize how ask-ing around about his father could get her hurt or worse—killed. This was the woman he'd been falling in love with for months, afraid to tell her the truth for fear of losing her. Now he might lose her to his lie or worse to a killer—unless he could find the killer first.

Earlier he'd been ready to go back to the motel and sleep. Instead he headed for the general store to check out what Marjorie had called the Hate Board, feeling as if time was running out. Maybe he would find a name on that board that would give him a clue to who might hate Vi Mullen the most. He had to find the killer.

AVERY EATON RESEMBLED the other members of her family, all dark hair and blue eyes, every one of them pretty or handsome, with an air of privilege and entitlement, Luna thought. Avery seemed young for her age and distracted for a woman about to get married.

"You must be excited?" Luna said. "Your wedding is coming up fast."

Avery seemed distracted as she nodded and smiled while Luna began to wash her hair.

"Have you thought about how you're going to wear your hair for the wedding?"

"Not really."

As she was working the shampoo into Avery's hair, she noticed a spot where a chunk of it was missing. She inspected the spot surreptitiously. It appeared that the hair had been pulled out by the roots.

"Did something happened back here?" she asked, touching the bare spot. "You're missing some hair. Did you get your hair caught on something?"

Avery reached back to touch the spot and Luna noticed a bruise on the young woman's wrist. There was a matching one on the inside of her upper arm the size of fingertips. Someone had grabbed her hard enough to leave bruises.

"I have no idea how I did that," Avery said. "It will grow back, right?"

"It should." Luna started to mention the bruises, thinking Avery might open up to her. It wouldn't be the first time that someone had poured her heart out to her.

But before she could, two of Avery's friends came into the shop. Avery's demeanor changed instantly as the talk turned to the wedding.

It wasn't until Luna was almost finished blowing out Avery's long hair that her friends left.

"Maybe you can put my hair up for my wedding to hide the spot back there?" Avery asked. "Also, could you come out to the ranch to do it for the wedding?"

"Sure, I'd be happy to. I'll make sure you look even more beautiful on your wedding day."

Tears filled the young woman's eyes. She hastily wiped them away. "I just have to get through the wedding," she said more to herself than Luna.

"An emotional time, huh?"

"You have no idea." For a moment, Avery chewed on her lower lip as she stared at herself in the mirror.

Luna had to ask. "Cold feet?"

Avery quickly shook her head. "Jory and I have been

going together since junior high." She gave a slight shrug. "Our dads predicted we would marry when we were born. We were inseparable as kids with our ranches so close together. Some things are just meant to be. At least that's what Jory says." But the smile on her face at the mention of Jory looked genuine.

Luna nodded and thought of Jaxson. "You've never dated anyone else?" Avery shook her head. "My parents were like that," Luna said quickly, not wanting to dim the light that had come back in the young woman's eyes at the mention of Jory Price. "They'd always said it was meant to be from the first time they met."

"Are they still together?" Avery asked hopefully.

"My mother died, but if she hadn't, they would have been together. My father never remarried. I doubt he ever will. My mother was the only one for him." She didn't add that she wished her father would find someone. She hated that he was alone, even though he seemed happy enough.

Then again if Lawrence Declan had someone, he might not worry so much about his daughter.

Luna considered broaching the subject of the bruises with Avery, but told herself to tread carefully. Clearly Avery loved Jory. But if he was responsible for the bruises, she wanted to tell her that Jory's behavior wouldn't change after the marriage.

Avery grew quiet as she settled her bill and confirmed her hair appointment for her big day. Luna would be styling her hair the morning of the wedding—now out at the ranch.

After a moment, Luna carefully asked, "Everything okay…?"

"Of course. I'm just a little jittery," Avery quickly answered. Too quickly.

Luna hoped Avery was really okay as she said that she'd never been to the Eaton Ranch and was looking forward to it. She was hoping to show Owen Henry's photo around while there. But she'd also be looking to see how Jory acted around Avery.

Luna worried though that if she saw more bruises, she would have to try to keep Avery from making a huge mistake—even if it meant being thrown off the ranch.

CHAPTER EIGHTEEN

JAXSON DIDN'T HAVE to use the key Yarrow had left him. He found the back door of the store standing open—just as it had been the day of the murder. The crime scene tape had been taken down now that the techs were finished. But the acting marshal hadn't said anything about letting people inside the store.

His hand went to the weapon at his hip as he heard a noise like someone was throwing things around inside the store. He unsnapped his holster and moved deeper into the shadowy darkness. He hadn't gone far when he noticed movement in the small office off to the right.

"Finding what you're looking for?" Jaxson asked as he stepped through the open door to see a figure bent over, dragging out files from a cabinet, glancing at them, then throwing them onto the floor.

Vera shot upright, spinning around, crushing a thick stack of files against her chest. "Deputy, you startled me." Vi's twin sounded winded. "I was just trying to make sense of my sister's idea of filing."

"Looking for anything in particular in an active crime scene?"

Vera slowly put the stack of files down on the paper-strewn desk, dusted herself off and met the deputy's gaze. Clearly she had been going through everything in the office before Jaxson walked in.

"As Vi's twin and only living blood relative, I am now owner of the store and antique shop. It's all in Daddy's trust that he set up."

Jaxson had no idea if that were true. "I'm going to need your store keys until the acting marshal says you can have them." He knew Yarrow had interviewed both Vera and Axel and that the two of them seemed to be an item now. Both were prime suspects, possibly even more so after what Jaxson had just seen. He wondered what Vera had been looking for and if Axel knew she was down here.

He held out his hand, waiting. Face flushed with anger, Vera dug in her pocket, pulled out a key ring with numerous keys on it. She pulled off two keys, which Jaxson assumed were to the front and back doors. Vera tossed both keys on the desk rather than hand them to him and started to stuff the rest back into her pocket.

Jaxson knew that Axel and Vera had moved into Vi's house. They probably also had keys to the antique barn and anything else Vi owned. But he could at least keep them out of the crime scene for the time being. "Please tell Axel I'll need his in case he still has them."

"Why would Axel have keys? I'm sure Vi took them when they divorced."

"Does anyone else have keys to the store?" Jaxson asked. "People who have worked here?"

Vera shrugged. "All I know is that Vi was strict about who got keys. Always worried about people robbing her blind as she used to say. It's surprising that she even let me have my own key. Then again I was her twin." She glanced around. "Half of all this has always been mine. Now it's all mine."

"So you had keys to the store when you returned to

town. You could have been waiting inside the store when Vi unlocked the back door and entered—before she was murdered."

Vera laughed. "I told you. I wasn't even close to Buckhorn when Vi died. You're barking up the wrong tree, deputy." She pushed past him and headed toward the back door, avoiding the large gaping hole in the flooring of the storage area, and was gone.

Jaxson looked around the office, wondering what she'd been after. Who could find anything in this mess?

After closing and locking the back door behind her, he made his way to the small postal boxes set into a wall in one corner of the store.

Vi had been postmistress until last year when a post office had been built on the edge of town near the new hotel. She'd been relieved of her duties and hadn't taken it well, but then neither had the residents who'd been getting their mail conveniently at the store for years, Luna had told him. He was surprised that the boxes hadn't been removed yet. Probably not worth the expense.

Next to them he found the board that he'd heard about. There were a half dozen checks behind the plexiglass cover along with a half dozen notes announcing that certain people were no longer allowed to charge groceries and could only pay with cash.

He pulled out his phone, recognizing some of the names. Karla Parson, the woman who'd saved Vi's life, was on the board, he noted. Vi had written that Karla wasn't allowed to charge groceries until she paid her bill, which was months overdue.

Public humiliation, he thought and wondered how Yarrow's interview with the woman had gone since she too was high on the suspect list.

But it wasn't just Karla. There were dozens of comments that had apparently been posted on Vi's website *All About Buckhorn*, which she'd printed out and scrawled her responses on along with threats that amounted to her saying she knew everyone's secrets in town and she was going to tell.

He took photos of everything on the Hate Board. Then stepping closer, he got a photo of the check Yarrow had mentioned. *AJ Crest. Insufficient funds.* It took him a moment before he could place the name. Wasn't he married to one of the Eatons? Deanna Eaton?

KEN KNEW THAT he'd reached a new low. Hiring a kid to spy on Shar. What had he been thinking? Worse, there appeared to be something to find given that the kid's latest call had him returning home to set a trap for her. That too was a new low. Where was trust? Loyalty? Truth?

He told himself that he'd been hurt too many times before. The truth was that he'd been made a fool too many times before and that was what had really hurt. Did he love Shar? Some days. Did he want to spend the rest of his life with her? Apparently not since he hadn't asked her to marry him.

He'd thought about giving her a ring, making it legal; after all, she'd been living with him for months. He'd been supporting her pretty much from the start. She'd moved in and then lost her job. At least that was her story. She said she was looking for another job, but he hadn't seen much of that.

The point was they were living like husband and wife.

He was the breadwinner and Shar was... What was she? Not the little woman who stayed home and had dinner ready when he returned from work. He wasn't even sure she knew how to cook. He'd seen no evidence of it. With his odd, ever-changing schedule, he usually got home too late for a home-cooked meal—even if she had made one. Instead he often found fast food that she'd picked up on her way home.

But on her way home from where?

Well he would find out tonight. He'd called her earlier, telling her he wouldn't be back for a few more days, maybe longer. He'd lied because he wanted to catch her in the act. But as he reached the edge of town, he thought that it would be just his luck to find her home when he arrived. Not that he wouldn't be glad to find all his suspicions were for naught, but this could be the only night that she hadn't gone out this week.

He turned down the street toward his house, his headlights illuminating the quiet street. It was early enough that if she'd gone out, she wouldn't be back yet. At least that was his thinking. He really didn't think she would be so careless as to have a man over in his absence.

As he neared his house, he saw that her car wasn't in the driveway. She could have put it in the garage though. Closer he saw that it was dark inside the house. By all appearances, she was gone.

He drove around the block, parked and walked back. Opening the back door with his key, he told himself that he'd be waiting for her when she returned home. Surprise!

WHAT LUNA HEARD in Jaxson's voice when he called was more than exhaustion. It was defeat. He'd spent the day questioning suspects in Vi's murder and no doubt waiting for Amy's remains to be identified. Luna knew that she was probably also adding to his worries.

She thought of earlier when he'd stopped by the salon. There had been that moment... Her heart lifted like it were filled with helium. If Avery hadn't come in just then... Luna shook her head. She was determined to get the truth. The last thing she needed to do was let her heart lead her and Jaxson anywhere near her double bed upstairs. But she needed more of his help if she was going to find the truth.

"I'm just going to grab something to eat and go back to the motel," Jaxson told her.

"I make a mean grilled cheese," she said, needing to ask him more about his father. "I have beer to go with it."

He'd agreed but when she opened the door to his knock, she felt a moment of guilt. He appeared dead on his feet. She turned a ball game on the television and left him on the couch while she made them both grilled cheese sandwiches and opened two beers.

By the time she returned with their dinners, he was stretched out on the couch, asleep. She was debating letting him sleep when he opened his eyes and sat up.

As much as she wanted to pepper him with questions, she let him eat and finish his beer before she asked, "Is there anything you can remember about why your father left? Surely your mother must have mentioned what caused it."

He raked a hand through his hair. "You mean what she said? That he had to take care of something and then he'd be back for us? Or what I believe—that he just left because he didn't want to play house anymore. I mean, if he had loved my mother and me, he would have married her, he would have stayed."

"Something to take care of... Why then? He'd been with the two of you for how many years?"

Jaxson shrugged. "I think they were together before she got pregnant with me. So more than seven. But everything about him was sketchy. He was working as a carpenter but getting paid under the table. Looking back, I wonder if he wasn't wanted by the law."

"Or maybe it was his family he was running from. Then suddenly he had to take care of something, implying it was a family problem in Montana, right? Do you remember something happening, an argument, anything that happened before he left?"

He shook his head and sighed. "He made it all up because he just wanted to leave. Maybe he felt my mother was pressuring him to marry her. I don't know. I was *seven*."

"Can you tell me what you remember about him?"

Jaxson looked away. "Luna, I can't do this."

"I'm sorry. I'm just trying to—"

"I know you want to help." He picked up his Stetson and rose to walk toward the door. "I have an early day tomorrow and I really need some sleep."

She stood up as well. Their gazes locked across the small room. This was what he'd done with her since they'd met. Always hurrying off.

He looked contrite for a moment before he stepped up to her. "Thank you for the sandwich. It was really good." He leaned forward and kissed her on the cheek. As he pulled back, he looked as if he wanted to say something more. Instead he shook his head, looking miserable. "We'll talk tomorrow."

Luna nodded, knowing that she'd pushed too hard. She'd so hoped he might remember something that would help, because at this point she felt stuck, unsure where to go next. He wanted her to step away, but she couldn't for so many reasons. She was worried about Jaxson. But she was also hooked. She couldn't stop until she got answers.

"I'm sorry," she said as he opened the door to leave. A part of her wanted to call him back. So many times she had thought of the two of them in her double bed, curled together like kittens. Tonight she would have loved that warmth and affection. Wanted him. Needed him.

He must have felt it, despite being determined to stay away from her until Amy's murder was solved. He looked exhausted, both physically and emotionally. "You asked about dates," he said, stopping, his back to her. "My father left the night of his birthday. June 11. Amy was convinced the date meant something. So that's when she left—on that date years later—if that makes any sense to you. It sure doesn't to me." He sighed and, with a shake of his head, left.

Luna moved to the front window and looked out into the night. She felt restless, too full of questions and few answers, especially as to what the future held for not just Jaxson but the two of them.

Clouds hung low, cloaking the town in what felt to her tonight like a suffocating blackness. The wind had kicked up and now whirled dirt and dust about on the pavement outside her window. It was spring in Montana, squalls blew through, some with rain, some with snow.

If she hadn't heard the storm rattling the old apartment windows, she might not have looked out. She might not have seen movement across the two-lane blacktop. She might not have seen the figure standing on the other side, staring at her building. She couldn't tell if it was a man or woman as rain streaked the glass and the wind whipped it past the window.

The figure was tall, dressed in all black, face in shadow beneath the Western hat and slicker he wore. It was a man, wasn't it?

With a start, the head tilted back slightly. The person was looking right at her.

She quickly stepped back behind the curtain, surprised that her heart was pounding. When she looked again, the figure was gone.

As JAXSON LEFT Luna's apartment, he felt as if he had a guillotine hanging over his neck, the clock not just ticking but speeding up. If the lab could get DNA from the corpse or the clothing to make a positive identification, it wouldn't be long before the truth came out. Usually DNA tests took weeks, days he desperately needed to find out what had happened. But he couldn't depend on it this time. The state medical examiner was involved. Yarrow was being pressured to solve these murders.

Tomorrow he had to finish the list of names Yarrow had given him even though he sensed they were no closer to finding Vi's murdered than he was Amy's.

His heart pounded as the past kept replaying in his head. Hadn't he known Amy had come here following a trail that had gone cold years ago? She'd been so damned stubborn. So desperate, he thought, remembering how trapped he'd felt. She'd clung to him, begging him even as they both knew that he'd made a terrible mistake that night at the party. Even though he and Katie had agreed to break up before that night, what he'd done had destroyed his relationship with her.

He knew that Katie had thought they would marry someday. He'd thought they wouldn't last past high school. They needed to date other people in the separate colleges they were attending in the coming fall. He'd be busy with sports and studying. The last thing he'd wanted was the responsibility of a long-distance relationship. He'd been glad to hear that she'd found someone. He hoped she was happy.

While breaking up with Katie had hurt, the worst thing was hooking up with Amy. He'd never foreseen that one-night stand turning into such a nightmare. He kept thinking of Amy and his sick mother together. Lillian Gray had to have recognized the naked vulnerability in Amy, seen herself in the girl, the weakness and destructiveness born out of a need to be loved at any cost. Wasn't that why she told Amy her so-called love story, making out his father who left them to be some romantic cowboy hero?

What happened after that, he supposed, was inevitable. All the stories his mother had told Amy had put stars in her eyes. He remembered the way Amy's chin had jutted out, her back ramrod straight, defiance and hope distorting her pretty features. "I'll bring him back to you and your mother and then you'll…" Her voice had broken, shattering into silent sobs for a moment. "You'll love me."

Jaxson shook his head, trying to push away the memories of Amy and her silly little flowered suitcase. She'd taken it, along with both his money and his mother's that they kept in the house.

He could barely remember graduation—the day his mother took a turn for the worse and died soon after. With

Amy's disappearance and suspicion hanging over him, his life as he'd known it had been over. All he could think about was getting out of Blackfoot, Idaho.

He'd had the delusional idea that he'd find Amy and clear his name—and return. He'd taken the old pickup he'd managed to buy with what money was left in the bank after burying his mother and he'd headed for Buckhorn.

But by then even Amy's trail had gone cold.

Still he'd always known that she would turn up and the past, once it caught up to him, would take him down.

KEN WOKE WITH a start, surprised that he'd fallen asleep waiting in the dark house. He glanced at his phone. Just after 2:00 a.m. Still no Shar.

So what had awakened him. A noise?

He got up from the recliner and moved to the window. Her car wasn't in the driveway. What if she didn't come home all night? She could be at a friend's. She could have taken a trip. What if she'd decided to surprise him and drive over to Buckhorn and was now waiting for him at his motel?

Doubts threatened to drown him. What the hell was he doing?

He turned from the window. Should he drive back to Buckhorn tonight? He thought about calling Shar, but it was the middle of the night. He'd look like a fool if the reason she wasn't here was an innocent one. Worse, if she had gone to Buckhorn to surprise him.

Convinced he had to go back, that coming here like this had been ridiculous and beneath him, he picked up his jacket to leave when he heard a noise. It came from the back of the house.

Moving stealthily through the house, he stopped in the

kitchen to listen. Muffled laughter and the scrape of a key in the lock. More laughter. The back door was flung open, banging against the wall as two individuals stumbled in, both nearly falling down. He caught the smell of alcohol and cigarettes as Shar fumbled for the light switch and her male companion hung on to her, both unsteady on their feet.

In a burst of sudden illumination, the glaring overhead light came on. It took a few moments for the two of them to see him standing in the middle of the kitchen, watching them. He ignored the man who let go of Shar and took a couple of steps back. His gaze was on her face. She'd once been a looker, but cigarettes, alcohol and late nights had stolen much of her beauty.

Her blue eyes widened first in alarm at the sight of him and the realization that she'd been caught. Amusement replaced alarm as the alcohol found the humor in this unexpected turn of events.

The man had backed himself through the still-open door. He now slipped out, stumbling his way across the backyard to disappear into the darkness. Apparently he'd ridden with Shar. No car engine started. Ken felt relieved that he wasn't going to have to go after the man and arrest him for a DUI, because he *was* the frigging acting marshal and it was his job.

Shar leaned against the wall simply looking at him as if suddenly tired. Her mascara was running down her cheeks and her lipstick was smeared. The amusement had left her eyes, replaced by resignation.

With nothing to say, he went back to the living room, picked up his Stetson and walked out the front door. Around the block, he got into his patrol SUV and drove toward

Buckhorn. He had two murders to solve. He was the acting marshal and he had a job to do.

Thirty minutes outside of town, he had to pull over. To
his surprise, he was crying. Not about Shar, but about his
life. Nothing had gone the way he'd thought it would. He
still couldn't believe that he'd asked out Vi Mullen and the
tough-as-jerky woman had turned him down cold. Worse,
he couldn't believe the way he'd taken her rejection. As if
someone better was going to come along for her. It seemed
someone worse had come along instead.

As he wiped his tears, he felt weak with regrets and
hated this time of the night when even his thoughts were
dark. He didn't care who'd killed Vi. She could burn in hell
for all he cared. Yet he had to find her killer before Baggins got back from his honeymoon. That alone depressed
the hell out of him.

He told himself that he was a good investigator. His
problem was that he was piss-poor when it came to picking
the right woman. But that didn't mean that he had to spend
the rest of his life alone. He'd find someone who actually
cared about him. She had to be out there.

He felt a little better as he drove on down the road toward Buckhorn. It dawned on him that he should be able
to find Vi Mullen's killer since he and the killer had something in common. They had both wanted to kill the bitch.

WITH THE DRAWING of the keys secure with his friend Cody,
Johnny Berg had felt safe for the first time since finding
Vi Mullen's body. That's why he'd agreed to go out drinking with his friends after work. He just hadn't planned on
shutting down the bars and then going to a friend's for
late-night pizza.

With his life more back to normal, he was starting to believe that he could put the whole murder-killer thing behind him. He had his "insurance"—the envelope with the drawing in it safe. It made him feel so relieved that he wasn't sweating going back to the apartment house.

He felt almost bulletproof, he thought with a smile as he got out of his car and walked up the broken sidewalk. He usually didn't come home this late and was glad to see that there was a night-light glowing behind the curtains at Ethel's apartment. Also Gabe was apparently home for a while since Johnny had parked behind the other renter's car. He liked it when both of them were in the huge old building. Especially lately.

Feeling happier than he'd been for the past forty-eight hours, his earbuds in and rocking out, he opened the front door and started up the steps as quietly as he could so as not to wake Gabe. Ethel he wasn't worried about, because she would have her hearing aids out this late.

Even his job had gone well today. He was back being Johnny on the Spot, delivering packages faster than anyone else. Smiling to himself, he passed the second floor and started up the stairs.

Almost to his third-floor landing, he remembered that the overhead bulb had burned out again. The stairway grew darker the farther he climbed unsteadily upward. He was thinking about what it was going to take to replace the bulb. He didn't hear anything, not with his music blaring in his ears. Nor could he see anyone waiting in the deep shadows for him.

But he did catch a scent on the air—one different from the musty decay of the apartment house. It was so familiar and yet sent a shiver of dread through him. He stopped almost to the landing, frowning as he tried to place the smell and why it suddenly had his heart racing. He knew that scent. He wished now that he hadn't drank so much. His brain felt foggy.

It came to him in a rush. Horse liniment. On the heels of the realization came with it the memory of the last place he'd smelled it. Buckhorn General Store, the morning of the murder.

He started to take a step back when a figure darted out of the black shadows at the top of the landing. Sober, he might have had time to react before he felt the hard shove to his chest. Sober, he might have had time to turn off his music and might have heard the figure move before he was struck. Sober, he might have been able to catch himself.

He grabbed frantically for the railing, arms windmilling as he felt himself tipping backward down the stairs. Fighting to regain his balance, he clutched wildly for the old wooden railing. His fingers found purchase and just for an instant he thought he could catch himself.

In the next instant though, he felt the railing break loose with his weight. Even then he thought the fall probably wouldn't kill him. Until he looked up and saw his killer and the baseball bat. He flinched as he saw the bat swing at his head but didn't have time to duck away from the impact. The bat smacked him so hard on the side of his head that he barely had time to see stars before the darkness.

He fell backward, the broken portion of the railing he'd grabbed tumbling with him down the flight of stairs. He was already unconscious by the time he stopped falling.

CHAPTER NINETEEN

LUNA HAD DREAMED about Jaxson last night and had awakened with both a body and heart that ached for the man. In the past few days, she'd felt the two of them growing closer than they ever had before.

She'd looked into his gorgeous green eyes and seen a good man who'd gotten caught up in things when he was young that he had spent years trying to outrun. Yet she was still leery. He'd lied to her, broken her trust.

Even knowing why he'd lied still made her unsure. But she told herself that once they found out who had killed Amy, maybe then...

She didn't know. The first time she'd met him she'd been sure he wasn't her type. He'd walked into her salon before she'd even opened officially and yet she'd given him a haircut. When he'd wanted to pay, she'd told him that he was her first customer therefore it was free. She'd known he'd ask her to dinner, which he had.

Even then she'd thought he was too predictable.

The thought made her laugh now. The whole time she'd been seeing him he'd been lying and not just about who he was, but why he wanted to see her.

Could she ever trust him again?

She thought about the way they'd left things last night and felt guilty that she'd badgered him with questions, seeing how exhausted he was. She'd hated leaving things between them like that. Was that why she'd had the dream where they'd held each other, curled up in her double bed and fallen asleep in each other's arms?

Pushing away the reminder of waking up alone this morning, aching, she told herself she had to resolve how she felt about Jaxson Gray—and soon.

JAXSON HATED LEAVING Luna the way he had last night, but he'd been in no shape to talk about his father. He'd been too exhausted, too upset and too worried, especially about Luna. He should have known that she would take this challenge on the way she did everything—diving in headfirst without any regard for life or limb.

He'd never seen such determination. If anyone could find out the truth, it would be her. She would have made a good cop, he thought as he tried to concentrate on what Yarrow was saying about the investigation.

He'd heard the acting marshal return in the wee hours of the morning to the motel. He'd thought that Yarrow would have spent the night at his house rather than return that late and wondered what had called him home in the first place. He knew nothing about the man's life.

But Jaxson could see that the investigation was taking its toll on the acting marshal as well. Solving this would be redemption for the older deputy. But like him, Yarrow had learned little from those he'd interviewed over the past two days.

They'd put in long hours and were no closer to finding Vi's killer. When the acting marshal finished, Jaxson briefed him on his interviews, ending with finding Vera Carter at the store, clearly looking for something.

Reaching into his pocket, he pulled out the two keys

he'd taken from the woman and laid them on the café table between them. "I wouldn't be surprised if Axel and Vera have more keys."

Yarrow studied the keys for a moment before he asked, "Any idea what she was looking for?"

He shook his head. "Whatever it was, she didn't find it. Vera is apparently the legal heir. If true, she will have all the time she wants to find whatever it was she didn't find last night."

"This only makes the two of them look more guilty," Yarrow said.

"I got the impression that Axel wouldn't know she was down at the store. She seemed frustrated when she didn't find whatever it was. Vi was an odd duck. She could have kept money hidden in the store since apparently she worried about someone stealing from the business."

"How are you doing on your list?" the acting marshal asked.

"I still need to talk to Clarice Barber, a longtime resident. I thought about talking to Darby Fulton Cole, the editor and publisher of the local online newspaper, but she hasn't been in town that long. I was also going to see if Ike Shepherd was back. I'd like to see if their surveillance camera at the gas station might have captured our killer on it."

"Why don't you take Gertrude Shepherd, then," Yarrow said. "I need to talk to Earl Ray Caulfield and his wife. Let's meet here. Text me when you're finished." He rose from the table. "Good job."

Jaxson watched him go, surprised by the compliment. What would the acting marshal say though when he learned that his deputy more than knew the woman buried under the floorboards?

KEN HADN'T HEARD from Shar, not that he'd expected to. He'd caught her red-handed—so to speak. There wasn't much she could have said then or now. It was over. He hoped that when he did return home again, all sign of her would be gone. Knowing her, she wouldn't even leave a note.

He had texted the neighbor kid and told him his services were no longer needed and that he would pay him when he saw him, but that he was out of town for a while. Having tidied everything up, Shar would be quickly forgotten. Even though she'd cheated on him, she was easier to forget than Vi—which bothered him more than he wanted to admit. He kept remembering the expression on Vi's face the day he'd asked her out in the store.

"I wondered if you'd ever get up the nerve to ask me out." She'd been restocking a shelf and hadn't stopped what she was doing to even look at him. "Haven't you wanted to ask me out since grade school?"

"Junior high," he'd said truthfully.

She'd snorted. "Talk about taking your time."

"I guess that's a no." He'd started to turn away, embarrassed enough. But she hadn't let it go at that.

"Why would you think I'd want to go out with you?" she'd demanded, making him turn back to her.

"Now that you mention it, I'm wondering that myself."

She'd looked up then from her work. "You've always been so smug, haven't you, Kenny."

"No one calls me Kenny anymore."

"But you're still that sniveling little boy I remember who used to eat the glue."

"That wasn't me." He'd glanced around mortified that someone might be listening to this. "Really, Vi, I thought maybe you'd like to go out to dinner some time or go see a movie. Don't make a big deal out of it."

"Don't make a big deal out of it? You think I'm desperate for a date?" She'd laughed, a high-pitched fingernails-down-a-blackboard cackle. The memory of it still made him cringe. "A date with you, Kenny, definitely wouldn't be a big deal."

"Clearly I've caught you on a bad day," he'd said, anxious to get away from her.

"That's it, sulk away like you always have," she'd said, glaring at him. "Maybe if you'd had the balls to ask me out before now…"

"Someday, Vi…" he'd said, trying to control his growing anger.

"Someday, what, Kenny?"

"Someone's going to shut that mouth of yours for good." He'd turned to leave.

"It will take a man a hell of a lot better than you, Kenny Yarrow," she called after him.

He walked out feeling the heat of her words making him sweat. But it was his own anger that had his blood boiling by the time he reached his patrol SUV. The ungrateful bitch. He had wanted to grab her scrawny neck and choke the life out of her. It had been all he could do not to go back into that store and…

The memory had him breathing hard even now, even knowing that she was dead. What a hateful woman. The irony was that he'd wanted to go out with her because he'd thought they had something in common. Both alone. Both outsiders in their way. Both miserable.

He drove down a back street of Buckhorn, feeling that misery. He was on his way to talk to Earl Ray Caulfield and almost to his house when he got the call about Johnny Berg. He was in the hospital in a coma.

WITH SO MUCH going on, Luna had completely forgotten about horseback riding with Tucker Price. It wasn't until she got the reminder that he would meet her at the ranch at two o'clock that she realized she could leave early and stop by the Eaton Ranch.

She needed to talk to Tom Eaton. So far everyone she'd shown Owen Henry's photo to hadn't recognized him. But Tom Eaton had apparently employed Owen. It was possible that Jaxson's father hadn't even gone into town seventeen years ago. He could have stayed out on the ranch until whatever job he'd been paid for was over.

Which would mean that he might not have crossed paths with Amy Franklin. But with them both vanishing seventeen years ago, it definitely made her wonder if Amy had found a man who, for whatever reason, hadn't wanted to be found.

They knew now that Amy had made it to Buckhorn about the same time Owen had been working just outside of town. It would have been foolish to ignore what seemed obvious. What would have happened if Amy had tried to get Owen to return to Idaho? As obsessed as she'd been, would she have threatened him?

But that would mean that she'd found out something about him that she could use as leverage. Something that Owen would have killed to keep quiet?

Luna felt as she if were trying to connect dots that just didn't add up. Or was she just refusing to see the truth because she couldn't bear the thought that Jaxson's father was a killer—and what that would do to Jaxson.

She called him. His phone went to voice mail and she was glad. She left a message. "I'm sorry about last night.

I'm going horseback riding with Tucker Price this afternoon. While I'm out there, I'm going to try to talk to Tom Eaton about your father. I won't mention your name. Just wanted you to know."

After she hung up, she called back and left a second message. "I forgot I told Tucker the other day that I would go riding." She didn't think it necessary to add it was when Jaxson had been ghosting her.

After she left the message, she wished she hadn't. She didn't owe Jaxson an explanation. But at the same time, she wanted to be up-front and honest. It wasn't a bad idea either to let a deputy marshal know where she'd gone and with whom—just in case.

She checked the time and put her phone away. She liked Tucker. He had a great sense of humor and it wasn't like she and Jaxson had an understanding. Far from it. So why did she feel guilty?

Because Jaxson was the man she wanted to be with. He'd stolen more than her thoughts for so long and especially right now when she was scared for him. Maybe the coroner wouldn't be able to get a DNA sample from the mummified body or any of Amy's belongings. Maybe it would always remain a mystery.

Luna couldn't stand the thought that she wouldn't be able to get justice for Amy and clear Jaxson's name. She refused to believe she couldn't uncover the truth. She was her father's daughter.

She hurried upstairs to change for her date, putting on a Western shirt, jeans and boots. She sent Tucker a text. See you at two.

A few moments later, her phone chimed. Meet at the stables.

KEN DIDN'T THINK things could get worse—until the call came from Langstone.

"You heard about Johnny Berg?" the coroner asked, getting right to the point.

"I read the initial report from my deputy over there. A senseless accident. I heard he was drunk." Silence. "He was drunk, right?"

"Legally drunk, yes, but I have reason to believe it wasn't an accident."

Ken told himself that he didn't want to hear this. He felt bad about the kid getting involved in Vi's death. He didn't want to believe that the killer had gone after him. Ken had been so sure the kid was safe. Not to mention what this would do to his investigation if he had another murder.

"Are you telling me he tried to commit suicide by diving down the stairs?"

"When he fell, he grabbed the railing," the coroner said with obvious impatience. Ken knew that Langstone had never had much regard for him. "At first it appeared it had snapped from the force, but on closer inspection, someone had sawed through the railing to weaken it," Langstone continued. "If you've read the report, then you know that when Berg was found, the renter went back to his apartment downstairs to get his phone to make the call. He thought he heard someone on the fire escape before your deputies arrived. Believing it was an accident, he just assumed that Johnny had brought someone home with him and, after Berg fell, the person took off. Berg's girlfriend had been around a day earlier. The older female renter is deaf without her hearing aids in and because of the hour she didn't hear or see anything."

"While that sounds suspicious—"

"Berg had a blow to his head—not the kind you get from falling downstairs," Langstone said, speaking over him. "Add that to the tampered railing, the fact that he came upon a murder victim days earlier, and I'd say you have a premeditated murderer on your hands. The state medical examiner is still here. She agrees and called the state crime lab to send techs. We're treating the incident as attempted murder."

Ken swore. Vi's killer had thought the kid knew something and tried to kill Berg? He rubbed the back of his neck. He'd been ticked off at the kid for contaminating his crime scene. But he hadn't really thought Berg was in danger, had he?

"I told the deputy who caught the case. He didn't contact you?"

Ken had seen a couple of messages, but he'd ignored them. He'd been so sure Berg's fall was an accident, and the deputy thought he was better at this than he was and just needed to get back into his own lane.

"I'll send you my report," Langstone said, sounding disgusted. "But we don't need any more bodies stacking up, Yarrow."

He wanted to snap, *Baggins wouldn't be doing any better if he were here*, but he wasn't sure that was true. "Maybe I'd better come—"

"No reason to. We have it under control."

"What about the other remains found under the floorboards?" Ken asked since he knew that was why the state medical examiner was there, attempting to get a DNA sample from the mummified body.

"It's done. The state medical examiner put a rush on the DNA sample. The crime lab has promised a quick turn-around because we have a killer on the loose," the coroner said.

"You really can't believe that the body under the floorboards has anything to do with Vi's death," Ken said.

"The point is that we don't know. I just sent you the autopsy report. Female, age somewhere between sixteen and twenty. We know when the floor was replaced so we know she was partially buried under the floorboards seventeen years ago. She was killed by a blow to the back of the head. From the way the skull was broken, possibly by something like a hammer. Berg was injured by a blow to his head as well, although we believe it was an old baseball bat. One was found at the scene. I believe the crime techs will be able to find blood on it even though, like Vi's murder weapon, the killer tried to wipe it clean."

For a moment, Yarrow didn't know what to say. What if there was a connection between the young woman's death and Berg's? "So we should get an ID soon." He knew with the latest forensics techniques, they could get DNA out of a rock.

"Depends on if the sample was enough to be viable. Also, as you know, if her DNA is on file. We don't know who she is or how she ended up under that floor. But at least it is something."

Like Ken needed to be reminded that so far he had nothing. He'd checked the Montana database for a missing young woman seventeen years ago, but had found no female who matched. He hadn't looked through all the missing girls beyond Montana yet because he hadn't had the time. He hoped her DNA brought up a name. At least that would be a start in trying to solve at least one of the murders. The governor was still ragging on him to solve Vi Mullen's murder.

He realized that he still had Langstone on the line. "Thanks for letting me know about Berg," he said.

"You'll have that report soon," the coroner said and was gone.

Ken swore. Langstone thought he was in over his head and the coroner was probably right. As he started to pocket his phone, he got a call from the dispatcher.

"I have a young man on the line who says it's urgent that he talks to you," she said. "He says it's about Johnny Berg."

"Put him through."

CHAPTER TWENTY

His ANGER DIRECTED at himself, Jaxson tried not to lose his temper when he heard Luna's voice mails. He had only himself to blame, he thought after hearing that she had a horseback riding date with Tucker Price. Not that it made him any less jealous.

Yarrow had called to say that he had to go back to the office in the next town over. He would be in touch and for Jaxson to interview Gertrude Shepherd and also see if the filling station had surveillance footage of the store.

Jaxson found the woman in her garage working on an old Ford pickup. The hood was up and Gertrude, in a trucker's cap and green overalls, had her gray head under it.

"Mrs. Shepherd," he called as he approached. He heard the clank of a wrench and called again.

She stuck her head out, squinted at him for a moment, then went back under the hood. "If this is about Vi Mullen—"

"I need to ask you a few questions."

"Well, I need to get this motor done for my customer," she said without looking at him as she continued to work.

He would have liked to have had her undivided attention, but today he would take what he could get. "I understand you and Vi had an argument recently at the store."

Gertrude harrumphed.

"I also heard it got pretty contentious."

"Contentious?" She stopped what she was doing to glare

at him. "I wanted to throttle the old hag." She went back to work.

"I understand it was over...cat food?"

She stopped working again, this time coming up from under the hood to wipe her hands on a rag and face him. "It was over that bitch butting into other people's business. I set her straight and that was all there was to it." She studied him for a moment. "You think I killed her?" She laughed. "I could have snapped her scrawny neck if I wanted to. But I didn't. She wasn't worth it."

Gertrude started to lean back under the hood again but stopped. "If I had snapped her neck, I wouldn't have left her lying in her store. I'd have gotten rid of her body, and I wouldn't have left behind any evidence. You should be thankful that the person who finally did send her to hell wasn't that smart. I'm half hoping that he or she gets away with it."

"They were smart enough to wipe their fingerprints from the murder weapon."

Her keen blue eyes widened a little at that. "Were they, now? If you had any leads though, you wouldn't be here. So, other than wanting to see what might be on our security cameras, you're probably dying to know who I think killed her." She seemed to think for a moment. "None of those old hens from the café. Too timid. Also, I'm sure they all have alibis since they would be at their usual tête-à-tête that morning, right?" She glanced at the rag in her hands. "Whoever went down there that morning must have thought they could reason with Vi. If they'd gone there to kill her, they would have taken a weapon. Which means you're looking for someone who *thought* they could talk sense into Vi. Sorry, but is there anyone that delusional in town?" Her eyes narrowed at him. "You have already concluded that, I'm betting. Being Vi, she pushed a normally rational person too far." She tossed the rag aside. "Give Ike a holler. He's over at the house."

With that, she turned back to her pickup motor, dismissing him.

He thought about what she'd said as he walked to the small yellow house behind the gas station and knocked on the door. He agreed with her. Luna had hinted once that Gertrude was pretty cagey with a criminal mind.

Retired-FBI agent Ike Shepherd took only a few moments to answer the door. He was a big good-looking man in his early sixties. Ike smiled when he saw him. Jaxson had met him numerous times since Ike had come to Buckhorn to apparently sweep Gertrude off her feet. The two had run off to Vegas and gotten married not all that long ago.

"I was just looking at the surveillance camera footage," Ike said in his usual friendly manner. "Come on in. You'll want to see this."

He stepped into the nicely decorated house—so at odds with the grime of an auto repair garage and Gertrude herself when she was working.

Ike led him to his computer on a breakfast bar. He hit Play and Jaxson watched as the main drag of Buckhorn came into view. As he watched, he saw movement down the street in front of the salon.

Luna came out and headed straight to her flowerpot at the curb. Ike zoomed in. Luna was on her phone, bent over her flowers—just like Carson McCabe had told him. The wind was blowing her hair and the flowers. He could see the thunderstorm that had rolled through later that morning clouding up in the background.

Ike zoomed back out as a semi roared past, kicking up dust and dirt.

The figure wearing a large Western hat, long stock coat and boots seemed to appear out of nowhere the moment the semi passed.

Ike froze the screen.

Their head down and slightly turned away from the camera, the slicker collar up and snapped closed, it was impossible to see the person's face. Had they been aware of the security camera at the gas station?

Ike unfroze the screen and the video continued as a dust devil came down the street and the person bent against the wind and flying dirt before disappearing out of view. "Probably a man, but could be a woman. Sorry the resolution isn't better. Gertrude didn't even see the need for a security camera to start with."

The former FBI agent was right. Between the poor resolution and the figure being so bundled up, it was impossible to tell if it was a man or woman. If a woman, she was tall. Jaxson couldn't help thinking about Vi and how small and insubstantial she'd been against an ice fishing spear.

"Could I see that again?" Jaxson asked, heart in this throat at the thought of the killer caught on video.

"No problem. I'll send you a copy too. It's hard to tell exactly where the person came from when the camera caught them." He froze the screen right after the semi passed. "I'd put my money on that being your killer. But there's something else you need to see."

Jaxson could see the front door of the store standing wide open. He'd missed it the first time he'd seen the video because he'd been staring at the person in the slicker and Western hat.

But that wasn't all he noticed now. Luna. She had looked up and was now staring down the street directly at the camera—directly at the killer—and the killer had turned in her direction and appeared to be staring back.

He swore as Ike nodded. "Your girlfriend was still on the phone. Maybe it didn't register. But if we're right and that's your killer," he said, pointing to the screen, "then there is a good chance the killer saw her. Right after this, Luna goes back into the salon. Even if the killer didn't recognize her…"

"I know," Jaxson said around the lump in his throat. "She isn't hard to find."

With a copy of the surveillance clip now on his phone, he left, feeling weak with worry. He wanted desperately to see Luna. He tried her number. It went straight to voice mail. He left a message. "I need to see you ASAP. I think the killer saw you."

He was about to pocket his phone as he reached his patrol SUV when he got a text. Hoping it was Luna, he checked and swore. Yarrow.

Jaxson had to read the text twice. His hand holding the phone shook as he read it again.

Berg in hospital—critical. Coroner says attempted murder. Might have lead though. Heading to office. Crime lab has DNA sample from remains under floorboards. Expecting news soon. Talk later.

LUNA DROVE INTO the Eaton ranch yard. She didn't see anyone as she climbed out of her SUV and walked toward the sprawling white house with its wide front porch. Several white rockers sat in one corner of the porch. A quilt had been thrown over the back of one of them. She noticed that the seats had quilted pads on them and next to the rockers on a small table was a bouquet of fresh flowers.

A woman's touch, she thought as she rang the bell. Waiting, she looked around the ranch, wondering where everyone was. Several ranch trucks were parked out by the barn and stables. A newer SUV and truck among them. She rang the bell again and looked at her phone. She still had thirty minutes before she was to meet Tucker Price at the ranch next door.

She saw the curtain next to the door twitch. She'd never seen Bethany Eaton, but she'd heard that she was agoraphobic and hadn't left the house in years. Luna knew someone was home even before she saw the curtain move.

The door opened, but the woman standing there definitely wasn't Bethany Eaton. The woman was tall and thin and had a broom in one hand and a dustpan in the other.

"I was looking for Tom Eaton," she said to the woman, who still hadn't spoken.

"It's okay, Magda," a male voice called from somewhere in the house. "I'll be down in a minute. Show her to the drawing room."

The woman opened the door all the way and Luna stepped in. The first thing she noticed was more flowers in the well-appointed entry. The woman led her deeper into the house. The place was beautiful from the gleaming hardwood to the rich thick throw rugs and the woodwork and wallpaper on the walls.

Opening a door, the woman motioned for her to enter and then disappeared down the hall. Luna glanced into what Tom Eaton had called the drawing room. It appeared to be the formal living room. Like the rest of the house, it was immaculate with pretty touches that made it appealing.

She looked toward the back of the house. She could see the woman he'd called Magda out on a large deck at the back of the house using the broom and dustpan to clean up what appeared to be a spilled pot of flowers. Past the woman, Luna saw where everyone was. A huge tent was being erected some distance from the house next to the pond. The wedding. She'd let it slip her mind with everything else that was going on.

Luna was too antsy to sit. She could still hear Tom Eaton on the phone upstairs. She caught the scent of more flowers. She thought of Avery and wondered what it must have been like growing up here. Even this kind of splendor didn't protect a person from abuse. The scent of all the fresh flowers though was making her a little nauseous. She looked around for a bathroom. Not seeing one, she headed back toward the front of the house. There had to be one upstairs.

She climbed quickly. She could still hear Tom on the phone doing his best to end the conversation, but she really needed to splash a little cold water on her face. This wasn't like her. She found herself questioning why she'd come here. Did she really expect Tom Eaton to remember some cowhand who'd worked on the ranch almost twenty years ago?

Once upstairs she headed down a hallway and found a bathroom almost at once. Closing the door, she went to the sink and splashed her face with the cold water. It took a moment, but she began to feel better.

As she stepped out of the bathroom, she could still hear Tom on the phone. A little turned around, she headed down another hall. She saw a sunroom at the end of the hall that

glowed from the afternoon rays. The room drew her because of the array of colors on the furniture inside it as the
sun lit up the room.

But she hadn't gone far when a door opened, and a
woman stepped out. Startled, all Luna could do for a moment was stare. She knew at once who the woman was
from her bearing alone. Bethany Eaton was beautiful with
her dark hair so like Avery's and pale blue eyes against her
even paler translucent skin. She was much taller and more
formidable-looking than Luna would have expected of a
woman afraid to leave her house.

"What are you doing up here?" Bethany Eaton demanded. "This part of the house is off-limits. I'm sure you
were told that the caterers and staff were to stay on the
lower floor."

"I'm sorry," Luna said, seeing that the woman had also
been startled and now looked both angry and scared. "I'm
not with the caterers or the wedding staff. I was waiting to
talk to Tom on another matter. I had to use a restroom and
then I saw your beautiful sunroom. I apologize."

As she heard Tom finish his call, she quickly turned
and hurried back the way she'd come, barely reaching the
ground floor before he came down the stairs.

Tom Eaton was a large handsome, imposing man with
distinguished graying hair at his temples and Avery's smile.
"Sorry to keep you waiting." He held out his hand and Luna
introduced herself as she shook it.

She was still a little taken aback by her encounter with
his wife.

"You're the local hairdresser," he said. "If you're looking for Avery, she isn't here."

"Actually, I wanted to see you. I'm hoping you can help

me solve a mystery." He looked intrigued as she pulled out her phone. "Do you remember this man?" He took the phone. "He worked for you seventeen years ago."

"I'm sorry, but I've had a lot of people work for me over the years," Tom said. "Seventeen years?" He glanced at the photo and quickly handed it back. Had his eyes widened or had she just imagined it?

"His name was Owen Henry," she said, but Tom merely shook his head.

"What about this woman?" She took the phone back to flip to Amy Franklin's photo.

Tom Eaton took even less time to study this one. "Sorry. Did she also work for the ranch?"

Luna shook her head. "I knew it was a long shot, but I had to try."

It surprised her that Tom wasn't more interested in the mystery she'd mentioned. He seemed distracted. From his earlier phone call? Or by the upcoming wedding of his daughter?

Luna saw him look back up the stairs. She followed his gaze to see Bethany standing at the railing. She was holding a long-stemmed rose. At first, she appeared to be caressing the bloom, but then the bright red petals began to fall over the railing and drift down toward where Luna and Tom were standing.

"I'm sorry I couldn't help," Tom said, both of them still watching Bethany and the rose petals pirouetting down on them. "I need to see to my wife. If you wouldn't mind letting yourself out." He turned and rushed up the stairs as Bethany Eaton dropped the denuded rose and turned away.

CHAPTER TWENTY-ONE

SOMEONE HAD TRIED to kill Johnny Berg? Jaxson felt sick. Berg had seen the killer and now he was lucky to be alive. Hadn't Jaxson worried that something might happen? And now Luna had possibly seen the killer. He tried her number again. Voice mail. This time he didn't leave a message. She was out horseback riding. She was safe with Tucker Price, right?

He'd been worried about Berg, but he really hadn't thought the killer would go after the teenager, had he? He'd mentioned the possibility to Yarrow... He wondered how the acting marshal had taken the news. Yarrow would have to be heartless not to be upset and Jaxson didn't think that was the case.

What the hell? He'd thought that whoever killed Vi had done it spur-of-the-moment out of anger. But to try to kill an innocent young man to cover up the crime?

Jaxson swore, terrified for Luna, but hopeful that Yarrow was right and he had a lead. He thought about the rest of the text. Amy's DNA sample was at the crime lab. The state medical examiner had put a rush on it.

He felt the past closing in. Unless he could find Amy's killer, he was about to lose everything. But the one thing he couldn't bear losing was Luna. He reminded himself that he might have already lost her.

IT WAS A beautiful day for a horseback ride. Luna wished that her mind wasn't on everything but the bright blue cloudless sky overhead and the shimmering pine-covered mountains close by. She was still upset over what she'd seen at the Eaton house. Bethany had clearly been in pain and Luna feared it was all her fault. She'd heard that Avery's mother was agoraphobic, but she hadn't expected a woman of her obvious physical and economic stature to be so mentally fragile.

She'd seen that Jaxson had left her a voice mail, but there hadn't been time to listen to it as she'd hurried to the Price Ranch and parked near the stable.

She couldn't help looking over at the Eaton ranch house though, remembering her short conversation with Tom Eaton after she'd upset his wife. Had he recognized Owen Henry? Or had it just been her imagination that she'd seen a reaction?

Tucker was already inside the stable finishing saddling the horses. He smiled when he saw her. A lock of his blond hair hung over his forehead as he pushed back his straw cowboy hat and considered her. "I was afraid you'd forgotten about our ride."

She shook her head. "What a wonderful day for it. Can I help?"

"You know anything about horses?" he asked with a teasing grin.

"I know one end from the other," she said as she stepped closer to the horse he'd just finished saddling to let the palomino snuffle her hand before she rubbed the beautiful horse between his eyes. She'd taken riding lessons as a girl and had always wanted her own horse. Fortunately she had a friend she'd ridden with a couple of years ago. She hoped riding a horse was a lot like riding a bike and that she hadn't forgotten everything she'd learned.

He chuckled as he handed her the reins to a beautiful buckskin, and they walked their mounts out of the stable and into the bright warm sunshine.

"Excited about the wedding?" Luna asked as she realized the white tent going up behind the Eaton house appeared large even from here.

Tucker stopped to glance over at the Eaton ranch. "They better hope we don't get a storm before the wedding."

She realized that he hadn't answered her question. "Your brother must be getting excited," she said as she swung up into the saddle.

The sound the cowboy made was noncommittal as he mounted his horse. Luna found herself still looking over at the ranch. In the distance she saw a vehicle pull up and Avery Eaton run into the house. Had her father called her about her mother?

Apparently not, because a few moments later Avery exited the back of the house, walking fast toward the tent. Luna thought again about the patch of missing hair and the bruises she'd seen.

From the barn, a cowboy ran after her. Even from a distance, Luna could tell that it wasn't her fiancé, Jory Price. The two seemed to be arguing because when the man touched Avery, she jerked away before storming back inside the house. It was too far away to tell who the man was, but Luna knew that hat from when Carson McCabe came in for a haircut. Black with a hatband of silver conch shells that gleamed in the sunshine.

As if sensing he was being watched, Carson turned in her direction.

"I thought we'd ride up into the mountains," Tucker said as he drew alongside her, blocking her view of the neighboring ranch—and Carson McCabe. "You okay?"

"Sorry, just daydreaming. Avery asked me to do her hair for the wedding. I've never been out here before and had no idea the Price and Eaton ranches were so close together." She raised her gaze to Tucker's handsome face.

Tucker huffed. "A little too close, if you ask me." He quickly changed the subject. "I'd be happy to show you around after our ride." He grinned and spurred his horse.

Luna warned herself to be careful. She liked Tucker. But Jaxson already had a piece of her heart. She didn't want to lead either man on—especially now when she needed to be watching out for a killer.

ON THE HOUR'S DRIVE back to his office in the next town, Ken had plenty of time to think about the cases that were piling up. He needed a break in the worst way. If he could just get a handle on Vi's murder…

The young man who'd called was waiting for him, looking nervous and upset. Like Berg, he appeared to be in his late teens. Ken ushered him back to the marshal's office and offered him a chair, even though all he wanted to see was the letter he'd been told about on the phone. But first he had to know who he was dealing with. The teen's name was Cody Leigh. He worked at a fast-food joint in town, was saving money for college and had been friends with Johnny Berg as far back as he could remember.

"And you were drinking with him the night he was attacked? Neither of you were twenty-one at the time."

"It was at a friend's house. And only a couple of beers," Cody said quickly. "Johnny was good to drive home. That's why I don't believe it was an accident." He pulled an envelope out of his jacket pocket. "He was afraid someone was going to kill him. The same person who slayed that old lady in Buckhorn."

Ken bristled at the *old lady* comment. Vi had been his age. "He told you that when he gave you the envelope and made you promise to give it to us if something happened to him, right? Have you opened it?"

Cody nodded. "I thought it might be a joke. I didn't want to give it to you unless it wasn't."

Holding out his hand, the teen finally handed it to him. He saw what was written on the outside of the envelope before he opened the flap and read the contents, his pulse picking up with each word—not to mention the drawing.

"He wanted to be an artist," Johnny's friend said, his voice going froggy. "He was really good at drawing stuff."

So it seemed, Ken thought as he thanked Cody, tried to assure him that his friend would pull through and sent him on his way. Then he photographed the envelope and its contents, made copies of the drawing and put the original in a plastic evidence bag.

Finally they had a lead. Not that he wasn't furious with Johnny Berg. Why hadn't he come forward right away with this information? Keeping it to himself might have cost him his life and Ken a lot of wasted time.

He was getting ready to leave when he got a call from the coroner's office telling him he could pick up the victim's suitcase.

He texted Jaxson. Meet me at the motel.

JAXSON HAD JUST finished interviewing one of the suspects on his list when he got a call from Carson McCabe. He'd thought for sure that he wouldn't be hearing from the cowboy. "Carson," he said into the phone. He couldn't help sounding surprised.

"I'm not sure you're going to want to hear this, but I did see someone that morning," McCabe said quickly. "Not in front of the store, but down the street from the store. Luna Declan. I'd forgotten about it until a few minutes ago when I happened to see her over at the Price place and it reminded me."

The deputy's pulse jumped. "Luna? You saw her the morning of Vi's murder?"

"Yeah. When I was leaving the bar, I'd pulled up to the highway and I looked to the west. I saw her standing at the edge of the sidewalk in front of her salon next to that huge pot of flowers that she keeps out there. I could see that she was on her cell phone as she bent over, messing with the flowers like she was cleaning out the pot. As I started to drive away, a semi roared past, kicking up a cloud of dust. I remember her looking straight down the street in my direction. But I got the feeling that she didn't see me with that thunderstorm that was rolling in."

Luna had been outside on the street at the time that the killer might have walked out the front door of the general store. "Did you see her go back inside the salon?"

"No, when I left, she was still outside."

Jaxson could practically hear the cowboy's shrug. "Did you see anyone else? Someone crossing the street right behind the semi?"

"No. Like I said, I could barely see out of my one good eye and that semi kicked up so much dust…"

How could McCabe not have seen the killer? Because the killer had already passed behind the semi before the cowboy looked down the street and saw Luna? But then who had Luna been looking at on the surveillance video? Not McCabe. It had to have been the killer and the killer had been looking right back at her.

Jaxson thanked McCabe. Trying *not* to think about Luna horseback riding with Tucker Price, he called her cell. It went straight to voice mail again.

He pulled in front of the motel and parked next to Yarrow's patrol SUV.

LUNA DIDN'T LISTEN to Jaxson's voice mail until after she'd returned from her horseback ride with Tucker. She had turned off her phone after talking to Tom Eaton and not turned it back on. She'd been determined to enjoy being on the back of a horse for a little while and not worrying about Jaxson or these murder cases or what had happened earlier at the Eaton house.

It was one of those amazing Montana spring days that make people move to the state. Cloudless blue sky, sunshine and air that feels so fresh a person couldn't breathe in enough of it. They'd ridden out of the valley and up into the pines. Rocky cliffs jutted out above them as they took a trail to the top of one of the vistas.

"The view is stunning from up here," she said as they ground-tied the horses and walked to the edge of the mountainside to look down at the long valley. She could see Buckhorn in the distance. Closer she could make out the Price and Eaton ranch buildings. "Looks like they got the tent up." When Tucker glanced in that direction and said nothing, she asked, "How long have Avery and Jory been dating?"

Tucker pulled off his straw cowboy hat and turned his

face up to the sun for a moment. "Jory says he's been in love with her since they were kids. I guess he finally convinced Avery to marry him."

Had Avery needed convincing? "Are you and your brother close?" she asked, guessing they were not.

He put his hat back on before answering. "Off and on." Turning, he smiled over at her. "I love my brother but sometimes he doesn't have the good sense God gave him."

"You're the older brother by a couple of years, right? So I can understand if you feel like you need to protect him." She kept thinking about Avery's lost hunk of hair and her bruises. "I get the impression that you aren't for this marriage?" No answer, so an answer in itself. "Have you told your brother your concerns?"

Tucker chuckled at that. "Even if I did, he wouldn't listen. He thinks he has it all figured out, knows everything." The cowboy shook his head.

"If you have reason to be concerned—"

"Maybe I just think he's too young to get married." She didn't think that was it as he shrugged it off. "We best head back if you want to have a look around the ranch."

It wasn't until they reached the stables that she found herself looking over at the Eaton ranch house again. She didn't see anyone, but she couldn't help thinking about Avery and what Tucker wasn't saying.

After unsaddling the horses, they were headed for the main house when she heard a pickup come roaring into the ranch. The truck came to a dust-boiling stop just yards from them.

Jory Price jumped out. "I need to talk to you," he yelled at Tucker as he strode in their direction. He didn't seem to even see Luna and he headed for his brother like a heat-seeking missile.

"Maybe some other time for that tour," she said quietly to Tucker and veered away toward her SUV. She wondered what had Jory so worked up. He seemed furious at his brother. Did it have something to do with the wedding? With Avery?

It wasn't until she left the two arguing next to the ranch house and drove away that she pulled out her phone and listened to Jaxson's message.

JAXSON TRIED TO concentrate on the drawing of the set of keys, but after hearing about the attack on Johnny Berg and the coroner's suspicion that it had been attempted murder, he was even more afraid for Luna. If the killer had seen her out watering her flowers the morning of the murder...

He'd filled Yarrow in on everything he'd learned from McCabe and given him a copy of the video clip from the filling station's surveillance camera. Yarrow hadn't recognized the figure the camera had captured but was excited about the drawing of the keys.

The deputy stared at the carefully drawn set of keys, hoping his boss was right about this being the clue that would blow the case wide open. "No key fob, just two keys on a nondescript ring," Jaxson said, stating the obvious. "Those two keys definitely look like car keys back when you needed one for the trunk and one for the ignition. So an older model vehicle, a truck?"

"You have any idea how many older model pickups there are in this county?" Yarrow asked. "But I agree that the keys probably go to a truck since there are more trucks in this country than cars. You know what this means. We need to see everyone's key rings that we've already interviewed."

He'd been thinking the same thing. That and how much easier it might have been if there had been a fob on the key ring or something to identify the owner. "These don't seem like someone's primary keys. They don't look like they've hardly been used at all."

"I've thought of that," Yarrow said. "I also thought of what Dave Tanner told you. He had to pull some of the drinkers' keys the other night. McCabe used the extra set of keys to drive home since there was no one at the bar at that hour to let him in for the keys he uses all the time."

Jaxson was already nodding. "You're thinking someone else might have left there original keys somewhere like the bar and were using their extra set. I'll show Dave the drawing. Maybe we'll get lucky."

"There is something else," Yarrow said. "Berg left a note with the keys drawing, saying he remembered smelling something that morning in the storage area of the general store. He thought it might have been horse liniment."

Jaxson raised a brow. "That doesn't narrow it down given how many people around here have horses. Both the Price and Eaton ranches raise them."

Yarrow nodded. "But added to the video, the keys and what we know, it's another clue. I think we're getting close."

CHAPTER TWENTY-TWO

DAVE STUDIED THE drawing for a few minutes under the lamplight in his office at the bar before shaking his head. "The keys might be familiar, but I don't recognize them." He handed back the drawing.

"You're sure they can't be a set that you've confiscated at closing before?" Jaxson asked.

"Could be," the bar owner said. "I've definitely held on to keys that look like these. But most are newer vehicles with key fobs rather than keys. You don't see many car keys like this except for older models, right? I guess General Motors is still making a few models that require keys, Honda and Toyota on their lower-end models. That probably doesn't help."

"These keys don't look worn at all as if seldom used," Jaxson said.

Dave nodded. "If I had to guess, I'd say the keys belong to someone who owns an older model pickup. Which is an easy guess since there are a lot more pickups around these parts than cars and a lot of them are at an age where they are still running just fine but might look their age."

"Like some of the ranch trucks around that ranch hands drive into town," Jaxson said.

"Those for sure," Dave agreed. "But also some of these ranchers just refuse to spend what it costs for a new pickup as long as the old one still runs."

Jaxson knew that was true. "Well, thanks for the help." He started for the door, anxious to see if Luna was back from her horseback riding date, when Dave stopped him.

"I was just thinking that picture of those keys," the bar owner said as if it had just come to him. "You know, the ones you keep in a drawer when you can't remember where you put your other keys."

"Or when the bar owner took your first set so you couldn't drive home drunk and you had to bring in your old extra set," Jaxson said, seeing where Dave was going with this. "Do you have any keys that the vehicle owner hasn't picked up yet?"

Dave turned toward his drawer, opened it and dug around inside for a moment. The drawer appeared to have a variety of items that had been left at the bar sometime or another. He pulled out a single glove, a cigarette case, a pair of glasses and tossed them aside before he dug in the back of the drawer and held up a set of keys. "I have no idea how long these keys have been in that drawer."

Jaxson pulled an evidence bag from his jacket pocket and held it open for Dave to drop the keys in. There was probably little hope of getting a clear print off the keys from the owner. Not to mention it was a long shot that the keys matched the ones Johnny Berg had seen lying on the floor just feet from Vi's dead body.

Laying the closed bag down on the bar, Jaxson saw that there were four keys on this ring. A house key? The other smaller key could have been to anything. The two other keys were older model vehicle keys.

Holding his breath, he compared them to Berg's drawing. They matched perfectly.

He felt a jolt of excitement. Unfortunately there was

nothing on the metal ring that gave any indication as to what vehicle—or driver—they belonged to.

LUNA RETURNED JAXSON'S call on her way into town. "I'm on my way to my apartment if—"

He cut her off. "I'll meet you there."

By the time she reached town, he was waiting in his patrol SUV behind her apartment and salon building in the shade. It was cool in the shade and yet her skin prickled with heat. Or was it fear? She'd heard the urgency in his voice. Had the crime lab matched the DNA and identified Amy Franklin?

"What's happened?" she asked the moment he stepped from his patrol SUV, all long-legged and handsome even with his worried expression. She felt such a tug at her heart that her eyes burned with tears.

"I'll tell you upstairs," he said, glancing around the alley nervously.

Luna led the way, scared now. It had to be bad, given Jaxson's behavior. Once in the apartment and the door closed, she turned to him. "What's wrong?"

She watched him take a breath and let it out slowly before he demanded, "Why didn't you tell me that you were out on the sidewalk in front of your salon the morning Vi was murdered?"

Luna stared at him as she sat down, her legs too weak to keep standing. "What?"

He stepped to her, dropping to his haunches to squat in front of her, his hands on her knees. "You don't remember going outside in front of the salon that morning?"

She could hear it in his voice. Fear. She frowned and tried to concentrate. The morning Vi was killed. The morning her father called with the bad news about Jaxson. It came back slowly. Pruning the dead blossoms, her cell phone to her ear. "I did go out to my flowerpot that morning."

Jaxson rocked back before rising to pull a chair over next to her and sit down heavily. "Carson McCabe saw you out on the sidewalk tending your flowers. From where you were at the edge of the sidewalk, you could have seen both ways down the highway. You could have seen anyone who came out of the general store at that hour."

"What are you saying?" she asked, suddenly afraid.

He reached into his pocket and pulled out his cell phone. "The security camera down at the filling station picked up this." He handed her the phone.

She started the video, surprised to see herself on it, though some distance away. There she was pruning her flowers, phone to her ear. It brought back the shock of that morning's news from her father. While a painful memory, what she'd learned since was even more upsetting.

Suddenly on the video, she'd looked up as a semi passed through town. That's when she saw the person in a stock coat, the collar turned up against the wind and the coming spring squall. The person had turned to look down the highway—straight in Luna's direction.

To her shock, she saw herself looking right at the person. For a moment, she couldn't breathe, let alone speak. She handed back the phone. "I saw the killer?" Luna shivered and hugged herself, remembering the same figure standing across the street in the dark, staring up at her apartment a night later. Staring up at her. "But I don't remember seeing *anyone* that morning and it's too far away to recognize the person."

"McCabe said you looked right at him as he was pulling out from the bar parking lot, but he got the feeling you didn't really see him."

She shook her head. "I was on the phone with my father, and he was telling me…" She glanced up at him.

Jaxson groaned. "That I'd lied to you."

She nodded. "I was in shock. I was just going through the motions. I hadn't even remembered going out there that morning."

He turned away for a moment as if he had more bad news. When he turned back, she caught her breath, terrified of what he was going to say.

"The deliveryman who found Vi's body, he's just a teenager, barely old enough to get hired for the job," Jaxson said, sounding tired and disgusted and as scared as she felt. "He was attacked. The coroner thinks it was attempted murder."

She felt her eyes widen in alarm. "No, that's horrible. You don't think…"

"That Vi's killer saw him at the store the morning of the murder and was afraid he'd seen something and would remember? As it was, he did. Turns out he saw a set of keys on the storage room floor. He saw them on the way into the store out of the corner of his eye but hadn't remembered them until later. By the time he found the body and left, the keys were gone. The killer apparently had picked them up."

"I thought he didn't remember seeing anything. How do you know this?"

"He was scared that the killer might come after him," Jaxson said. "He left a drawing of the set of keys and a note with a friend that if anything happened to him…"

Luna sank down into a chair. She could see how upset

Jaxson was. He'd met the teenager Vi had once called Johnny on the Spot. She'd said it with some affection, which wasn't normal for Vi.

The killer had seen Johnny Berg and now Johnny was in a coma. The killer had seen her too and since Luna had looked right at the person...

"I think you should go stay with your dad for a while."

Luna stared at him. She was scared, but she wasn't going anywhere. "I'm not leaving."

"Your life is in *danger*," he said, sounding angry. "You have to go."

She shook her head. "If I leave town, that will only convince the killer—if I did see him or her—that I know more than I do. The killer tracked down the deliveryman. You think the killer can't find me at my father's?" She rose from the chair and started past him, but he reached for her hand.

"Then I'm staying here with you."

She looked from his hand holding hers to his handsome face and gave him a warning look. He hadn't earned the right to try to run her life—even if it was to protect her.

He let go of her hand. "I know. I pretty much blew it with you. But your anger and disappointment at me aside, you know I'm not dangerous."

She raised a brow, but she didn't move away from him. He had no idea how dangerous he was to her heart. Just his touch had sent a bolt of electricity through her. Being this close to him was killing her. She couldn't bear the thought of him staying in this small apartment with her.

"Luna, I'll sleep on your couch. Just until the killer is caught. Just until I prove to you that I can be trusted with your heart."

She desperately wanted to argue that she didn't want or

need him sleeping on her couch for numerous reasons—her desire for him being at the top of the list. She also liked to think she could take care of herself.

But she remembered the dark figure standing out in the storm as it had started to rain. It was the same person from the video, which meant if it was the killer, then the killer had seen her and was still watching her.

She thought about telling Jaxson, but knew that would only make him more adamant about her leaving town for her own safety. "Just find Vi's killer."

KEN DIDN'T KNOW how much longer he could keep this case. The governor was demanding that the state crime investigators be brought in if Vi's murder wasn't solved in the next forty-eight hours. Apparently Vi Mullen had been a large contributor to his campaign—just like the previous governor of the same party.

Forty-eight hours? He couldn't imagine solving this case that quickly since he and Gray had been working long hours and had little to show for it. But he also couldn't imagine that the state investigators would be able to solve Vi's murder any faster either.

What he desperately needed was a suspect. A viable suspect to appease the governor and buy himself more time before this case was taken away from him. If he could prove that Vera Carter or Axel Mullen arrived in town before the murder, then he would make an arrest. Unfortunately he thought the two might actually be telling the truth—that they hadn't reached Buckhorn until Vi was already dead.

He studied the video clip and the photos Gray had taken at the store of the Hate Board, as the said locals called it.

There was some nasty stuff on there. Was one of these residents Vi's killer and Berg's attempted killer?

But after a few minutes of cross-checking the names of the most-incensed residents who'd posted, he hit another dead end. Several were in wheelchairs or used walkers, and others had already been interviewed by either him or Gray, including Lynette Crest. Her son AJ's insufficient-funds check was still on the board.

His cell phone rang. Gray. "What's up?" He listened while the deputy told him what he'd learned from Dave Tanner at the bar about the keys. Ken had hoped that the drawing of the keys would be the lead that broke the case wide open.

Now it sounded like the drawing had only helped find another set of the same keys that had been in a drawer at the bar for who knew how long. Clearly they must go to a vehicle that wasn't driven a lot—or the driver had forgotten where he or she had left the other set of keys.

All the keys did was connect Berg's attacker to Vi's murder. Ken knew he should be glad that he had probably only one killer—and not two—running loose.

"You're saying that the keys Berg drew are a second set and the keys found in the drawer were the originals," he said. "Then this person been driving all this time with the second set?"

Gray shrugged. "Whoever left their keys at the bar hasn't bothered to pick them up for who knows how long. Maybe they have another vehicle they drive most of the time and this is a spare car—just like the keys. All we have to do is find the vehicle. If the keys fit…"

"Yeah," Ken said. "Hang on to the keys, but in the meantime, they released that suitcase that was found under the floorboards. You interested in seeing what's inside?"

THE SMALL FLOWERED suitcase lay in the middle of a sheet of plastic as Jaxson was let into the motel room.

"You up to this?" Yarrow asked. "You're looking a little green around the gills again."

"I'm fine," Jaxson said. But he was far from it, as the acting marshal threw him a pair of disposable gloves.

"I don't suspect we'll find anything of interest. We can only hope there will be some clue as to who this girl was since no purse was found with her remains." Yarrow turned to him. "Open her up."

He could feel the older man's gaze on him as he reached across the plastic. He'd expected to find the zipper rusted, but mummification, he'd learned, required a dry closed-in space. Like under floorboards. The zipper made a purring sound as he unzipped his way around the bag and then lifted the lid.

An old musty smell rose from the suitcase. He recognized the blouse lying on top and quickly took it out and laid it on the plastic. There wasn't that much in the suitcase, but then again Amy hadn't brought much to his house when she'd conned her way in. It seemed that she hadn't gone home for more clothes before disappearing.

A pair of worn jeans, a black skirt, several pairs of underwear, no bra other than the one she'd been wearing apparently. There was an old sweatshirt of his, the Blackfoot Athletic Department logo so faded it was unreadable.

He set it aside. There was only one more item in the suitcase. He picked up the T-shirt; one Katie had given him. It was navy with the silhouette of a football player going up for a touchdown catch on the front.

Jaxson had a sudden flash of the day she'd given it to him. He'd just found out he was being offered a full ride to one of the colleges he'd hoped to attend. He remembered the tears in Katie's eyes as if she knew that once they went away to college, the two of them would be over. As it was, they had ended even sooner.

As he carefully lifted the T-shirt from the suitcase, something inside it rustled. He froze, and his gaze shot to Yarrow who was standing over this scene, arms folded. Reaching inside, he pulled out several notepad sheets of paper that Amy had obviously hidden there. He got a glimpse of Amy's swirly handwriting and was about to set them on the plastic when Yarrow reached for them.

As the acting marshal read what was written, he let out a curse. "These are blackmail notes."

Jaxson rose, his heart a sledgehammer in his chest. He tried to breathe as Yarrow handed him the top one. Amy's curlicued handwriting was at odds with the threatening nature of the notes. He let out a breath. It looked as if Yarrow was right and she'd been practicing writing blackmail notes.

To his father? With a relief that made his knees weak, he saw that she hadn't written anyone's name at the top of the sheets. Who had Amy been trying to blackmail for five-thousand dollars—the same amount Jaxson's father had allegedly been paid by Tom Eaton?

AGAINST JAXSON'S PROTESTS, Luna got some extra bedding out for him and put it on the couch. She'd given him an extra key to the door downstairs and to her apartment without further argument.

All the time she'd tried not to think about what it would be like having him this close. If she'd dreamed about him last night, tonight would be worse.

Jaxson had insisted on making dinner, frying up the rainbow trout she had taken from the refrigerator along with sweet potato fries, Luna's favorite, and a small salad. They'd eaten on the couch, watching the local news.

She'd gotten the feeling that neither of them wanted to talk about the murders or the future. She tried not to think about the video he'd shown her and the person she'd looked right at and hadn't really seen the morning of the murder. There was no doubt it was the same person who'd been standing across the street, watching her apartment.

Common sense and that memory had made her accept him staying with her. But for how long? Until the killer was caught? How long might that take—if ever? She tried to concentrate on the forecast.

Afterward she insisted on doing the dishes since he'd cooked. To her surprise, he hadn't made a big mess of her kitchen. Then again the man had been on his own for a long time. He'd apparently learned to take care of himself—just like she had.

She took her time cleaning up the kitchen. By the time she finished, it was late. She could tell that Jaxson wasn't any more comfortable with this than she was. He looked exhausted and yet there was that spark of chemistry that flickered between them.

"I'm going to call it a night," she said. She loved nothing better than to go to bed and read a book. It helped her relax and finally to sleep. "Is there anything else you need?"

His gaze met hers for an instant too long. "I'm fine," he said, dropping his eyes. "Please don't worry about me.

I'll try not to get in your way." He looked at her again. "Or make you uncomfortable."

She didn't know what to say about that. But *uncomfortable* was the wrong word for what he made her feel. "Good night then," she said and stepped into the bedroom part of the small apartment and closed the accordion folding door that divided the space.

Later, after a shower and changing into one of the soft large T-shirts she slept in, she climbed into bed, wondering if he was already asleep. She worried about him. It was only a matter of time before there was a DNA match and the truth about the remains under the store floorboards came out. As exhausted as he was, that must make sleeping difficult.

She picked up her book, but couldn't get into it, so she finally turned out the light and lay in the darkness, thinking about the cowboy cop in the other room. She could hear him breathing.

"Do you miss football?" Luna asked, pretty sure he wasn't asleep.

He answered at once, sounding surprised. "Why would you ask that?"

"Because I talked to one of your former assistant coaches when I was in Idaho. He said you were a natural and could have gone on and been famous."

She heard the amusement in his voice when he said, "That was a lifetime ago, Luna. I don't even remember that kid with his big dreams." He was quiet for a few moments. "What I wanted more than anything was to get away from my problems."

"Your mom."

"I know that sounds awful."

"No, it doesn't. I'm sure her unrealistic belief that your father would return was hard to live with. But still it must have been hard to give up on a possible football career to look for Amy."

Silence, then, "I thought I'd find her, clear my name and still be able to go to college in the fall. But when I didn't find her, I realized I couldn't go back. That part of my life was over and... I was relieved."

That surprised her and she said as much.

"You have no idea how many what felt like unrealistic expectations I had on me from my coaches, my teachers, my mother, Katie. They all saw their version of my future as if they were already invested in it. When I didn't go back, I felt like a burden had been lifted off my shoulders. I was...free even with Amy's disappearance hanging over my head. I had options for the first time in my life. I became a cowboy and I liked it. I still do. Apparently it's in my blood since my father was a cowhand for most of his life. At least that's what he told us."

"Did you decide to become a lawman to find Amy?" she asked, moving so she could see him through the crack where the folding door didn't quite close. He was lying on the couch, his hands behind his head.

"Maybe at first, but I like the job. Most of the time. Although I do miss being on the back of a horse." She saw him nod. "I'm still a cowboy at heart."

She felt that grin all the way to her toes as if he'd just stolen another piece of her heart. She felt that old yearning become an ache inside her.

"I didn't ask," he said in the other room. "How was your horseback ride with Tucker?"

She hesitated, then answered honestly. "I would rather it had been with you. Good night, Jaxson."

Rolling over, she told herself again what a bad idea it was for him to stay here. She'd never been more aware of him just on the other side of that flimsy folding door.

CHAPTER TWENTY-THREE

THE NEXT MORNING Ken decided it was time to talk to AJ and AJ's boss and father-in-law, Tom Eaton. The drive from town to the ranch was a pleasant one until he got a text from Shar. He'd had to pull over to read it all. She'd apparently made it while under the influence. It was an angry diatribe. The gist of it was that he worked too many long hours, especially at night, and that he never took her anywhere. So basically the fact that she'd found someone else was his own fault.

He didn't respond to it. However he knew that it wouldn't be over until she got to tell him to his face what she thought of him and he got his house keys back. But in the meantime, he had more important things to think about.

Pulling into the ranch, he spotted the huge white tent in the backyard behind the house and was reminded that Jory Price was marrying Avery Eaton this coming weekend. He parked and got out, taking in the huge house with its wide front porch. He'd bet Tom Eaton was glad to be marrying off his only other daughter to a Price instead of a Crest. The union would bring together two huge ranches and their families. Who knew if AJ Crest would even still be around if the marriage to Deanna Eaton was really on the rocks.

Climbing the steps, Ken crossed the porch and knocked. The man who opened the door was striking from the gray at the temples of his dark hair to the expressive light blue eyes and classically cut features. "Mr. Eaton? I'm Acting Marshal Kenneth Yarrow. I'd like a minute of your time."

Tom Eaton seemed startled for a moment as if a marshal were the last person he expected to find on his doorstep. But he recovered quickly. "Marshal Yarrow, please come in." He opened the door wider and stepped aside. "I'm assuming this has something to do with my son's fight the other night at the bar?"

"No, actually," he said as Eaton led him to a small living room and offered him a seat. "It's about Vi Mullen's murder."

Eaton looked surprised as he waited for Ken to sit before he took a seat. "I knew Vi. Anyone from the area did, but only as a passing acquaintance. I'm afraid I wouldn't have any information about her murder."

"I wanted to ask about your son-in-law, Alan Crest." He couldn't miss Eaton's change of expression from helpful to guarded.

"AJ?"

"Are you aware that one of his personal checks was posted on a board in the general store after it came back because of insufficient funds?"

Eaton groaned softly and raked a hand over his face. "I suppose it's no secret that AJ has been…struggling."

"I understand he's married to your oldest daughter, Deanna, and that he lives here on the ranch and works for you. Is that correct?"

The man hesitated for a few moments too long. "Sadly, the two are having some marital problems, that I'm sure they will resolve. But what does that have to do with Vi's murder?"

"Did you ask Vi to take the check down?" Ken probed.

Another hesitation, this one even longer. "I considered it, but I try to stay out of my children's trials and tribulations. Marriage…" He seemed to hesitate. "It isn't always easy."

Ken had heard that Tom's wife, Bethany, was agoraphobic and never left the house, hadn't for years. That must make things difficult in a marriage. "You didn't confront Vi then?"

"I wouldn't say that. I suspect you wouldn't be here unless you'd heard that I did get into an argument with Vi a few weeks ago." He sighed. "I paid an overdue bill for AJ and Deanna. I didn't appreciate the lecture on parenting that came with it."

"Did your wife confront Vi as well?"

He shook his head. "Bethany doesn't leave the ranch."

"Not ever?" Ken asked.

"Not for years."

"What about Deanna? I would think she wouldn't want that bad check on the Hate Board."

Eaton shook his head. "I doubt she would care, truthfully. She does all the cooking and helps run the ranch. Things like what someone in town might be saying about her doesn't bother her. She has two kids to chase after and helps me run the ranch. She has more important things on her mind, as do I."

"Doesn't her husband help?"

"AJ works the ranch. He's a good hand. Probably a better hand than a husband. Is any of this really helping with your investigation, Marshal?"

"What happens if your daughter and son-in-law divorce?"

With a sigh, Eaton said, "Not much. He'll still work here, live here, help take care of the kids."

"Your daughter is okay with that arrangement?" Ken had to ask.

"She and I have discussed it." He chuckled. "Like I said, Deanna doesn't worry about anything but the ranch."

He was finding this hard to believe. "Even if AJ were to remarry?"

Eaton laughed. "Deanna would be happy to have another woman help in the kitchen. I can assure you, Marshal, we're easygoing, us Eatons. Not much ruffles our feathers. Certainly not someone like Vi Mullen."

"But AJ isn't an Eaton," he pointed out and rose. "Can you tell me where I can find him? I'd like to talk to him."

LUNA HAD A break between clients. Earlier today she'd had a thought. She knew that Vi had gone through numerous workers in both the general store and the antique barn. She usually hired young people who were looking for a summer job since that was when the most help was needed. Tina had often worked the antique barn, while Vi had worked alongside her employees at the store.

By Memorial Day and the unofficial beginning of Buckhorn tourist season, Vi would have hired a half dozen young people. Most didn't last for one reason or another—Vi being one of those reasons often.

But since it was still early, Vi hadn't had any help coming in the day she was murdered.

When it came to stocking and inventory, she turned to Lars Olson.

Luna figured that Jaxson or Yarrow had already talked to Lars, but she thought she'd give it a try anyway. She found him in the town shop, sharpening his chain saw blades. As she stepped from the sunshine to the cool darkness, she felt a shiver and looked over her shoulder behind her. No one was following her, so why had she felt as if there was?

She blamed Jaxson for his warnings about how dangerous moonlight investigation could be.

Lars turned and seemed surprised to see her standing in the shop doorway. He was one of her regulars, but he'd skipped a few appointments lately and his untrimmed hair was starting to show it. As if suspecting that's why she'd stopped by, his hand went to his thinning head of hair. "Is it really that bad?" he asked, only half joking, she thought.

"Could use a trim, but that's not why I'm here." She stepped into the shop with all its oily equipment smells and pulled out her phone. "Have you ever seen this man?"

Lars wiped his hands on his overalls before he took her phone. He stared down at Owen Henry, then shook his head. Before he could hand back the phone, she touched the screen and brought up Amy's photo.

"How about her?" She saw the change in his expression. "You've seen her before."

"Wow, it's been years, but I would swear she came into the store looking for work. The only reason I remember is that kind of hangdog look in her eyes—and how could anyone forget that dress she's also wearing in the photo? That threadbare dress with those huge flowers on such a petite girl? She looked like someone who could use a job and probably a decent meal." He shook his head. "If she came looking for either a job or a meal from Vi, she went away disappointed. Who is she?"

"You're sure she was looking for a job?"

"That's what Vi said later when I asked about her. I'd seen the girl later walking down the street, carrying her suitcase. Seems like it had flowers on it as well. She must have liked flowers."

"You didn't see her again?" He shook his head. "Did Vi say anything else about her?"

"You know Vi, she wouldn't have anyway, but one of the ranch hands putting down the storage room floor called to her."

Her pulse jumped. "The day you saw this girl, the storage room floor was going down?"

He frowned. "Must have been, huh. I'm surprised I remembered that. It's been years. I thought about catching up to her, offering some money, but didn't for fear that she would think I wanted something from her. You haven't said who she is."

"Just a missing girl, an old cold case that caught my eye," Luna told him. "Thanks for your help."

"Too bad Vi isn't alive, then again she probably wouldn't remember. This time of year, a lot of young kids start showing up, looking for summer jobs."

Luna couldn't hide her excitement as she left the town shop. Lars had remembered Amy. He'd been able to put her at the general store—while the storage room flooring was being put down. He'd confirmed it by mentioning the time of year—the same time as now—before the tourist season began and about the time Amy could have arrived in town from Idaho.

She texted Jaxson. I have news.

KEN FOUND AJ CREST out by the barn unloading a hay truck with two other ranch hands.

"Acting Marshal Kenneth Yarrow," he said, announcing himself. The three men all stopped what they were doing to look at him. "AJ Crest? Would like to ask you a few questions. Is there some place we could speak privately?"

The other two shot him looks as AJ jumped down from the back of the flatbed. "We can talk in the stables." He led the way as if he'd been expecting this, Ken thought.

The stables were cool and dark as AJ led him inside. "We shouldn't be interrupted in here," the ranch hand said, turning once out of earshot of the others. "What's this about?"

"Mind if I record this?" He didn't wait for a reply as he pulled out his phone. "Vi Mullen. You ever argue with her?"

"Me and everyone else in town."

"What was it about?"

He huffed. "Like I can remember."

"Maybe your check that bounced? She didn't take it down from that board of hers," Ken said. "That must have embarrassed you."

"I didn't ask her to take it down. My mother did. And embarrass me?" He chuckled. "Believe me, nothing could embarrass me at this point. It's no secret. My dirty laundry is hanging out there for anyone who wants to see it. My wife emptied our checking account after catching me with another woman. It's an old story, Marshal. One I'm sure you've heard before."

"Where were you the morning Vi was killed?"

AJ looked surprised. "You think I killed her?" He laughed and shook his head. "I was right here on the ranch. Anyone can verify it, including my wife and father-in-law. We were in the kitchen when we heard the news from one of those busybodies in town who called. None of us were surprised except maybe my mother-in-law. She was definitely the most upset over it. Sent her right back to bed, but that's where she spends most of her time anyway. So I suspect if she'd been looking for an excuse, she found one."

"She's agoraphobic, I understand?"

"If that means she hides upstairs, then I guess she is."

Ken thanked him for the information, then he asked, "Where is the truck you usually drive?"

Outside Ken took the keys he'd gotten from Jaxson and climbed inside AJ's pickup. He tried the keys. They didn't fit.

He thanked the ranch hand and left. If AJ had a violent temper, the acting marshal hadn't seen it. Nor did the man seem that upset about the check on the Hate Board at the store.

But his mother, Lynette, on the other hand was another story.

JAXSON GOT LUNA'S text and headed straight for her salon. But when he got there, he found a note on the door that read Back Soon. He headed down the street toward the café, thinking she might have needed her late-morning coffee. Also, Yarrow had suggested he talk to Earl Ray Caulfield, a local war hero who most people in town thought of as the de facto mayor.

He hadn't gone far when ahead he saw two cowboys coming down the sidewalk toward him. The last person Jaxson wanted to run into was Tucker Price or his buddy Carson for that matter.

Jaxson tipped the brim of his Stetson as he passed them and tried to keep his expression neutral. Most everyone knew he and Luna had been dating regularly. Tucker would have known that when he asked Luna out. He tried not to let that anger him, but it must have shown on his expression.

"I don't think the deputy likes you stealing his girl-friend," he heard Carson say and laugh. Jaxson caught the smell of alcohol as they passed on the street.

"Shut up," Tucker said, and Jaxson heard a short scuffle break out behind him, but he didn't turn around. He didn't want to get into it with either cowboy when they were sober. He especially didn't when they'd been drinking.

He wanted to put as much distance as possible between himself and Price.

Luna wasn't anywhere to be seen in the café, but Earl Ray was waiting for him in his usual booth when Jaxson joined him.

"Coffee or a cola?" Bessie called from the kitchen. When he declined his usual breakfast, she said, "I have banana cream pie, your favorite."

"Thanks, Bessie, but I won't be staying that long." He kept thinking about Tucker and Carson. He hoped to hell that they weren't driving. But they'd been headed down the street toward the bar. He figured the two had already finished off a six-pack on their way into town.

"What can I do for you, son?" Earl Ray asked.

Jaxson could understand why the man was the most beloved in town. He was always cheerful and ready to help anyone in need. "Were you around when the new flooring was put down in the storage room at the store? It would have been seventeen years ago from what I've been told. Do you recall who did the work?"

Earl Ray nodded. "I remember Vi being upset about the dust and the noise. Seems it was a couple of ranch hands. I was just thinking about that. I'm pretty sure AJ Crest put down the floor. He had a couple of young cowhands working with him. Not sure, but they could have been Tucker

Price and Carson McCabe. You know Carson's father is the Eaton ranch manager and AJ is married to Tom Eaton's daughter, Deanna."

"You really think it was Tucker and Carson. They would have been awfully young," Jaxson said.

"Just boys, but they'd probably been wielding hammers since they were toddlers out there on the ranch. I'm pretty sure it was those three, with AJ in charge and the other two doing the grunt work. Have you spoken to them?"

"Not about this. I'd heard the job was done by local ranch hands, but I didn't have any names before."

"Is this about the remains under the floorboards?" Earl Ray asked quietly.

Jaxson nodded and pulled out his phone. He showed Earl Ray the photos of his father and Amy.

"Luna showed Bessie and I these," he said, handing back the phone. "Sorry, neither looks familiar. Wait a minute." He took the phone again. "The girl. There is something about her. I kept thinking of her after Luna showed me her photo. Think I might have bought her something to eat at the café. This time of year, we start getting stragglers coming through town either looking for work or heading somewhere on a shoestring. I often help them out with a meal—and advice," he added with a laugh.

Earl Ray looked again at the girl's photo. "There is definitely something about this one," he said with a shake of his head. "Desperation? I can't remember her story, but I think I was worried about her."

Jaxson thanked Earl Ray and left the café. As he did, he checked the text he'd gotten on the way here. Luna had news. He started down the street toward her salon when he saw Carson and Tucker in front of the bar next to a ranch truck. Dave appeared to be having a serious discussion with the two of them.

Jaxson knew trouble when he saw it. He hesitated only a moment before he hurried down the street to see what was going on. He already had a pretty good idea he knew.

BACK AT THE MOTEL, Ken studied the report from the crime lab on Vi Mullen's murder, hoping for something concrete he could use in his investigation. The problem was that the store had too many fingerprints of everyone who ever touched the boxes in the storage area. So basically a dead end since there was no way of knowing if the killer's prints were among them.

As for the lone bloody partial footprint, the lab had concluded it was made by the worn sole of a cowboy boot. They could only guess at the size, but estimated it could have been a female with size nine. Or a man's size ten to twelve. So basically an average man's foot size or a little more than average woman's.

His cell phone rang and he saw it was the crime lab. Had they discovered something more? Something that might actually help him solve these cases?

He could really use some good news right now. There was so much pressure from the governor to turn the entire investigation over to the state boys. It was almost a temptation. Let them try to figure this all out.

But he wasn't ready to give up. He couldn't blow his chance to prove to everyone what he could have done as marshal—if they hadn't overlooked him. True he had gotten thrown more than one murder—and a mess of a case. However right now he was feeling optimistic. With Gray's help and whatever the lab had for him, he thought they might actually solve it all.

He quickly picked up. "I was just reading your report. Not much to go on."

"No," the lab tech said. "Not on that victim, but I do have good news on the remains. We were able to match the DNA to a missing teenager from Idaho. She disappeared seventeen years ago. The coroner had estimated her age at the time of death from somewhere between sixteen to eighteen. She was days away from her seventeenth birthday the last time she was seen. Her name was Amy Franklin. She was a junior at Blackfoot High School."

"Any living relatives?"

"Her mother is the one who called the police that she was missing. She is still alive and needs to be notified. I'll text you the information."

Ken tried to feel relieved. At least he was making some progress on the second victim. But he still had no idea how this Amy Franklin had ended up under the floorboards or what she'd even been doing in Buckhorn.

Maybe her mother might have some idea.

CHAPTER TWENTY-FOUR

TUCKER PRICE SAW the deputy coming and stepped back from the ensuing argument. Jaxson saw him try to warn Carson McCabe, but the ranch hand was standing nose to nose with the bar owner. The argument looked as if it was about to turn physical.

"What's going on here?" the deputy asked loudly.

"Just trying to stop these boys from driving drunk," Dave said without looking at him. He was still facing McCabe, who apparently wasn't giving an inch. He glared at Dave, both hands bunched into fists. Clearly he was looking for a fight—often alcohol-fueled if history was repeating itself.

"I can settle this argument real quick," Jaxson said. "You want a ride in the back of my patrol SUV, Carson?"

For a moment neither Dave nor Carson moved. Then slowly the ranch hand opened his hands, flexing his fingers, before he stepped back and turned to the deputy.

"Just having a little disagreement is all, Deputy," McCabe said.

"Then hand over your keys to Dave and call someone out at the ranch to come pick the two of you up," Jaxson said.

For a moment he thought the ranch hand was going to argue the point. But he sighed, smiled and said, "Waste of time since we haven't had that much to drink, but I guess I'm not being offered an option, am I, Dave?" He reached into his pocket and dropped his keys on the ground at Dave's feet—ignoring the man's outstretched hand.

"What is it about you, Carson?" Dave said. "You want to get eighty-sixed from the only bar in town?"

"Step back, McCabe," Jaxson ordered as he moved between the two men. Carson was still looking for a fight. Jaxson wouldn't have been surprised if the ranch hand attacked the bar owner the moment he reached down for the keys lying on the ground.

Picking up the keys, the deputy shook his head at McCabe. "Best make that call." He looked past him to Tucker Price who was leaning against the ranch pickup. "You're not planning to drive anywhere, are you, Price?"

Tucker shook his head. The two men locked gazes for a long moment. If Jaxson had wondered how long Tucker Price had been hoping to come between him and Luna, he no longer did. There was challenge in the rancher's expression.

"Don't the two of you have work to do out on the ranches?" he asked, pulling away from what he knew could easily become another standoff.

Not to mention that right now he and Luna weren't exactly together. His own fault, he thought with a curse. With his future up in the air, he couldn't be sure he could repair the damage he'd done, but he was going to damn well give it his best shot. He didn't need Tucker stepping in.

Then again Luna could date anyone she pleased.

Tucker made a call for a ride and Jaxson and Dave went into the bar.

"I don't think they're going to give you any more trouble today," he said as the bar owner went behind the bar and he took a stool. He figured he'd better stick around until the two outside were gone. "Mind if I see those keys?"

Dave handed them over. Since it was an older ranch truck, the key ring looked a lot like Johnny Berg's drawing, but with more keys. He handed it back.

"Did you ever find the owner of that set you found in the back of your drawer?" Jaxson asked.

"Not yet. I suspect whoever left them just had more keys made at the hardware store over in Lewistown. Or used their spare set." He offered him a beer, but the deputy declined, saying he was still on duty. "Any closer to finding Vi's killer?"

Jaxson shook his head. "We've spent days interviewing people. Right now it seems impossible that there is a solution in all of it. And yet, I know how this works. Suddenly there is a thread that connects a string of clues together and wham! There's your killer. Or it becomes a cold case because there are just enough missing clues that there appears to be no thread and the case goes unsolved."

At the sound of the bar's front door opening, they both turned to see Jory Price and a ranch hand from the Price spread. Dave tossed Jory the keys. "Can you get your brother home?"

Jory made a face but nodded as he caught the keys.

"McCabe shouldn't drink," Jaxson said as Jory and the ranch hand left.

"He is a mean drunk," Dave agreed as he stepped behind the bar. "But I suspect there is more to it. Have you met his old man? I've heard he's hard to work for and probably even tougher on his own son." He shrugged. "It's why I haven't eighty-sixed Carson. Yet."

"You're probably too nice to own a bar," Jaxson said,

smiling, as he climbed off the stool. He thought of Luna's text. Now that things had settled down here, he was anxious to see what she'd found out. He just hoped she was back at the salon by now. He didn't worry about her as much during daylight, but he still worried.

KEN SAW THAT he'd gotten a text with the information about Amy Franklin's next of kin. He wasn't looking forward to telling Amy's mother that her daughter's remains had been found. When Shar called, he was almost relieved to put off the other call. Still he considered not taking his former girlfriend's call.

He'd figured by now she was either with the man she'd brought to his house after the bars closed that night or she'd picked up someone else at the bar where Ken had met her.

He'd thought of that first night often since the awkward scene at the house. It hadn't surprised him that she was running around on him. He'd caught the last act of an argument between Shar and some man at the bar that night. The man who she'd called Bud had slammed her against the bar, threatening to kick her ass.

Bud had clearly been looking for a fight and Ken had been ready to give him one. But once he'd pulled his badge, Bud had backed off, storming out, saying it wasn't the last Ken or Shar would see of him.

Shar had gone to the ladies' room, cleaned up and came out appearing none the worse for wear. She'd taken a stool down from him and thanked him, back ramrod straight, a determined look on her face. Buying her a drink had seemed like a nice thing to do. She'd thanked him politely with a nod and a smile, and they'd both enjoyed their drinks and the music for a good ten minutes before she moved down to pull up a stool next to him.

He'd known the kind of woman she was even before they left the bar together. She'd moved into his place the same way she'd moved down the bar. The woman had a lot of practice at moving in—and on.

So why was she calling? "Hello?"

Silence, then, "It's me... Shar." He said nothing, waiting. "I'm sorry. You were nice to me, and I was... Well, we know how I was. I really need to see you. It's important. I don't want to do this over the phone. Also, I still have the key to your place. I figured you might want it back."

"You could have just left it at the house."

"How's the investigation going?" she asked.

He sighed and realized that he'd missed having someone to go home to who would ask about his day. "Confusing. We've collected a lot of information, but I can't see how any of it ties together and leads us to the killer. Killers, actually."

"There's more than one?"

"Two bodies almost twenty years apart so I'm assuming two killers, but you never know."

"You sound tired. Call me when you're coming home. I'll meet you at the house. Don't worry—no drama. I wouldn't bother you, but it's important. Also I hate leaving things the way we left them." She let out a nervous laugh. "Is that okay?"

He wasn't sure if he believed there wouldn't be drama. Or that she just wanted a more adult parting. It didn't seem her modus operandi. Maybe she really was sorry. Maybe she really did have something important to tell him.

Not that he had any intention of taking her back. He wasn't a complete fool. He disconnected, not sure how he felt. Confused more than anything. He couldn't imagine why she wanted to see him. It had to be more than an apology and a goodbye. Maybe she thought he would weaken. Not likely.

But closure would be good. He texted Jaxson. Have to run home. See you in the morning. He told himself he needed a break from the case. He wasn't getting anywhere with Vi Mullen's murder. He'd been waiting, hoping for a DNA match on the mummified body before worrying about the cold case murder.

He also needed to get his key back from Shar. A conciliatory ending between them would be nice.

Ken hoped he wasn't making a mistake as he called Shar back. "I'm headed home now."

"That's great," she said, sounding pleased. *Too pleased?* "Call me when you're almost to town. I'll meet you at the house. I have something for you."

"Shar—"

"Don't worry. It's not a bribe, Marshal."

"Acting Marshal."

She chuckled. "But for how long? Once you solve this case… See you later."

He disconnected, feeling better than he had in a long while and warning himself against the feeling. People didn't change. He knew that firsthand. He needed to be very careful tonight.

Armed with the information he needed and a good hour's drive, he called Naomi Franklin to tell her the news about her missing daughter.

LUNA CHECKED HER appointment book, glad to see that her day was almost over as Darby Cole was leaving. She'd just got through showing the newspaper woman the photos of Owen and Amy. Darby hadn't recognized either, but she hadn't been in Buckhorn long. It had been a long shot that the journalist might have any knowledge of Owen or Amy.

Before the salon door closed, a woman stepped through. Luna turned and felt a start. It took a moment for her brain to tell her that it wasn't Vi Mullen standing in her doorway.

The woman laughed. "Identical twins, but I'm guessing you've got that now."

"You must be the Vera Carter I've been hearing about," Luna managed to say, even though her heart was still pounding as if she'd seen a ghost.

"Don't believe everything you've heard about me," the woman said, stepping in to let the door close behind her. She even sounded like Vi. "I was hoping you could do something with my hair."

She'd just been thinking about closing early but wasn't about to turn down the number one suspect in Vi's murder investigation. "What did you have in mind?"

"Apparently Vi and I had the same exact haircut."

"Darn close," Luna agreed.

"Then let's fix that," Vera said with a flourish as she whipped off her jacket, hung it on one of the hooks by the door and headed for the chair. "Maybe something like yours," she said as she sat down and gazed at Luna behind her in the mirror.

"A pixie cut?"

"Why not?"

Luna spun the chair around, opened the cover on the sink and turned on the water as Vera lay back.

"So did you know my sister well?" the twin asked with a smile.

"We got along." Cocking an eyebrow, she asked, "Are you looking for her killer?"

"Not hardly," Vera said. "Just curious. I've heard Vi had trouble making friends."

That was putting it mildly, Luna thought. "Did I hear that you're planning on selling everything, including the store, antique barn and her house?" she asked as she began to shampoo Vera's short dark bob.

"I can't believe the way news travels in this town. As Vi's only true heir, I have a lawyer working on it." She must have seen Luna's surprised expression. "Oh, haven't you heard? Tina isn't even a blood relation to Vi. Only in Buckhorn would babies be switched. Vi's daughter was stillborn. The county nurse had just delivered a baby from Earl Ray's wife, Tory, who'd kept her pregnancy a secret even from him. Didn't want kids. I get it. So the county nurse switched the babies."

Luna was stunned. "So Earl Ray is Tina's father." She thought of all the times she'd seen the two of them together as she rinsed Vera's hair and massaged in the conditioner. "How long have they known?"

"A while now, I guess."

"What does that mean as far as Vi's house and businesses?"

"Our Daddy set up everything in a trust so neither of us could sell without the others approval. He knew Vi would never sell and leave. But Vi's gone."

That was fortunate for Vera, she thought as she rinsed Vera's hair, wrapped it in a towel and spun the chair around.

"I heard you've been dating the deputy who's investigating the case. He and that acting marshal getting any closer to finding the killer?"

"Not that I've heard," Luna said as she began to cut the woman's hair. "I heard you were the number one suspect though."

Vera laughed heartily. "First time I've been first at anything."

"If it wasn't you, then who do you think did it?"

"I wish I knew. I suppose you don't like having a killer in town, huh."

Luna finished the cut, added some product and blew the short pixie dry. As she spiked it with her fingers, she asked, "What do you think?"

"I love it," Vera said. "I've needed a change for a long time."

She wondered if Vera hadn't left her hair exactly like her twin's for the shock value when she hit Buckhorn. "You really didn't get to town until Vi was dead?" she said, handing Vera a mirror so she could see the back of her haircut. "Quite the coincidence."

Vera studied the back of her head with the hand mirror. "No one believes me that I just had this feeling that I had to get to Buckhorn." She smiled and handed back the mirror. "I saw you asking that newspaper woman about some photos on your phone?" Luna realized that Vera must have been standing near the open doorway of the salon longer than she'd thought. "Is this about Vi's murder?"

"No, it's about a cold case."

"Well, let's see them," the woman said and held out her manicured hand.

Calling up the photo of Amy first, she handed her phone to Vera, who glanced at the girl and handed back the phone. "Don't know her."

"This is from seventeen years ago, so you weren't in

town," Luna said. Still Vera held out her hand to see the other one. She pulled up Owen Henry's photo, expecting the same result, but clearly Vera was curious—and pushy to boot.

She handed her phone over, wondering why she was humoring the woman. Because Vera Carter didn't take no for an answer—just like her sister, Vi.

KEN PUT THOUGHTS of Shar out of his head as he called the dead girl's mother to give her the horrible news. Naomi Franklin answered on the third ring.

"Mrs. Franklin, I'm Acting Marshal Kenneth Yarrow. I'm calling you from Buckhorn, Montana. I'm afraid I have some bad news. It's about your daughter, Amy."

She made him repeat his name. Her voice was rough. A smoker's voice. "If this is a prank call—"

"It's not, Mrs. Franklin. Your daughter's remains have been found."

He'd expected her to break down. Instead he heard her swear.

"After all this time? After years of wondering where she was, what she was doing? I figured she was dead or she would have called for money, you know? She really is dead?"

"Yes. I'm so sorry to have to give you this news."

He heard her sniff and then take a drink of something before she asked, "What happened to her?"

"That's what we are trying to find out. But apparently she was killed not long after she disappeared from Idaho."

"She's been dead all these years? Then why am I just hearing about this now?" she demanded.

"Whoever killed her hid her body. It was only recently

discovered. I heard today from the crime lab after they matched her DNA that you provided the police with when she went missing."

"You're telling me someone *murdered* my daughter?"

"Given that her body was hidden, we are investigating her death as a homicide," he said.

"Well, I can tell you right now who did it. That boyfriend of hers. He disappeared right after she did. I figured they were either together or that he killed her and was on the run. Told the police but they had bigger fish to fry. Said my daughter probably just ran away from home. She was always doing that, but this time felt different. I knew the boyfriend did it." She sniffed. "I knew."

"What boyfriend was that?" he asked.

"Jaxson Gray. Everyone was so high on him just because he could throw a football. I never trusted him."

What the hell? Ken thought he'd heard wrong. "I'm sorry, can you spell that name for me?" She spelled both names. No mistake.

"Can you give me a description of him?" He listened as she described his deputy. "You told the police about this when your daughter disappeared?"

"I just told you I did. Like they could have cared."

"Did they talk to her boyfriend… Jaxson?"

"He swore he had nothing to do with it. Told them some story about her taking off to find his no-count father. Amy always was a handful. Her father and I couldn't do anything with her. She'd been living over at his house. We just thought, fine, let him deal with her."

He kept thinking about the deputy's reaction when he'd seen the mummified body in the hole in the floor. "You assumed he knew where she had gone?" Ken asked, his thoughts falling all over themselves.

"Amy wasn't legal age. Figured they had run off to get married. Didn't have to run off—we would have signed. Anything to get her out of our hair. But I guess things didn't go as planned. Why else would he kill her?"

Good question. If he had. Ken again thought of Jaxson's reaction when he'd seen the remains and swore silently. Seeing Vi with what looked like a giant fork stuck in her chest hadn't even made Jaxson twinge. But that girl's mummified body had sent him looking like he was going to pass out.

Now it made sense. All this time Jaxson had known exactly who was in that makeshift grave. He'd known when they went through the girl's suitcase. Ken swore. His deputy had kept his mouth shut the whole time. To cover up his crime? To buy himself time? Surely he knew his name was going to come up in the investigation once they had the DNA.

"I'll have to get back to you, Mrs. Franklin, when her remains will be released for burial."

"I'm not paying to have her shipped all the way back to Idaho. You just do whatever you do with them. We had to put that girl behind us years ago. There won't be any burial. She chose the path she took. We've been mourning that girl for seventeen years."

Ken was still in shock as he disconnected. The mother's reaction alone had his head spinning. But hearing Amy's boyfriend's name... Jaxson Gray? Realizing that his deputy had known this whole time... He couldn't wait to get his hands on Jaxson. Ahead he saw the outskirts of town.

He was half tempted to turn around and drive back to Buckhorn, find Jaxson, cuff him and throw him in the back of his patrol SUV and haul his butt to jail if for nothing more than impeding his investigation.

Calm down. You're in no shape right now. You'll do something rash. Better to wait. Jaxson wasn't going anywhere. If he were going to run, he would have done so the moment he saw the girl's remains.

Tonight Ken would finish things with Shar, tidy up his personal life. He would deal with Jaxson tomorrow.

CHAPTER TWENTY-FIVE

LUNA WATCHED VERA smile down at Owen's photo. "Handsome, huh," she said, trying not to be annoyed at the woman leering at Jaxson's father.

"He was my favorite of the two for sure." Vera started to hand back the phone.

"Excuse me?" Luna said, taking her phone. "Are you saying you *know* Owen Henry?"

"Not as Owen Henry. Back then everyone called him O.H."

She stared at Vera. Was the woman pulling her leg? "How did you—"

"O.H. and I were close because we were both black sheep of the family. I hung around Eaton Ranch growing up mostly to stay away from my twin—but also away from work in one of the shops owned by our parents. O.H. and I hung out because his older brother, Tom, was a lot like Vi, always giving him trouble, and once Bethany came into the picture…" Vera rolled her eyes. "You can imagine how she treated her father-in-law's love child."

Could any of this be true? "Wait, Owen was an Eaton?" Luna thought about the five grand Tom had given him seventeen years ago. Maybe Owen hadn't worked for the money. Maybe it had been money to send him on his way again.

Hadn't Owen told Jaxson's mother that he had to take care of something with his family and then he'd be back for her and Jaxson? What had happened that he'd never made it back?

"If that's true, why isn't his last name Eaton?"

"Because he was the love child of Thompson P. Eaton, Tom's father."

Luna still wondered if Vera was making this up as she went along. "Love child? Who was his mother?"

Vera shrugged. "But once O.H. found out that Thompson was his father, he suspected it was Marianne Price from the ranch next door. They were a little too cozy after her husband died. You really haven't heard any of this? I suppose a lot of it wasn't common knowledge and it has been years." Vera settled in, clearly happy to pass on such good gossip.

"I'm sorry, I'm confused," Luna said. All this was way before her time since she hadn't lived here long.

Vera spoke more slowly. "Tom's father, Thompson P. Eaton, brought home a newborn baby that he said he'd found. He didn't want the infant to have to go to social services, his story, so he pulled some strings and his wife, Linda, raised O.H. along with their son, Tom. They named him Owen Henry. Thompson had wanted to adopt him and give him his last name for obvious reasons since the kid was really his with some woman who'd allegedly worked on the Price Ranch next door. Linda got wise and hit the roof, so the baby was just Owen Henry and they never adopted him. Almost sixty years ago, it was easy to get the kid a birth certificate in that name if you were Thompson P. Eaton."

Luna was trying to make sense out of all this. "So O.H. is an Eaton."

Vera continued as if she hadn't spoken. "O.H. was raised alongside his older brother, Tom, but everyone treated him more like a hired cowhand. Years later he found out the truth. He and his father argued and O.H. left the ranch. He'd already been in trouble with the law, so no one went looking for him. It was all hush-hush. I'm sure Tom was glad to see his half brother go." Vera narrowed her eyes. "Why are you asking about O.H. now anyway?"

Luna had to think fast on her feet—fortunately it was something she was pretty good at. "Someone told me that they thought he was in Buckhorn seventeen years ago— about the time the new flooring was going down at the store. I thought he might know who did the work."

"Oh, this is about the remains that were found," Vera said as if losing interest. "I really doubt O.H. knows anything about that. Vi was never a fan of his. She would never have hired him to do the work." She rose to leave.

Luna was thinking about what Clarice had told her. "Why wasn't she a fan of his?"

Vera shrugged. "He wasn't wild about her either." Pulling a wad of bills from her purse, she paid Luna and said, "Too bad it wasn't easy like it is now to get DNA results. O.H. could have hired a lawyer and maybe gotten half the Eaton Ranch and while he was at it, some of the Price Ranch as well, if I'm right about who his real mother was. Not that O.H. would have done it. Tom and his snooty wife, Bethany, would have made his life miserable, and I can't see either Tucker or Jory welcoming O.H. with open arms. That's probably why he left and never came back."

Vera started for the door, but then stopped. She turned, frowning as if she'd thought of something. "Seventeen years ago, you said? That was about the time Thompson died. Maybe O.H. *did* come back. Everyone knows the ranch was left to Tom, the only son the old fart acknowledged. If O.H. came back wanting his share, I'm betting there were fireworks. Just the hint of a scandal would have sent Bethany into a tizzy." Vera started as if another thought had struck her. "You know, I bet that's what happened. It would explain why Bethany turned into a house mouse—afraid to even go outside—about that same time." She shrugged.

"That's how long she's been agoraphobic?" Luna asked in surprise. Vera nodded as if deep in thought. She reminded herself that she shouldn't trust that Vera had based any of this on fact. Also the woman hadn't lived here in years. "You know a lot about the people of Buckhorn and the area for someone who's been gone for so long."

Vera smiled. "I left, but I kept up with the gossip. I have an *inside* source at the Eaton Ranch. Want to know what goes on in a household? Ask the housekeeper." Vi's twin laughed. The laugh was eerily too similar to Vi's. "Trust me, Magda hears and sees *everything*. Someday I bet she will cash in on all she knows. I would love to see Tom's and Bethany's faces when she does." With that, Vera laughed and left.

Luna was seldom shocked by what people told her. This was a first. Jaxson's family really was from here? Because of that, it made sense why he had returned all those years later after his father died to mend fences with his brother and get his inheritance. What had happened when he'd shown up at the ranch seventeen years ago to find out his father had left him nothing?

She thought of Tom Eaton. How would he have reacted to his half brother's return? Or Bethany, for that matter? Luna figured the five grand Tom had paid him pretty much said it all. But that didn't explain why Bethany no longer left the house.

The bell over her door jangled. She turned and smiled, glad to see Jaxson.

WHEN JAXSON ENTERED the salon, he found with relief that Luna had returned. "I have news," he said. "Any chance you're finished for the day?" he asked, not wanting to be interrupted as someone walked slowly past on the sidewalk and waved to Luna.

She told him to lock the door behind him and they headed upstairs.

"I can tell you're anxious to tell me, so you can go first," he said, smiling at her.

"I talked to Lars Olson. He remembered Amy. Remembered that flowered dress and her flowered suitcase," she said excitedly. "She came into the store and talked to Vi. Lars later asked Vi about it and she claimed that Amy had asked for a job. But Lars seemed to think there was more to it."

"Like what?"

"He wasn't sure, just that Vi had been upset." She saw his expression. "What?"

"Who knows what Amy might have said to Vi. Maybe she'd been trying to blackmail Vi." He told her about what they'd found in Amy's suitcase.

"Blackmail notes?" she said in surprise. "But what could she have on Vi? She couldn't have been in town long."

"Amy could have overheard something. She was clever that way, always working things to her advantage. The blackmail notes were generic, as if she was practicing her blackmail technique." He raked a hand through his hair as he paced the small apartment. "What if she tried to blackmail my father?"

"About what?"

Jaxson shook his head. "She would have needed money. I doubt she had much and getting to Montana would have drained what cash she had, I suspect." He saw her change of expression.

"I showed her photo to Earl Ray. He thinks he remembers buying her a meal."

"She left Idaho a good week before I did. I have no idea how she got here. I drove so it took me one long day."

"If we knew exactly how long it took to remove the old flooring in that part of the storage area and replace it, we might have some idea," Luna said. "More than likely Vi would have known. The information is probably somewhere in Vi's office."

"From seventeen years ago?" He shook his head. "She probably paid the cowhands in cash so it wouldn't even be on the books. Even if she didn't, seventeen years is a long time to keep that kind of information."

"Once we know who put the flooring down—"

"It might have been Tucker Price and Carson McCabe," Jaxson said. "They were both young, but Earl Ray says they would have been working with AJ Crest, who was possibly overseeing the job." He could see this news surprised her.

"Now we just need to know when," she said excitedly. "But even so, we won't know exactly when Amy or your father arrived in Buckhorn. Or when your father left. We're assuming he left right after cashing the check Tom Eaton gave him."

"Amy couldn't have been in town that long," he said. "I came looking for her after graduation—a week or so later. I had a vehicle. She apparently took a bus or hitchhiked. So she couldn't have been more than a few days ahead of me."

That he'd missed catching up with her by such a short time made him ache. Maybe everything would have been different if he had.

He looked at Luna. But maybe he would never have met this woman. He would have had no reason to come to Buckhorn, Montana, if his life had gone according to plan.

"If she had been in town long, I would think more people would have remembered her. How long were you in Buckhorn?" Luna was saying.

"Just forty-eight hours, then I heard about a job down south in Wyoming and headed there. Once I saw how small Buckhorn was and asked around about Amy, I knew she wasn't in town. I figured she'd never made it. Or had gotten sidetracked, hooked up with somebody..." He shrugged. "I wouldn't have put it past her to forget all about this quest of hers, forget about me, my mother, everything, when it became too hard."

"Instead, she was here about to blackmail someone," Luna said.

"If she hadn't already." He met her gaze. "I suspect whoever she blackmailed killed her."

"The question is who and why? What could she have found out about someone in town that quickly?" Luna asked.

"That was the thing about Amy. All she would have to have done is overhear a conversation. She might have met someone on the bus here. She was quick that way. Sneaky. Yet she looked so...innocent. People underestimated her."

"Still no word on a DNA sample?" Luna asked.

He shook his head. For days he'd been waiting for the axe to fall.

"That must have been hard, going through her suitcase."

"It was. She hadn't just stolen what little money we had at the house, I found an old sweatshirt of mine and a T-shirt Katie had given me that she'd taken. The sweatshirt was faded enough that the school logo was hard to make out. But, Luna, eventually it is all going to come out about my connection to her." He shook his head. "I'm a lawman. I'm withholding important evidence. I wanted time to try to solve this, but time has run out. I need to tell Yarrow." He rubbed the back of his neck.

"I can see how hard this is on you," she said.

"None of that matters," he said quickly. "It's you I'm worried about. Please, Luna, be careful. Amy was pretty streetwise and believed she could handle just about anything. She certainly underestimated whoever she tried to blackmail."

"JAXSON, THERE IS something else I heard today," Luna said as if hesitant to tell him. "Considering the source, I hate to repeat it. But if there is any truth in it…" She told him about Vera wanting to see the photos she had been showing around on her phone. He listened without comment until she finished.

Shaking his head, he said, "I have a hard time believing it."

"So did I, but it makes sense."

"But it also puts my father in Buckhorn at the same time as Amy who we know was blackmailing someone and gives him a motive for murder."

"I know it looks bad for your father—but only if he didn't want anyone to know. Why would he care? He'd been done wrong by not just his father but his brother. If anyone didn't want the truth coming out, it wasn't your father."

"Do you realize what you're saying?"

"That Tom and Bethany Eaton have more reason to keep O.H. a secret."

"If Marianne Price was the mother, then both Tucker and Jory have motive for not wanting it to come out, but murder?"

It did seem a long shot.

That sat in silence for a long while, both apparently lost in their own thoughts. She couldn't help but be aware of the man. Being this close to him, feeling as she did...

"Are you ever going to forgive me?" he asked.

She felt her heart do that little bump in her chest. "I want to."

He sat up straighter, those green eyes of his boring into her. "I'm in love with you, Luna Declan. I know you don't want to hear that right now, but it's true."

The oven timer went off, signaling that the pizza she'd put in earlier was done. Luna rose from the couch, but he reached for her hand before she could escape. A shiver of desire raced from his warm large hand and through her bloodstream. Being this close and not ending up in his arms was pure hell.

"You say you don't trust me, but I don't believe you," he said quietly as he made slow agonizing circles with this thumb at the center of her palm. "If you really thought I was a murderer, you wouldn't allow me to be here with you."

It was true and they both knew it. But even worse was trying to pretend that she didn't feel the bolt of electricity that arced between them even when they weren't touching.

"The pizza," she said, her voice breaking as she pointed toward the kitchen, and he let go of her hand.

In the kitchen, she grabbed a hot pad, pulled out the pizza and setting it down, leaned against the counter. She wasn't sure how much of this she could take.

He came up behind her. She didn't move, didn't even breathe, as he pressed close enough that she could feel his breath on the bare skin of her neck. She felt tears burn her eyes as she leaned back into him. He put his arms around her, resting his head against hers.

Since she'd learned of his deception, she'd spent days investigating him and holding him at arm's length. He was right. She trusted him with her life. But her heart?

She slowly turned in his arms to face him. Looking up into that handsome face, she surrendered. She was a woman who'd gone to Idaho because of him. She'd let him move in under the guise of protecting her. She'd also been trying her best to keep him out of prison. She was a woman in love.

"Tell me," he said. "Tell me to stop and you know I will." He slowly bent toward her until their foreheads touched.

She held her breath for a moment before she tilted her head back and looked into his eyes. *Last chance.* She closed her eyes, her lips parting as his mouth found hers. Heat rushed along her nerve endings to turn molten at her center. Her arms went around his neck, their bodies closing the gap between them and escalating the desire they'd both been fighting, running hot inside them.

They clung to each other as if a fierce wind had blown through the apartment and if they let go, they might never find each other again.

THE NEWS ABOUT his deputy had shaken Ken more than he wanted to admit. He'd come to appreciate Jaxson's intelligence and keen eye. He'd also begun to trust him and had been glad that he'd chosen him to help with the investigation. Jaxson was a hard worker, curious and resourceful. Ken didn't want to believe this, but he couldn't forget the deputy's reaction when he'd looked into the crawl space where the floorboards had been removed and seen the mummified body.

He swore. Jaxson hadn't just known the woman. He'd *dated* her. *She'd lived with him at his mother's house.* Jaxson had been questioned by the cops in her disappearance, then he'd disappeared as well—not long before Amy Franklin had gone under the Buckhorn General Store floorboards.

Had Jaxson been in Buckhorn seventeen years ago? If so… Ken tried to see the cowboy deputy as a killer. Even if Jaxson hadn't been in Buckhorn at the time Amy Franklin went under the floorboards, why hadn't he said something?

For the obvious reason. He'd either killed the girl or he feared he would be blamed. Had he been trying to solve her murder as well as Vi's all this time? Or busy covering up his part in it?

Ken swore. He'd thought he knew the deputy, but this proved that he didn't. Jaxson was smart. Maybe he thought he could get away with murder.

That thought rattled Ken and made him question everything the deputy had said since these cases had begun. He thought back to when they'd gone through Amy Franklin's suitcase. Jaxson had been surprised by the blackmail notes hidden in the T-shirt. Or had he?

He felt disappointed, knowing what he had to do. First thing was getting the deputy off the case. Second, was contacting the Blackfoot, Idaho, police and getting as much information as possible on the missing person case—and if they had even more incriminating evidence that Jaxson might have been involved. Third, interview the deputy and get his side of the story before he cuffed him and arrested him. No matter what, Jaxson was off the Vi Mullen case. Off the force.

Ken realized that by tomorrow he would be detaining his own deputy. How was that going to look to the higher-ups? At the very least, this would bring into question his abilities as even acting marshal. There was no way he could keep the state investigators from taking over after this. He didn't stand a chance of ever being marshal here and he could thank Jaxson Gray for that.

JAXSON DREW BACK to look at Luna. His heart was pounding. He'd been afraid that she would push him away. Not that he would have blamed her. But instead she was holding on to him the way he was her—as if neither of them ever wanted to let go.

He'd been pushing her away for months, terrified of getting too close. Yet each time he was around her, he felt himself becoming more enchanted with her, wanting her and needing her. Unable to think of anything else.

She was so confident, so independent, so sure of her future and where she fit in it. He on the other hand had been running scared for too long. But when he was with Luna, he was able to believe that he might have a future—one that he couldn't imagine without her.

"I want you." His voice sounded rough with emotion. "I have wanted you for so long. I've never felt like this before. I've never wanted anyone like I do you."

He saw the answer in her eyes even before she leaned up to kiss him and whispered, "I'm yours."

The bedroom was only feet away, but it could have been miles the way they tore at each other's clothing. There was a desperation as if this might be the only night they would ever have together.

PRESSING HER AGAINST the counter, Jaxson lathed her naked breasts with his tongue, sucked the hard tips into his mouth before biting down gently on her turgid nipple.

Luna groaned in ecstasy as she arched against him. Her hands roamed over his body as if imprinting the feel of his warm skin and strong muscled contours on her memory. His hands caressed her stomach, the inside of her thighs, spreading her legs apart to find that pleasurable spot that made her legs grow weak. At his touch, she came almost at once, crying out at the waves of pleasure from his tongue.

He worked his way back to her lips, leaving a trail of kisses along her naked body. When his mouth found hers again, he deepened the kiss as he lifted her, swinging around to set her down on the table. She took in his naked body. The man was beautiful. She grasped him, guiding him to her, needing him inside her to fill that ache she'd had for him for far too long.

She let out a gasp as he filled her, their bodies molding as he began to move in a rhythm as old as time. She rocked as he held her, taking her higher and higher, the pleasure again growing and growing, until she cried out. Her head fell back, her breath ragged, as he buried his hands in her hair and groaned with his own release.

Luna looked into his beautiful face as she watched him catch his breath, his gaze on her, questioning. Did she regret it? Not a chance. She smiled at him as her heart seemed to fill with helium.

Sweeping her up, he carried her into the bedroom, dropping her on the bed and falling in next to her. They curled together as outside thunder rumbled and rain streaked the window glass. Spring in Montana, one minute it was sunny and warm, the next it might be snowing, but Luna loved it. Just as she did this man next to her.

They didn't speak of it, but they both knew there was

much worse than a storm coming. Tonight though, they were safe and together and that's all that mattered.

As KEN DROVE down his street, he realized he hadn't called Shar to let her know he was almost to town. He told himself he just wanted to finish this with her, but in truth, right now, he was thankful for the diversion. He didn't want to think about the shitstorm his arresting his deputy would bring down on not just him but the whole department.

His earlier good mood had vanished by the time he pulled into his driveway. With a curse, he realized that he'd have to wait for Shar. He should have called her. Maybe it was for the best. Was he really in the mood for some tearful goodbye? And goodbye was all he had to offer her.

Getting out of his car, he heard the sound of a vehicle roaring up the street. He turned, thinking it would be Shar, and if so, she was pissed. This was going to be drama-rama.

But the vehicle that came to an exhaust-boiling stop at the edge of his driveway was a tricked-out pickup truck. The man behind the wheel jumped out yelling, "Where the hell is she?"

Ken recognized him from the bar the first night he met Shar. Before he could speak, Bud pulled a pistol from behind him and pointed the business end of the barrel at his head.

"Where is Shar?"

"She doesn't live here anymore," Ken said, trying to quickly assess the situation. Only a fool would pull a gun on a marshal, even an acting one. If the man thought Ken was just a deputy, this was still a fool move. A desperate one since Ken was clearly wearing his uniform jacket. Was the man on something?

"You need to put the gun away," he said calmly, thinking he would diffuse the situation, then haul this fool's ass to jail. He was in no mood for this. A night behind bars would do the man good.

"You don't tell me what I need to do," Bud said, waving the pistol at him. "She said she was coming here to get back together with you. That you invited her."

Ken shook his head. "That's not what she told me. She was only going to stop by to return my key. That's all it was because we are definitely not getting back together."

"Bullshit," the man spat, and he saw what he'd feared in Bud's eyes. The damned fool was going to pull the trigger—unless Ken could get the gun away from him right now.

CHAPTER TWENTY-SIX

IT WAS HARD for Luna to leave Jaxson the next morning. They'd made love again last night and again this morning. While taking their time, the end result was just as powerful as it had been in the kitchen yesterday.

Wrapped in his arms, she'd felt a strange sense of completion. Not that she'd ever needed a man to feel complete. Yet, with Jaxson, it felt so right, as if she had been waiting for him. As if she had needed him and still did.

It was an odd feeling for a woman hell-bent on being independent. She'd prided herself on being able to solve whatever problem arose. She had felt that there wasn't anything she couldn't do on her own—if she set her mind to it.

Now, as she looked at Jaxson lying in her double bed with only a sheet thrown over his thighs, she felt an ache more powerful than anything she'd ever felt. She didn't want to leave him. Not today. Not ever.

"I'd feel better if you called Avery and canceled. Knowing what we do, I don't like you going out to the ranch," he said. He'd pushed himself up onto one elbow as he watched her dress.

She couldn't cancel for so many reasons, she thought, remembering the woman's bruises. "I can't abandon Avery on her wedding day. All we know is what Vera told me and I'm not even sure about that."

"Which is what worries me," he said. "Luna, I know

you. You won't be able to help yourself. You'll have to find a way to verify the information and, if true, it could put you in danger."

"It's a *wedding*," she told him. "There will be probably a couple hundred people or more around. It's not like I'm going to be out there alone. Anyway, I'll be fine." She told herself that she was fine before Jaxson. It annoyed her that she was more worried about her safety now because of her feelings for him.

"You didn't deny that you're going to try to verify the information about my father," he pointed out, giving her a side-eye.

She had to smile. Dang but he looked so gorgeous lying there, their lovemaking seeming to radiate in his face. And that grin of his… She didn't dare get too close to the bed or she'd be back in it—and be late to do Avery's hair before the wedding.

"I'll be careful," she promised as she grabbed her case with everything she would need and headed for the door. "I'll call you when I'm finished."

JAXSON HAD KNOWN he couldn't stop her, but he'd had to try. He got up, showered and shaved. The whole time he found himself smiling. Last night had been incredible. This morning hadn't been bad either. He felt better than he had for a very long time. He loved Luna and he was pretty sure she felt the same way.

Both of them knew though that the future was still up in the air. He wouldn't be free until Amy's killer was caught and he was cleared. What if that never happened? He told himself that he couldn't let himself go there. He'd involved

Luna. He'd wanted desperately to solve this case for her sake as well as his own.

But it was time to come clean with Yarrow—no matter what happened. He was the law. He had to own up.

As he got dressed, he realized he hadn't heard from Yarrow. He thought about calling him, but he needed to do this face-to-face. It was Saturday. Were they really taking a day off from the investigation? That didn't sound like his boss.

Something Luna had said kept nagging at him. Once in his patrol SUV, he drove down behind the Buckhorn General Store and let himself inside the back. The gaping hole where Amy had been found almost made him change his mind.

He wondered if the store would ever open again. He couldn't see Vera running it. The storage room floor would have to be fixed. Would the blood ever come out of the worn wood that hadn't been destroyed?

In the office, he looked around at the mess Vera had made. He had no idea where to even start. Pulling out Vi's chair, he sat down, starting with the files she had piled on the desk.

The problem was that he didn't know exactly what he was looking for. He told himself he'd know it when he found it.

NOT FAR FROM the ranch, Luna's cell phone rang. She saw that it was her father and picked up, knowing he wouldn't be calling unless he had news. She'd told him she was doing the bride's hair today out at the Eaton Ranch. This must be important for him to call.

"What have you found out?" she asked without preamble.

"I know you have the wedding today, but I thought you'd

want to hear this right away. Owen Henry." She held her breath. "I found him."

"You mean you found his death certificate," she said, not as elated as he sounded.

"No, he's alive. I found him."

Luna let out a shocked breath. "How is that possible? You said he hasn't held a job or had a driver's license or even a bank account in seventeen years?" She was trying to imagine where he could have been all this time without any record of his whereabouts.

"There's a reason why he seemed to have dropped off the face of the earth," her father was saying. "He joined a group of anti-government, survivalist militia members on a ranch in northern Idaho. I talked to an FBI agent I know who's been monitoring the group. The intermountain west is a hotbed of these groups, with Montana even leading Idaho. They've been stockpiling weapons. There is a BOLO out on their leader, but he never leaves the compound. The FBI doesn't want another Waco, so right now they're waiting."

"Owen Henry is definitely a member of this group?" She knew there were groups like this in Montana and that the FBI had been keeping an eye on. She remembered her father talking about one years ago, the Freemen over by Jordan. "Where in Idaho?"

"Luna. Even if you could get into the compound, you aren't going."

"There must be some way to talk to him."

"It's possible that the agent could get Owen out. It wouldn't be easy and would put him in danger."

"Wait, agent? Are you telling me…"

"He's been working undercover for the government.

There'd have to be a damned good reason to pull him out now."

"He's wanted for questioning in a cold case murder. Isn't that good enough?"

"Not in this explosive climate," her father said. "Until you can prove that there is a connection to him and the deceased, there is no way the FBI is going to go in after him. These are dangerous people. The FBI isn't going to get involved without solid proof."

"Then I'll have to find it," she said. "I have to go. Thanks." She disconnected. She still couldn't believe the news. *Owen Henry was alive.* Jaxson's father was alive. She reminded herself that Jaxson hadn't wanted to find his father. He wouldn't be pleased to know that Owen had joined an anti-government group of survivalist militia members in Idaho, who were considered armed and dangerous—even as an undercover informant.

But Owen might be the only person who knew what had happened to Amy. Unless Luna could find a connection between Owen Henry and Amy Franklin, she wouldn't be talking to Owen Henry—and neither would Jaxson—even if he had wanted to.

Luna slowed for the turn into Eaton Ranch. The place was a flurry of activity as florists and caterers and wedding planners prepared for the day ahead. She parked and carried her case toward the main house, debating calling Jaxson with the news. She wasn't sure how he was going to take it and decided it would be better to tell him later.

The front door was standing wide open, so she didn't bother knocking, just walked in like everyone else. She put down her case and walked to the back of the house to look out at the tent she'd seen erected the other day. It really was huge. A group of people were putting out chairs in row after row where the actual nuptials were to take place.

She started to turn away when she spotted Avery near the barn with a cowboy in what appeared to be an ugly confrontation. Not the groom, she thought, or there might not be a wedding at all.

Avery tried to leave, but the cowboy grabbed her and shoved her back against the barn wall. Luna felt her pulse jump. The bruises, the missing hair on the young woman's head. She started to push out the door, no longer willing to let this go any further.

But she'd only taken a couple of steps when she saw that it wasn't the intended groom, Jory Price. It was his older brother, Tucker.

That moment of stunned clarity made her stop. She pulled out her phone and called Avery's number as she turned back to the house. It rang three times before Avery answered, sounding breathless and close to tears.

"Hi, just wanted to let you know that I'm here. Early, I hope that's all right," Luna said, her heart in her throat. She had no idea what Avery and Tucker were fighting about, but the sight of his fury and the way he'd slammed Avery against the barn wall had her shaking with her own anger inside.

"Great. Why don't you go up to my room? It's the second door on the right at the top of the stairs."

"See you there." Luna disconnected and walked back to the house without looking in the direction of the barn until she was inside. When she looked back, she saw Tucker striding across the yard, head down, shoulders bent as he headed toward his own ranch house.

She didn't see Avery and assumed she needed a few minutes to pull herself together. What had the two been arguing about? Luna's first thought was that Tucker was trying to keep her from marrying his brother. If so, then Tucker and Avery had some history. Some disturbing history given the signs of abuse and what Luna had just witnessed.

It shocked her. She kept thinking of the cowboy who'd taken her on the horseback ride. But then she remembered when they returned to the ranch and how his younger brother, Jory, had come roaring up, angry and upset and needing to talk to him.

Would there even be a wedding? she was wondering as she climbed the stairs. It was quiet up here, none of the hustle and bustle on the lower floor. She opened the door to the second bedroom on the right. The room was huge with a canopied bed and a sitting area with a breathtaking view of the ranch and the mountains beyond. The room was decorated for a princess, a Western one, but still royalty.

Luna had heard that Avery was her daddy's pride and joy and that Tom Eaton had spoiled her. Funny, but Luna didn't see that. If anything, the young woman seemed trapped. Had there never been any question that she would marry one of the sons of the ranch next door? Maybe the question had only been which one?

At a sound behind her, Luna turned. "Just give me a few minutes," Avery said as she closed the door and, keeping her head down, her long dark hair hiding her face, hurried into the adjoining bathroom.

JAXSON COULDN'T BELIEVE all the paperwork Vi had kept. Scraps of paper with notes written on them, old payment sheets, years of inventory records. He dug through it, wondering if he wasn't wasting his time. If there was something here, he certainly hadn't found it.

He started to put a stack of papers he'd gone through back into the file cabinet when a bill for lumber caught his eye. Putting the stack of papers aside, he picked up the bill. Hardwood flooring. He glanced at the date. Bingo! It was for the replacement flooring in the storage area.

There were several sheets of paper stapled to the back. He quickly flipped through them and found what he was looking for. In what he assumed could only be Vi's scrawl was an itemized list of expenses. There down the list was the amount of money paid to the workers who'd installed the flooring. Three names were there: AJ Crest, Tucker Price and Carson McCabe. Crest had gotten the lion's share since the other two had just been boys and hired hands.

Along with the list was the date of the final payment. June 17—six days after Amy had left Idaho. Somewhere in between her body had gone under the floor. He flipped over the invoice to the last sheet attached to the packet. It was from a notepad. The only thing written on it was a phone number.

The number didn't ring a bell, but it seemed odd that the note had been stapled to the flooring bill. He put it aside and replaced what he'd taken out of the file cabinet. Looking around, he wondered again what Vera had been looking for.

He couldn't see Vera or Axel taking over the running of Vi's businesses. There was a rumor going around town that Vera already had feelers out with a plan to sell everything.

Had Yarrow turned the store over to her? Where was Yarrow? He realized it was strange that he hadn't heard from him all morning.

As he started to leave the office, he noticed something.

He stood studying the back wall. Strange Vi didn't have a safe, he thought as he stepped to the tall, wooden shelving that took up the entire wall. It would be impossible to move since like everything else it was filled with boxes of paperwork and dust, he noted.

Starting to turn away, he noticed that a box on one of the shelves had disturbed the dust. He lifted it out. Behind it was a good twelve-inch size spot on the wall where it appeared the Sheetrock had been patched.

But when he touched it, the piece of Sheetrock moved. He could see a corner of the paper had been peeled back. Grasping the paper, he pulled. The square of Sheetrock fell out and he found himself looking into a gaping dark hole.

WHEN AVERY CAME out of the bathroom, she was still flushed but dry-eyed. "So what are you thinking for my hair? My mother says it should be up. My father thinks it should be down." Her voice broke.

"It's your wedding, Avery. Why don't you sit down here and we can talk about it." She pulled out a chair at a large dressing table, turning it to face the mountains.

Luna stood behind the chair and smoothed Avery's long hair when she sat down. She didn't know where to begin so picked up a brush from the dressing table and began to work her way through the mass of hair. The last thing on her mind was how to fix Avery's hair for the wedding.

"I'm a good listener if you need to talk," she said as she brushed. Silence. "I saw you with Tucker." She felt Avery tense. "I'm not telling anyone if that's what you're worried about. I'm just…concerned." Still nothing from the bride-to-be. "Is he the one who pulled out your hair?"

The chair shook with Avery's first sob. As she bent

over in heart-wrenching tears, Luna released the woman's hair and waited. It took a few moments before the crying stopped and Avery pulled her hands away from her face.

"I can't get married," she said on a choked breath. "I can't do that to Jory."

Luna had to ask. "Are you in love with Tucker?"

Avery swung partway around in the chair. "No," she said fiercely. "No."

"But he has something on you." She saw the woman swallow and look miserable. "Some other man?"

"It was just a couple of times. A mistake." She started to cry again, but stopped herself. "I don't know what I was thinking. I love Jory."

"But Tucker found out and now he doesn't want you marrying his brother."

Her laugh was sharp and bitter. "He doesn't care about his brother."

Luna could see Avery making up her mind as to whether to tell her the rest. She took a guess, "He wants you for himself."

Avery seemed surprised. "Not to marry me. He's blackmailing me into sleeping with him. Payment or he'll expose me. He's always flirted with me. He said he always thought it would be the two of us—not his baby brother."

"What do you want to do?"

She shook her head. "I don't know." She began to cry again.

"Jory must have noticed the bruises and asked you about them," Luna said.

"I've kept them hidden from him. We haven't…" She shook her head, but she didn't need to finish. They hadn't slept together. Probably waiting until after the wedding. She wondered whose idea that was.

"Even if you go through with the wedding, I doubt Tucker will stop blackmailing you. If anything, I suspect he'll get worse. He could hold this over you for the rest of your life."

"I know."

"You have to tell Jory before the wedding. Tell him everything—especially about Tucker blackmailing you—and why." She saw Avery swallow, her eyes wide with fear.

"He'll hate me," she said through her tears.

"I doubt it. Is the other man Jory's best man?" Luna asked.

Avery looked surprised again. "How did you…"

"Just a guess. You might need a whole new wedding party."

She got up from the chair and looked out at the tent and all the activity. "My father will kill me if I cancel the wedding."

"I wouldn't worry about him right now. Once he knows what Tucker's been doing, I think he'll understand." Luna certainly hoped so. "If you want, you could call Jory and have him meet you here in your room so you two can have some privacy. I'll wait downstairs."

"I doubt I'll be needing my hair done after this."

"If Jory really loves you, he'll be hurt, but he won't want to lose you. If he doesn't love you enough, then you're better off without him," Luna said. She thought it was the kind of advice her father would have given her. Not that she would have wanted to hear it. "It's up to you. But it seems like the sooner Jory knows, the sooner Tucker won't have any power over you. And frankly Tucker should be arrested for what he did to you."

Avery dried her tears and nodded. She pulled out her phone and Luna picked up her case to leave the room. "Jory, I need to talk to you. Now. No, it can't wait. Can you come to my room at the house? Please." Her voice broke. "Hurry." She disconnected as Luna reached the door. "Will you wait downstairs?"

"No matter what happens, I'll be here. Lock your door after he arrives. Don't let anyone disturb the two of you so you can talk."

Luna went to the top of the stairs to wait. She considered taking the time to find Tom Eaton. She definitely had questions that only he—or his wife, Bethany—could answer. Not that she wanted to upset Bethany on her daughter's wedding day.

Guests would be arriving in two hours. The bride's attendants would be here soon too, she thought. Before Luna could consider going to look for Tom Eaton, Jory Price came in the front door and ran up the stairs, taking them two at a time. He looked scared as he hurried down the hall to Avery's room.

Staying where she was, Luna waited, hoping Jory was the kind of man who would stand by his woman. She couldn't help but think of Jaxson. All he'd done was lie to her. She hadn't exactly stood by him.

It hurt that he'd lied. Trust was huge for her. If she couldn't trust Jaxson, then she couldn't have him in her life. The thought made her heart ache. Would Jory feel the same way? Would he call off the wedding?

Luna heard raised voices and crying. She waited anxiously, her heart aching for Avery and afraid Jory would

burst from the bedroom and take off down the stairs to an-
nounce that the wedding was canceled.

"What are you doing here again?"

She spun around, coming face-to-face with Tom Eaton.
"I'm here to fix Avery's hair for the wedding." Not that she
thought there would be a wedding given what she'd heard
outside the bedroom door.

"Why are you standing out here in the hallway, then?"
he demanded.

She could tell that he was worried Luna was going to
upset the mother of the bride by being on this floor again.
"I have a little time. Besides I wanted to ask you about
your...brother, Owen Henry."

The name alone made Tom look around as if he feared
she'd been overheard. "Come with me." He turned on his
heel and led the way down the stairs and around a corner
and a hallway into what she saw was his office. He closed
the door behind them. "I don't know where you heard—"

"You recognized his photo when I showed it to you.
He's your *brother*."

"I don't know that for a fact," Tom said, going around
to sit behind his large desk.

"Then why did you give him five-thousand dollars?"
She saw him start.

"How did you—"

"Do you know where he is?" she asked.

"No. Why are you asking me about him?" he demanded.

"His son has been looking for him." It wasn't quite true,
but true enough.

"His son?"

"Deputy Jaxson Gray."

Tom rocked back in his chair and seemed at a loss for

words. "I don't understand why you would bring this up on this day of all days," he finally said. "My youngest daughter is getting married."

Maybe.

"You're as bad as the reporters who felt they had to know all about the trouble O.H. had gotten himself into. Fortunately that time the government was involved so we were able to keep a lid on it."

Government was involved? Luna had a feeling that she now knew what that meant. Had Owen made a deal that required him to go undercover?

"So I have to ask, what business is this of yours?" he demanded. "I thought you were a hairdresser?"

"Jaxson and I are…friends. I've been helping him track down his father. But you don't deny he came back here to the ranch seventeen years ago and you paid him five-thousand dollars?"

"I don't have to answer any of your questions," he said, getting to his feet so abruptly that his office chair banged into the bookshelf behind him.

"Would you rather an officer of the law ask the questions? Owen Henry disappeared shortly after you paid him off."

The ranch owner looked stricken. "I don't know where O.H. is. He was here, but that was the last time I saw him." He rubbed a hand over his face. "I really can't do this today." He met her gaze. "If you're here to fix my daughter's hair for the wedding, then you need to do it and leave. I won't have you disrupting what should be my daughter's most memorable day."

He showed her out of his office. As she stepped out, she thought she saw Bethany disappear down the hallway. Back upstairs, Luna slowed as she neared Avery's bedroom door, wondering if there was still going to be a wedding or not.

The bedroom door was standing open. Hesitantly, she peered inside. Empty? She stuck her head in. "Avery?"

AT FIRST JAXSON thought the hole in the wall was empty. He turned on the flashlight on his phone and shone it into the darkness. Something glinted against the tarnished silver of what appeared to be a large metal box.

Putting his flashlight on the shelf so he could see what else might be in there, he pulled out the box and looked deeper. Nothing.

The box felt too light. The lock on the front had clearly been tampered with. Whatever had been in here was gone, he thought even before he opened it.

AVERY CAME OUT of the bathroom, a washrag over her face. She pulled it down to look at Luna. Her eyes were so swollen, her face flushed. "I'm getting married." Her voice broke. "Jory's angry but he still loves me." A sob escaped. "He wants to spend his life with me." She looked as if she was going to cry again.

Luna rushed to her. "Of course he does," she said quickly. "So let's get you ready. First things first, you need to call downstairs and see if we can get some cucumber slices and tea bags for your eyes. Don't worry, you are going to be a beautiful bride, I promise."

By the time Avery's attendants were to arrive, the puffiness around her eyes was gone. "You're a miracle worker," she said, giving her a large tip. "Thank you so much."

Luna shrugged it off. "Just part of the job." She left Avery to her attendants.

Out in the hall, she shifted her case, hoping that Avery and Jory made it as a married couple. She had to admire him for not chucking the relationship.

She kept thinking about what Tom Eaton had said. The government was involved in whatever trouble Owen had gotten into? She found a quiet corner and called her father.

After quickly filling him in on what Tom Eaton had said, she asked, "What kind of trouble could he have gotten into that the government was involved—and kept it quiet?"

"Let me see what I can find out," her father said. "I'll get back to you. But I'd suggest you get out of there."

She couldn't have agreed more. Pocketing the phone, she didn't hear anyone come up behind her. Didn't register that anything was wrong until she felt the prick of a knife blade in her side and heard a voice whisper, "Make a sound and I will kill you."

CHAPTER TWENTY-SEVEN

JAXSON HAD BEEN digging through Vi's records for what seemed like hours when he found the hidey-hole in the wall with a metal box in it. He figured it was what Vera had been looking for since he was pretty sure at one time it had been full of money. Someone had emptied it.

All that was in the bottom of the metal can was a sheet of paper folded in half. Maybe one of them had left an IOU, he joked to himself.

He started to unfold the paper when his cell phone rang. It was the main number at the marshal's office in the next town. Had Yarrow gone home for some reason? He hadn't mentioned it earlier. He quickly picked up. "Gray, here."

"Deputy Jaxson Gray?" The voice on the other end of the line sounded official. He felt his pulse jump.

"Yes?"

"I'm calling about Acting Marshal Kenneth Yarrow?"

"Yes, who is this?"

"I'm with the state police. I'm calling to inform you that Marshal Yarrow has been shot and taken to the hospital. He is in critical condition. The doctors are afraid he isn't going to make it. They've taken him into surgery. DCI will be contacting you regarding your ongoing investigation."

The Division of Criminal Investigations would be taking over. Jaxson hung up in shock. Yarrow was fighting for his life after being shot? By Vi's killer? Someone else? *What the hell?*

He'd forgotten about the paper in his hand until it slipped from his fingers and fluttered to the floor. As he reached to pick it up, still shocked at the news, he saw that a photograph had apparently fallen out of the folded sheet of paper.

The paper was blank. He tossed it aside and looked at the photo. The shot had been taken from inside the store and some distance away, so it wasn't that easy to make out the two figures. It was as if the person with the camera was hiding.

He held the photo up to the light and felt a start as he recognized one of the two figures being photographed. Amy. She was wearing the clothing she'd been found dead in. She was looking in the direction of the camera—unlike the other person, a figure much taller in Western clothing with a dark bobbed haircut and a hammer in her hand.

Behind the two he recognized the storage room—and the dark shadow where the flooring hadn't completely been replaced. He drew the photo closer, his heart pounding. Bethany Eaton?

LUNA FELT THE tip of the knife blade cut through her shirt. A trickle of blood ran down her side.

"We're going out the side door," Bethany whispered at her back. "Trust me when I say I have nothing to lose. I will kill you. At this point, what's another dead body?"

She could hear the music coming from the tent. The wedding would be starting soon. People rushed past them, no one paying any attention to the older woman who appeared to be leaning on Luna for support as they crossed the manicured lawn headed in the direction of the Price ranch house.

But as they neared, Bethany pointed her toward the stables. The woman's hand wasn't steady. Luna kept feeling the bite of the knife, the trickle of blood, a constant reminder of how easy it would be for the the knife to sink into her if she tried to break free.

"Why are you doing this?"

"To protect my family."

"You're going to miss your daughter's wedding."

"I wasn't going anyway. After you upset me, I told Tom I couldn't possibly face all those people. You played right into my hand."

"You aren't agoraphobic."

"No, but it has worked well for me for years. My family has gotten used to me not being around. They don't question my movements and the house is large enough that I can come and go freely. Tom and Avery know better than to bother me. Deanna is busy running the ranch with her father. No one notices when I'm gone or if one of the older ranch pickups is missing as well. The ranch hands are constantly coming and going on a place like this. All I have to do is dress like one of them."

"People know I'm out here fixing Avery's hair for the wedding," Luna said.

"It will be hours before you're missed," Bethany said and stuck the knife in a little harder, making Luna wince in pain as more blood ran down her side.

Luna realized now that she'd seen the woman the morning of the murder and again standing outside her apartment. What's more, Bethany had seen her. "Why did you kill Vi?"

"She'd been blackmailing me for years. Said she was putting away a little nest egg separate from her businesses and probably Axel's prying eyes. She wanted me to contribute to it." Her tone reeked of bitterness. "She really thought I would keep paying her more and more as time went on."

"Blackmailing you? Because of your brother-in-law, Owen Henry?"

They had reached the stables and Luna saw that two horses had been saddled. There was a Just Married sash tied to each. Apparently the wedding couple were planning to ride off into the sunset. Or riding into the reception.

"Don't call O.H. that," Bethany snapped, giving her a jab with the knife. This one almost doubled her over. She pushed Luna face-first into the stable wall, using her weight to hold her there. Then Bethany shoved a pair of plastic zip tie handcuffs at her, the knife now digging into her back.

Luna's shirt was soaked with her own blood and now stuck to her side. She was afraid to attempt to try to wrestle the knife from the woman, telling herself to wait, that she would get a chance to free herself even as she put the cuffs on in front.

She felt Bethany move behind her, the pressure of the knife coming off her back—but just for an instant as the loop of a rope was dropped over her head and pulled tight around her neck, cutting off her air.

Luna instinctively grabbed for her throat to relieve the pressure. She felt the knife did deeper into her flesh.

"Do that again and I'll end this right here," Bethany snapped.

"What are we doing?" Luna asked as she fought for air but didn't dare reach up again to try to get her fingers under the rope. The woman pulled the loop tighter. She could feel it digging into her neck as Bethany dragged her over to one of the horses and began to wind the other end of the rope around the saddle horn.

"You're going to get on your horse. If you do anything to try to get away, I will jerk you off your horse and drag your body until you wished you were dead." She dug the knife blade into Luna's back one last time before she swung up into the saddle with the other end of the rope attached. "Get on your horse," she commanded, jerking the rope, throwing Luna off balance, the rough rope cutting into her throat. "Now."

She looked into Bethany's face and reminded herself that the woman had put an ice fishing spear through Vi. Luna's only chance of getting away was to bide her time and believe that she would get the opportunity to best the woman. Her story didn't end here, she told herself as she thought of Jaxson. They'd only just begun. She couldn't bear the thought that they would never get the chance to see where these feelings between them would lead.

ONCE IN THE SADDLE, Luna had fought to push away her fear and remain calm as Bethany led her up the road away from the ranch houses. She kept the rope around Luna's neck taut. No one saw them. Everyone was inside the tent at the wedding.

She had to think. Bethany probably wouldn't be missed— just as she'd said. She'd been a ghost for years. Why? It had to be more than Owen Henry coming back into the Eatons' lives seventeen years ago.

Bethany had loosened the rope on the saddle horn just enough so that Luna wasn't being choked, but not enough that she could try to get the lariat off her neck. She realized she still had her cell phone. If she could call Jaxson... She eased the phone out of her pocket and tapped his number.

With a silent cry, she saw it go to voice mail. Leave a message. She thought quickly of what to say.

"Bethany, you let Vi Mullen blackmail you for seventeen years just so no one knew that Owen Henry was your husband's half brother? That's as silly as you stealing Price Ranch horses to take me up into these mountains to kill me. You really can't think that you can get away with this." She fumbled to pocket her phone, afraid she would drop it in her hurry to hide it.

Bethany reined in, shaking her head, clearly angry. For a moment, Luna thought the woman wouldn't answer. Worse, that she might pull her from her horse and make good on her threat to drag her to her death.

"You have no idea what that man did to my family by coming back and bringing that horrible girl with him," Bethany spat out as she slowed her horse next to Luna's. "He swore he didn't know her. That she was apparently a friend of his son's." She made a rude sound. "*His son.* Next another bastard would end up on our doorstep if it was up to that conniving little bitch. She was worse than O.H."

Luna felt a jolt. Blackmail. The blackmail notes Jaxson had found in Amy's suitcase. "Amy Franklin?"

HIS HEART A hammer in his chest, Jaxson turned to quickly search for the flooring invoice and the note in Vi's handwriting stapled to the back. The phone number. Bethany Eaton. His pulse clanging like a bell in his head, he quickly dialed the number, praying that he wasn't too late.

It rang three times and he was about to hang up when it went to voice mail and a female voice said, "This is Bethany Eaton, I can't come to the phone. Please leave a message."

Luna. She was out at the ranch. He glanced at the time.

She should have called by now. Maybe she'd gone to the wedding or the reception and couldn't call because she hadn't left. He tried to make excuses so he didn't have to face his worst fear. He started to call her number when he saw that she'd left him a voice mail.

She was fine, she *had* called, everything was okay, he told himself as he hit play. He listened, terrified by what Luna was telling him. Bethany had her. The message ended. She was taking Luna up into the mountains to kill her.

Heart in his throat, he tried her number as he headed for the door. The call went straight to voice mail, but by then he was in his patrol SUV headed for the Eaton Ranch.

"I TOOK CARE of Amy and her schemes. AJ was overseeing the new storage room floor at the store so Vi had given him a key. I sent him and his crew home for the day, telling him Vi asked me to meet her there. But it was that foolish girl I was meeting to pay her off." Bethany laughed. "It wasn't quite the payoff she expected. I covered the floor joists to hide her body with a few boards I nailed down." She glanced over at Luna. "You think I'm heartless?" She scoffed at that. "I'd never hurt anyone before that. I locked up the store and went to the bar. Tom came to get me later that night. The bar owner back then had taken my keys and wouldn't let me drive in my condition."

"AJ didn't notice the next morning that you'd added a few boards?"

"Apparently not. Nothing was ever said. No one noticed the body. I knew I could find what I needed in the store to keep the body from smelling. I was married to a rancher, remember?"

Luna thought of the set of keys the killer had dropped

in the storeroom the morning of the murder. Jaxson had speculated that they were a spare pair. Then the originals had been found in a drawer at the bar. Dave said they could have been in that drawer for years. Seventeen years?

"That's when you became agoraphobic," Luna said, just as Vera had speculated.

"I couldn't believe what I'd done and then Vi Mullen called me to tell me about her retirement fund she was working on. I didn't know she was still in the store that night."

Luna felt sick to her stomach as they rode into the tall pines, the afternoon sun weaving its rays through the branches. As they began to climb the mountain, she listened to how Vi had hidden, taken one of her disposable cameras off a shelf and got a photo of Amy and Bethany— Bethany about to swing the hammer that killed the girl. "She didn't try to stop you?"

"She said it happened too fast, that she never dreamed I would do it." She scoffed. "She told me that she would keep my secret. The floor was finished. No one would find the body, and no one would miss the girl. Unlike me, she'd been smart enough to take the girl's purse from out of the hole so if she was ever found, no one would know who she was."

"Vi had the girl's purse? If you had placed an anonymous call to the cops, they would have thought Vi killed her." Vi would have realized that and gotten rid of the purse since she didn't need it. She had the photo.

Bethany rode in silence for a few moments. "Except for that damned photo and others of me dragging the girl's body over to the hole and dumping her into it. Vi sent me copies of the photos and threatened to go to the police. I had no choice but to pay her blackmail for all these years."

Luna felt a chill move through her body even in the warmth of the afternoon. "Why did you wait seventeen years to kill her?"

Bethany seemed confused by the question for a moment. "I should never have started paying her. As it was, I had to tell Tom the truth. How else could I get the blackmail money? He was so furious. He never forgave me. Said I should have paid off that girl the way he had O.H." She scoffed. "We had a different way of dealing with things. I would have never given O.H. a dime."

"You would have killed Owen too?"

Bethany swore. "I didn't have to kill him. All I had to do was make an anonymous call to the FBI since I knew that he had a standing warrant against him for some anti-government property destruction when he was younger. But that girl? She would have bled us dry. Tom still thinks it was the five-thousand dollars he paid O.H. that kept him away." Her laugh was eerily frightening.

Luna felt nauseous as she remembered the teenage deliveryman who'd found Vi's body. "You tried to kill Johnny Berg."

"Who?"

"The deliveryman who almost caught you the morning of Vi's murder."

"Oh, him. He was merely a loose end." She waved it away like a pesky fly. "That blow to his head should have killed him. If he ever comes out of the coma, I doubt he'll remember anything. Unlike you, snooping around, asking questions."

"I don't understand," Luna said truthfully. "You know you can't get away with this. Jaxson knows I came out here today. I promised to call him when I was finished with Avery's hair. When I don't call—"

Bethany brought her horse up short with a curse. "I forgot about your damned phone. Give it to me."

Luna cringed at the error she'd made. She worked the phone out of her pocket again. Once Bethany knew that she'd called Jaxson... She fumbled the phone. It fell to the ground, making the ranch woman swear again.

"I'm sorry," she said, seeing the fury in the woman's eyes as the rope was pulled tighter. "It's these cuffs."

Bethany looked at the phone lying in the dirt for a moment, then spurred her horse. Luna had to quickly do the same to keep from being pulled from the saddle. If she ended up on the ground, she knew what would happen.

"It doesn't matter," Bethany said. "It's all going to come out. You asked why now? I was sick of everyone wanting a piece of what Tom and I have built. O.H., Vi and even Magda. After all these years, my housekeeper is threatening to tell what she knows." Shaking her head, she said, "It has to end."

"Killing me won't make it end," Luna said.

Smiling, she said, "You're right. You're simply a diversion."

They had reached an opening in the trees. Bethany brought her horse up short. Luna could see nothing but wide-open country and blue sky ahead at the edge of what appeared to be a cliff. "This is where we part company."

CHAPTER TWENTY-EIGHT

JAXSON ROARED INTO the Price Ranch, coming to a dust-boiling stop just feet from the stable. As he jumped out, Tucker came out of the door to yell, "What the hell?"

"Where's Luna and Bethany?"

"Probably still at the reception. I came over to see if the horses were ready for the bride and groom and—"

"They were gone," Jaxson finished, pushing past him into the stables. He could see that Tucker had a horse saddled and was working on another. "Bethany has Luna." He grabbed the reins.

"Wait, what? You can't—"

Jaxson pushed him aside and swung up into the saddle. "Luna is in trouble. Bethany plans to kill her. I've called for backup." But he knew backup wouldn't be able to get there in time. "Tell them where I've gone."

With that he spurred the horse and shot out of the stables for the mountains. He had no idea how long they'd been gone except for the message Luna had somehow managed to leave him. He rode hard down the wide path toward the mountains. He could see fresh tracks in the dirt. Two horses. Neither moving at a gallop. That meant he might have a chance to catch up to them, to get there in time.

The thought had his heart seizing in his chest. He had to stop Bethany. He couldn't lose Luna. Not now. Not ever.

LUNA STARED AT the cliff ahead of them and saw what the woman had planned for her. She tried to keep the growing panic out of her voice. "Bethany, there is no way you can get away with this." She wished with all her heart that it were true. But she needed more time. The rope was cutting into her throat. She eased her horse closer to Bethany's to take some of the tension off it. The older woman didn't seem to notice.

"Tom will have left me everything I need on the other side of the mountain. I will disappear. I have money put away. I let Vi believe I was broke, but I am far from it and Tom will get me more when I need it."

"What kind of life will that be away from the ranch and your family?"

Bethany laughed and let go of the length of rope she'd been holding. It sagged against her horse's flank. "Freedom. I never wanted to be a rancher's wife to begin with. I was born for something better."

"Still, I don't understand how you can just disappear."

"They'll find my horse and enough evidence that they will believe we both died here. Tom will take care of Magda and the deliveryman if he survives. See, I have it all planned. I *will* get away with it. I fooled everyone into believing I was agoraphobic. Once I'm away from here, I'll become the person I was supposed to be."

"Sounds like you have it all worked out—if you can trust Tom." She saw Bethany's slight hesitation and continued, "I really doubt he's happy with the way you've handled things, not to mention all these years of having an almost-invalid wife—at least when other people were around. This would be his perfect opportunity to be rid of you."

Bethany shifted in the saddle. Several loops of the rope

came off the saddle horn, but she didn't seem to notice. "Tom wouldn't do that. He loves me. Anyway, I'd make sure he'd go to prison for helping me."

There was slack in the rope now with their horses close. Luna feared that she wouldn't have time to get the rope from her neck though before Bethany spurred her horse and took off. She eased her horse forward a little more, hoping the woman didn't notice as she tried to distract her.

"You're that sure it wouldn't be his word against yours?" Luna said. "Because from where I'm sitting, he doesn't have any blood on his hands. He let you do all the dirty work, didn't he?" She saw that she'd struck a nerve. "He didn't try to kill Johnny Berg, you did. Nor is Tom here now."

"My husband wouldn't double-cross me." But Luna heard the sliver of doubt that had crept into her voice. "I've heard enough. Let's just get this over with," Bethany snapped and spurred her horse.

Luna had only seconds. She grabbed the length of rope between them, praying it worked. She didn't have time to claw the rope from her neck so she did the only thing she could. Taking the extra rope that had been falling between them, she flipped it into the air so the loop dropped over Bethany.

As Bethany's horse lunged forward, the rope caught her in the chest and tightened so quickly that the woman didn't have time to realize what was happening before she was jerked off her horse.

The moment Luna had flipped the slack rope into the air, she'd let go to try to get the rope from around her neck. She'd barely gotten her fingers under the rope when she too was pulled from her horse. She plummeted to the ground behind Bethany and instantly realized her mistake.

Even with her fingers under it, the rope around her neck was too tight for her get it off and now Bethany was tangled in it. Bethany's horse spooked with the two of them caught in the rope behind the mare, and ran in what appeared blind fear toward the cliff.

JAXSON RODE UP over a rise and saw the dust first. Racing across the open area, he couldn't believe what he was seeing. One horse stood yards away, saddled, reins hanging down. The other was kicking up dust as it dragged what looked like a body behind it. No, two bodies, he realized as he spurred his horse after the runaway mare.

He knew in an instant that the only way he was going to be able to stop the horse was to catch up to it and try to rein it in. The mare had veered away from a large rock at the top of the cliff but was now running dangerously close to the edge of the drop-off.

He leaned over his horse, snapping it with the reins, terrified that he couldn't reach the mare in time. Worse, if he failed in what he planned to do, they would all be going over that cliff. He drew alongside Luna and Bethany, but couldn't tell if either of them were still alive. He concentrated on gaining on the horse. A little closer. Just a little closer. As he came along side it, he could see the wild-eyed horse wanting to flee—and the only way was over the cliff.

Jaxson grabbed the side of the bridle, the horse jerking its head wildly. He quickly snugged the bridle to his thigh as he drew the horse away from the edge of the cliff and finally brought the lunging mare it to a stop.

He had to keep hold of the bridle as he unwound the rope from the saddle horn and then released the mare. She jumped away but didn't run far now that she wasn't dragging two bodies behind her.

Leaping off his horse, he ran to Luna. At first he couldn't tell if she was still breathing. He loosened the rope from around her neck. Her hands were bleeding from where she'd held it away from her neck. Everywhere else the rope had touched her skin was burned and bleeding as well.

"Luna," he cried, ready to do CPR when she let out a gasp, then another. He knelt beside her, wishing he could help her breathe. Tears streamed down her dust-coated face at the sight of him as she tried to smile. He pulled out his pocketknife and cut the plastic cuffs from her wrists, which were also bruised and bloody. The sight of her injuries made him draw in his breath to hide his own pain. "You're going to be all right."

After long moments, she caught her breath and wheezed out one word, "Bethany?"

He looked over at the ranch woman just feet away, tangled in the rope. The horse had dragged her first through the sagebrush and rocks. She'd gotten the worst of it, protecting Luna in a way she'd never planned. He didn't need to check her pulse to know that she was dead. Her head must have hit a rock because part of her skull was open, her eyes staring blankly up into Montana's deep blue sky.

Bethany Eaton was gone, dying as brutally as she had killed.

CHAPTER TWENTY-NINE

LUNA HAD BEEN in the middle of a glaze when her father called. Jaxson and her father hadn't wanted her to go back to work so soon. But after everything that had happened, she'd needed her work more than ever.

She was wearing a turtleneck to cover up the injuries to her neck. The doctor said that where the rope had cut into her skin would eventually heal, though in some places she might have scars so she might want to see a plastic surgeon. Luna wasn't worried about those scars. It was the ones inside her from almost being killed that she needed to repair first.

That horrible day was a blur. She remembered the sound of the helicopter, its blades spinning in the sky above her, but recalled little of the ride to the hospital. Jaxson had tried to block her view, but even now she had trouble forgetting Bethany's damaged skull and those vacant eyes.

Her phone rang again. Seeing it was her father, she answered, telling him that she would call him back in a few minutes. He'd been calling now almost every day for weeks, worried about her even though she kept telling him that she was fine.

Jaxson had been just as bad. Fortunately he was busy helping the state police finish the investigation and visiting Acting Marshal Ken Yarrow, who was still in the hospital in an induced coma.

Johnny Berg had come out of his coma. He had some memory loss, but the doctors said he should have a full recovery because he was young. He'd even be able to return to work soon. Knowing that the killer was dead definitely helped in his recovery, the doctors said.

With Luna's testimony, the officers went after Tom Eaton who'd broken down. He'd confessed all, swearing he was only trying to protect his wife and his family. The keys Dave had found in the back of his drawer at the bar had fit perfectly into the ignition of the pickup Bethany always drove. The extra set she'd dropped the day she killed Vi Mullen had been found in her purse. Dave had recalled seventeen years ago, Bethany coming into the bar one night acting strangely. She'd drunk too much and he'd had to call Tom to come get her. He hadn't remembered taking her keys.

Dave did remember that it was the last time he'd seen her in town. It was assumed that was the night she'd killed Amy Franklin and covered her body with more floorboards. Like the day Luna saw her after Bethany had killed Vi Mullen, the woman had been wearing a long duster over her bloody clothing.

"Had Tom left a vehicle and everything Bethany needed to escape the day of the wedding?" Luna had asked Jaxson days after the incident.

"He had. If she'd been able to get to the car, she would have been long gone by now."

And Luna would have been dead. That was the thought that haunted her deep in the night. But when it did, Jaxson would hold her, reminding her that she was alive and safe in his strong arms.

He'd saved her life, but even before that she'd known she

couldn't live without this man. She could forgive him any-thing when he looked at her with those green eyes of his. He loved her and showed it in every possible way—especially in her double bed, she thought, and felt her face heat. Last night they'd talked about the future and the children they both wanted and the life they would have.

She felt excited, knowing that that future was here in Buckhorn.

She finished and stuck her client under the drying ring before stepping into the back to return her father's call. "I'm fine, you really don't have to call me every day," she said without preamble the moment he answered.

"Do you think Jaxson would like to see his father?"

"What are you saying?" Luna asked, heart in her throat.

"We might be able to make that happen. Let me know."

CHAPTER THIRTY

JAXSON LISTENED TO everything Luna had found out about his father. It explained so much about why Owen Henry hadn't married his mother, why he'd come back to Montana, hoping to fix things with his family, and where he'd been all these years.

When she'd finished, he knew he had to see his father again. He told himself it would be one of the hardest things he ever did—and he'd been right.

Earl Ray had handled everything via Luna's father, including setting up the cloak-and-dagger meeting in a cabin up in the mountains. Jaxson would never forget the rush of emotions he felt when his father walked through that door. He hadn't known what his reaction would be. He'd spent so many years hating his father for what he'd done to him and his mother.

But as the man came through the door, their resemblance to each other so strong even with his father graying, it had startled him. He'd moved as if propelled by his mother as he stepped into the man's arms.

Earl Ray reminded them that they didn't have long, and they'd sat down across the table from each other and his father began to talk.

"I dreamed of returning to the ranch with you and your mom, but I was a man on the run. First, I had to make things right with my father. Thompson P. Eaton wasn't the kind of man who forgave easily. I'd joined an anti-government group right out of high school. That to Thompson was the worst form of blasphemy. The group turned out to be not what I expected, but I'd gotten in deep enough that I was wanted by FBI. That's when I went to Idaho, met your mother, fell in love and we had you."

"Then you left us."

His father nodded, sadness in his green eyes that were so like Jaxson's own. "I had this dream of returning to the ranch and I couldn't let go of it. But I couldn't bring the two of you up there until I'd settled things with my father. I had to be careful because of the warrant so it took me a while to reach Montana. Unfortunately, things didn't go as planned there. My father had died. My half brother, Tom, wanted nothing to do with me. Being the bastard son of Thompson Eaton, I had no right to any part of the ranch. Tom said he'd give me five-thousand dollars if I'd leave town and never come back. I took it, planning to return to Idaho, my tail between my legs.

"But before that could happen, I was picked up by the FBI. They offered me a deal. Prison or go undercover at this two-thousand-acre encampment in northern Idaho run by an anti-government group."

His father met his gaze. "I think even then I knew there would be no going back. But I told them the only way I'd do it was if they checked in on you and your mom and money was sent to the two of you."

"But they would have let you go at some point over the years?" Jaxson said.

Owen nodded. "By then you were doing great in school and sports. I feared going back to you might put the two of you in danger. The feds had been depositing money in your mother's account. They offered me another deal. Another militia group they were concerned about. They needed intel from inside."

"At some point you could have left," Jaxson argued. "You could have let us know you were alive."

"It's not that easy to leave and your mother knew I was alive because of the money that was sent."

"Did you meet Amy Franklin?" asked Luna who had been sitting quietly in a corner.

He shook his head. "Earl Ray filled me in, but sorry. I never saw her. Seventeen years ago, I was in a compound in Idaho, reporting to the government how arms were being bought and amassed, and what the group was planning next."

"It sounds dangerous," Luna said.

Owen nodded. "That's why it is almost impossible to come and go. But don't worry, I'll be fine. This time."

"Don't you want a…real life?" Jaxson asked.

"It doesn't get much more real than this," his father said with a bark of a laugh. Then his eyes filled with tears. "I'm in too deep, son. As much as I'd love to walk away, to spend the rest of my life being near my son, I would just be jeopardizing your life." He shook his head.

"So you know nothing about Amy Franklin's death or Vi Mullen's," Luna said. "Or that your half brother is on his way to prison."

"Tom tried to reach out to me via my government contacts. He told me that he wanted to offer you at least part of the ranch. Take it, son. Rightfully, it should be yours."

"I'm a deputy marshal now."

"Your choice. But the land would be there if you want it."

"How dangerous is it, you coming here?" Luna asked.

"It's fine, but I need to get back." He looked at Jaxson. "I'm so proud of you, son. I can't tell you how much I regret missing you grow up. Or how often I thought of you and your mother. The two of you were the loves of my life. Inside this group, I'm at least doing something to make up for the mistakes I've made. Maybe one day I'll get to see my grandchildren."

Luna got up to give them some privacy. As she and Earl Ray walked out, she looked back. Owen Henry had pulled his son into his arms again. They stood like that for a long time.

VERA CARTER SMILED to herself as she drove out of town at the break of day. Normally she wouldn't be up at this ungodly hour. But today she was celebrating.

She looked in her rearview mirror as Buckhorn, Montana, began to vanish behind her. "So long," she said to the image. "Thanks for the memories." She laughed, still amazed that after years of not getting a break, her luck had finally changed and in a big way.

Unfortunately she had Vi to thank for that. Her twin's death had made Vera a lottery winner. As the legal heir, everything her sister had amassed had been sold. Anticipating a possible legal battle at some point down the road on behalf of her own daughter, Vera had put a lot of the funds into a trust for Jennifer to help pay for her continued care and supervision in the mental health care facility where she was imprisoned. As trustee of the account, Vera would have access to the funds. It wasn't like Jennifer would ever be released, but Vera didn't want some well-meaning Buckhorn resident taking her to court on Jennifer's behalf.

That had tied up all the loose ends, she thought, reach-

ing into the passenger seat. She patted the huge purse full
of Vi's secret retirement fund money she'd finally found
in her sister's office. It was more than enough, but in case
Vera ran out, she could always come up with excuses to
dip into Jennifer's trust.

Ahead was nothing but open highway. For years she'd
lived in her twin's shadow, but no more. She was one of a
kind for the first time in her life. She couldn't believe the
way things had worked out. She'd sold everything, including the house that Axel would soon be waking up in. He'd
think she'd just gone off to see her local drug dealer and
probably wouldn't get worried for hours.

The Realtor was scheduled to come by later this afternoon to give him the news. He had twenty-four hours to
vacate the house so the new owners could start renova-
tions. She'd sold the house to a wealthy couple who loved
the view and the seclusion, but hated everything Vi had
done inside the house and planned to gut the entire place.

Vera thought her twin had to be turning in her grave.
This latest would have her spinning like a cyclone.

She could just see Axel's face when he heard that he'd
been bamboozled not by one twin, but two. It made her
laugh. He'd be livid, but what was he going to do? Get in
his beat-up pickup and come after her? She had her pass-
port in her purse. Once she moved the money into foreign
banks, she would join it and start spending.

Vera was thinking she'd start somewhere in the south
of France when suddenly a deer came flying up out of the
barrow pit directly in front of the SUV. Instinctively she
swerved, missing it by a hair and blowing one of the front
tires. She fought heroically to keep the vehicle on the road,
but lost control.

She would never know exactly how many times the SUV rolled before it crashed at the bottom of a deep ravine and exploded.

But at one point, her purse came open as the SUV rolled. The last thing she saw were hundred-dollar bills floating in the air around her before she saw nothing at all.

KEN YARROW OPENED his eyes and seemed surprised that the first person he saw was his deputy sitting in the chair next to the hospital bed. He blinked. "Jaxson?" His voice was a dry rasp from lack of use.

The deputy started and rose quickly to come to his side. "You're awake."

Yarrow was looking around as if confused. "How long?"

"You've been in an induced coma for almost a week. Welcome back."

He closed his eyes again. "What happened?"

"You were shot. Do you remember any of it?" He'd been told that a woman named Shar had called the ambulance and the police after finding Yarrow shot and bleeding in his driveway. A former boyfriend of hers was picked up not too far from Yarrow's house. The woman had saved his life.

Ken opened his eyes again. "I do remember that I needed to talk to you, but can't remember why," his voice broke. Jaxson got him some water and a straw and handed it to him. "Just that it was important," he said hoarsely after taking a drink.

"Whatever it was, it may no longer be important." He told his boss everything that had happened. It had made him question again whether he was cut out for this work.

His boss looked as if he couldn't believe the way it had all shaken out. "You solved the murders." He coughed and took another sip of water. "Maybe you really will be a US marshal someday."

Jaxson laughed. "Not in the cards. For the time being, I'm happy as a deputy marshal." Tom Eaton had contacted him, telling him that his lawyers were drawing up papers that would give Jaxson one-third of the ranch, free and clear. He figured Tom was trying to make up for a lot of wrongs from his past, but probably also worried that he might sue for half of the ranch.

He'd said he would talk to Luna about it and get back to Tom, but he was touched and thought the offer more than generous.

Right now though he had other things on his mind. Marshal Leroy Baggins would be returning from his honeymoon next week and Jaxson was going to ask for some time off to reevaluate things. He'd spent so many years with Amy's disappearance hanging over him, that his decisions had been made based on knowing that one day she would turn up—probably dead and that he would be the number one suspect.

Now that he was free of that, all he wanted was Luna and the life he could see for them together here in this small Montana town in the middle of nowhere.

"Anyway," he said, "I'm never leaving Buckhorn. I've asked Luna Declan to marry me."

"The hairdresser?"

He chuckled at that since Luna was so much more. He still couldn't believe how close he'd come to losing her. "She said yes, so we're getting married. I hope you're well enough to attend the wedding. The doctor said you should be able to go back to work before long," he told Yarrow, who surprised him when the man shook his head.

"Not going back."

"Well, you don't need to make that decision now," Jaxson assured him. "You almost died. Give it a little time."

"No, I'm quitting. I'm done."

"What will you do?" he asked the older man.

Yarrow smiled. "Anything I want to."

The doctor came in to check on his patient. As Jaxson was leaving, he passed a woman in her early fifties. He overheard her asking what room Ken Yarrow was in. She carried a bouquet of flowers and what looked like a box of candy.

It made Jaxson smile as he walked away.

At the mental hospital, Jennifer Mullen sat staring blankly straight ahead. She seemed to be in her own world now, unreachable since her escape weeks before and return to the mentally insane ward. Not even being told about the death of her mother and her aunt Vi seemed to register. Nor was she interested in anything that was going on in Buckhorn, her former hometown.

Still the orderly had brought her down to the lounge. He'd put her scrapbook in front of her even though she hadn't seemed to notice. He'd also made some copies of articles about Buckhorn, Montana, that he thought she might want. She used to paste them into the scrapbook for hours on end. But she hadn't had an interest in doing it now for a very long time.

He missed her, he thought, as he sat down in a chair across from her so he could watch the clock and take her back when her time was up. Picking up the latest article, he turned it where she might see it. "Look at this, Jen. It says here you are one rich lady. Your mother left you a bunch of money. It's waiting in an account for you." He didn't tell her why the story had hit the news. He knew the doctor had tried to tell her about her mother's and aunt's deaths. She'd deal with that if she ever came back from wherever she'd gone mentally.

"Just think, one day you might be released from here. Rich. You could buy anything you wanted. Imagine that."

Her expression didn't change, but he thought he caught a glint in her blue eyes. Dr. Moss kept saying that he could rehabilitate her. That there was good in her and one day she might walk out of here.

"You might drive away from here someday," he told her. "In some fancy car. I can see you in a convertible, the top down, your hair blowing back." He smiled, hoping it happened, but doubting either of them would be leaving here, especially in a new expensive convertible.

But if anyone could, it would be Jen, he told himself as he put her scrapbook and the articles away for next time and led her down the hall to her appointment with Dr. Moss.

THE SUN ROSE over the mountain, the rays making the dewdrops on the pine needles glisten. There was a scent in the air, a promise of warmth and blue cloudless skies ahead. It was spring in Montana, just days away from Memorial Day weekend and the start of tourist season in the town of Buckhorn. There was excitement and expectation on the cool breeze as Luna opened the door of her salon. Her petunias were flourishing in the large pot out front.

She carried a large pitcher of water, but stopped in the middle of the sidewalk to breathe in the day, unable not to smile. Buckhorn had come alive again after the long winter and short spring. She waved to a couple of the shop proprietors out getting ready for the steady stream of travelers who would soon be coming down this highway in search of the real Montana.

Down the block, Luna waved to Bessie and Earl Ray in front of the café. When she glanced the other way, she saw the new owners of the Buckhorn General Store hard at work. Windows were being washed and awnings going up. Summer was just a blink away and everyone was getting ready.

Luna glanced at the engagement ring on her finger and felt the excitement and expectation fill her to floating. She felt as if her life was just beginning and there was nowhere she wanted to be but right here in Buckhorn with Jaxson.

"Good morning," he said as he came up behind her and took the water-filled pitcher from her. "I wondered where you'd gone."

She smiled as they stepped out to the curb, looking at the petunias that now filled the pot, overflowing with color. Lately she couldn't quit smiling. It wasn't just the start of the town's true season that had her feeling this way. She met Jaxson's gaze as he finished watering her precious petunias and stepped to her for a kiss.

"You're going to have the whole town talking," she warned him as the kiss ended.

"The whole town is already talking about us," he said with a grin. "Most of them will be at our wedding. I finally get to meet Lawrence Declan." He'd visited with her father on the phone since saving her life. Luna wasn't at all surprised that the two men had bonded.

So much had happened. She'd come so close to dying. But all she could think about was that Jaxson was finally free of the past. His father wouldn't be at the wedding—

but she knew they would be in his thoughts always. Jaxson finally knew the truth. She'd seen the change in mind. He was stronger, yet at the same time gentler. He was finally free to be the man he wanted to be.

"Ken was telling me that you once said you wanted to be a US marshal," she said. Ken Yarrow had recovered from his gunshot wound and retired. He had promised to be at the wedding even though he was thinking of leaving the county, maybe even leaving the state. He said he needed to make some changes in his life. "A US marshal?"

Jaxson laughed. "I was just pulling his chain. He figured I had my eye on the marshal position." He shook his head. "I'm happy right now being a deputy marshal."

They'd talked late into the night about Tom Eaton's offer of one-third of the Eaton Ranch. They both felt it was more than generous. It would be a wonderful place to raise their children. They planned to go out to the land today to decide where they were going to have their house built. Luna knew he was as excited as she was.

"I like being a deputy," Jaxson said as he waved to Mabel Aldrich who was headed down to the café for the morning get-together with her other women friends. "But I feel as if my roots are calling me." He turned to meet Luna's gaze. "There's a lot of cowboy in me, Luna."

"Don't I know it," she said, snuggling against him as they walked back inside.

* * * * *

Get 4 FREE REWARDS!

We'll send you 2 FREE Books plus 2 FREE Mystery Gifts.

FREE
Value Over
$20

Both the **Romance** and **Suspense** collections feature compelling novels written by many of today's bestselling authors.

YES! Please send me 2 FREE novels from the Essential Romance or Essential Suspense Collection and my 2 FREE gifts (gifts are worth about $10 retail). After receiving them, if I don't wish to receive any more books, I can return the shipping statement marked "cancel." If I don't cancel, I will receive 4 brand-new novels every month and be billed just $7.49 each in the U.S. or $7.74 each in Canada. That's a savings of at least 17% off the cover price. It's quite a bargain! Shipping and handling is just 50¢ per book in the U.S. and $1.25 per book in Canada.* I understand that accepting the 2 free books and gifts places me under no obligation to buy anything. I can always return a shipment and cancel at any time by calling the number below. The free books and gifts are mine to keep no matter what I decide.

Choose one: ☐ **Essential Romance**
(194/394 MDN GRHV)

☐ **Essential Suspense**
(191/391 MDN GRHV)

Name (please print)

Address   Apt. #

City   State/Province   Zip/Postal Code

Email: Please check this box ☐ if you would like to receive newsletters and promotional emails from Harlequin Enterprises ULC and its affiliates. You can unsubscribe anytime.

Mail to the Harlequin Reader Service:
IN U.S.A.: P.O. Box 1341, Buffalo, NY 14240-8531
IN CANADA: P.O. Box 603, Fort Erie, Ontario L2A 5X3

Want to try 2 free books from another series! Call 1-800-873-8635 or visit www.ReaderService.com.

---

*Terms and prices subject to change without notice. Prices do not include sales taxes, which will be charged (if applicable) based on your state or country of residence. Canadian residents will be charged applicable taxes. Offer not valid in Quebec. This offer is limited to one order per household. Books received may not be as shown. Not valid for current subscribers to the Essential Romance or Essential Suspense Collection. All orders subject to approval. Credit or debit balances in a customer's account(s) may be offset by any other outstanding balance owed by or to the customer. Please allow 4 to 6 weeks for delivery. Offer available while quantities last.

Your Privacy—Your information is being collected by Harlequin Enterprises ULC, operating as Harlequin Reader Service. For a complete summary of the information we collect, how we use this information and to whom it is disclosed, please visit our privacy notice located at corporate.harlequin.com/privacy-notice. From time to time we may also exchange your personal information with reputable third parties. If you wish to opt out of this sharing of your personal information, please visit readerservice.com/consumerschoice or call 1-800-873-8635. **Notice to California Residents**—Under California law, you have specific rights to control and access your data. For more information on these rights and how to exercise them, visit corporate.harlequin.com/california-privacy.

STRSMAX22R3

HARLEQUIN
PLUS

Try the best multimedia subscription service for romance readers like you!

Read, Watch and Play.

Experience the easiest way to get the romance content you crave.

Start your **FREE TRIAL** at
<u>www.harlequinplus.com/freetrial</u>.